The Raven and the Witch Hunter Omnibus: Volumes 2-4

H. M. Gooden

Published by H. M. Gooden, 2019.

Also by H. M. Gooden

The Dragons of the North
Mai's First Date

The Raven and the Witch Hunter
The Raven and the Witch Hunter: The Spirit of Big Bear
The Raven and the Witch Hunter: The Wedding
The Raven and The Witch Hunter: Honeymoon and Full
Moon Blues
Wendigo

The Rise of the Light
Fiona's Gift
Dream of Darkness
The Stone Dragon
The Phoenix and the Witch
Dragons are Forever
The Raven and the Witch Hunter

Standalone

The Raven and the Witch Hunter Omnibus: Volumes 2-4

Watch for more at https://www.hmgoodenauthor.com/.

To my readers.

Thank you for joining me on another adventure.

You are the inspiration for my stories,

I couldn't do this without you.

BIG BEAR
CHAPTER 1

B y the time Vanessa arrived at work, she was officially late. The detour to the library to drop Emma Jane off had added almost twenty minutes to her drive. Luckily, when Vanessa arrived, her coworkers were so relieved that she was alive after the recent deaths that she didn't get yelled at, or even unofficially reprimanded. The director, Bill Holland, even came over personally to make sure she was prepared for shooting the moment she entered the warehouse.

Vanessa reassured him, offering him a brave smile. "I'm okay. This week has been...unexpected," she said. Shaking her head, she looked at him. "How are you doing? How is Mr. Montgomery?"

Vanessa wasn't sure she really wanted to know, but after watching Mr. Montgomery collapse the previous night she was confident that he was going to need mountains of therapy at the bare minimum before he could move on, or even return to the set. She shuddered when she recalled the sight of Elaine Montgomery, the witch who'd been stealing the youth and life of several people on set, melting into a puddle of goo. Apparently when you're thousands of years old, you decompose more quickly than those with a normal life span.

Bill sighed, rubbing his forehead as he turned to look at the set, which was much quieter than usual. "I didn't know her well, so it's more of a rude shock than it is personally difficult. The shoot has been set back with the police investigations still ongoing and delaying everything, and of course, everyone's devastated about the death of the other cast and crew." Bill laughed humorlessly, dropping his hand from his face. "Ha! Listen to me. Investigations!" He shook his head and looked at Vanessa. "We can't use the areas where they found Elaine or Sandra, but we're already behind, so we need to work around them somehow. I'm glad you came at least. If you hadn't, we'd have been even more backed up."

Vanessa tilted her head. "The show must go on, right?"

She allowed a somber expression to cross her face, explaining the quip when she realized it may have come across as insensitive or worse, heartless. "Work helps me push the loss and sadness down for a bit, so I'm glad we can keep going. I'll be in makeup and then I guess it's back to the dumpster again?"

Vanessa winced as she recalled the day before, when Sandra had done her makeup. Bill gently clapped her on the shoulder.

"That's the spirit! Find Rebecca. She'll show you what we're using today for the makeup trailer and it'll be Joanne who gets you prepped for your scene today. See you in twenty."

He patted her shoulder one more time then walked away. Vanessa bit her lip, then turned to go and find Rebecca as instructed.

For the rest of the day she was called 'brave', 'courageous', and 'strong' by everyone she passed or spoke to but was uncomfortable accepting their accolades. She knew the truth. Not only was she not a victim, no matter what the witch's intent had been, but she was also the reason the producer's wife had been found decomposing on the floor. The entire day was an awkward mix of praise and hard work and by time it ended, Vanessa had never been happier to go home.

However, the moment she walked into her apartment she felt a disturbance in the air. She wasn't sensitive the way Cat, her sister, was, and had never had dreams or read auras, but she could feel the air moving around her. She knew instantly that someone else was in her home.

"Hello?"

She entered cautiously, not removing her shoes in case she needed to make a quick exit. Her heart began beating faster, until a familiar laugh came from the living room, surprising her but also instantly filling her with relief. Vanessa rounded the corner of the kitchen and looked into the living room, confirming her suspicions about who the owner of the laugh was when she saw the woman sitting on the couch laughing at something on her phone.

"Oh my God! Evelyn! What are you doing here?"

Vanessa swept her sister's best friend up in a hug and twirled her around. It was only possible because Evelyn was diminutive in comparison, standing about five feet four inches tall and a buck twenty soaking wet, while Vanessa had several pounds and almost seven inches of height on her.

Evelyn laughed, squeezing Vanessa back tightly before protesting. "Okay, girl! Down! I'm happy to see you, too. Now put me back on my feet, if you please."

She sounded amused, but her voice still featured the no-nonsense tone Vanessa had grown to love over the years.

"What are you doing here? Not that you're not always welcome, of course," said Vanessa, quickly reassuring her.

Before Evelyn had found out that she was an ancient goddess, she'd spent most of her free time with Cat, both in the apartment in San Francisco and at their houses back in Valleyview. When they were all learning about what they could do with their new-found powers, they'd practiced together a lot. Yet after a difficult battle in Scotland, Evelyn had been busy trying to understand her own life. Finding out she was an ancient African goddess who'd lost her memory would have been overwhelming for anyone, but in addition to that giant box of turmoil to unpack, Evelyn had also discovered her true love was the ancient earth god, Robin Goodfellow, who had helped them more than once in their fight against evil. Consequently, she hadn't been around as often to hang out over the previous year and Vanessa missed Evelyn almost as much as Cat did.

Evelyn shrugged, sitting down on the couch and tucking her legs underneath her. "I had a feeling you needed my help."

She stretched out her arms on the back of the cushions, looking relaxed and at home.

Vanessa sat across from her and leaned in.

"Okay, now you have me curious and hopeful. What do you know that we don't?"

Evelyn smiled mischievously. "What don't I know, *cher*? You know I can see dreams and read things from people and their emotions. I knew from the moment Emma Jane came through my door, on her search for the next in a long line of bad guys, that you'd be needing help from me in the near future."

"Yes, please!" Vanessa exclaimed, shamelessly adding, "whatever help you can provide, I'm all over it." Changing subjects, she continued. "But first, tell me what you saw. Emma Jane said you sent her to me, saying we could help each other and that I was in danger, but absolutely nothing else that was helpful."

Evelyn raised an eyebrow, acknowledging the statement in her typical, nonchalant fashion.

"That's true. I didn't want to give the whole thing away at that time. I just gave her enough information to get her where she needed to go. I didn't say anything to you or Cat because I didn't want to influence events any more than necessary."

"Wait a minute, does that mean Cat knew you were coming? Are you the help she said might show up today?"

Evelyn raised a shoulder. "Probably, although you never know with her either, do you?" Evelyn chuckled, then took pity on Vanessa. "Okay, yes. We've been talking since Emma Jane showed up on her mission. As I'm sure you're aware, you probably could have dealt with this particular bad guy without her help, especially if I'd given you and Cat a heads-up. The entire situation was just a strange convergence of location and events. But..."

Evelyn paused for dramatic effect and Vanessa felt frustration bubbling up. She was grateful when Evelyn finally continued. "I did see a completely different opportunity here, a bit of a star-crossed thing, as you've surely discovered by now. Which is why, my friend, I came to see you today."

Vanessa flopped backwards, banging her head dramatically on the couch a few times before rolling onto her side and putting a hand on her hip. "Oh god, yes! I'm so incredibly frustrated right now. First I had to deal with Emma Jane trying to run away because she was being all noble and trying not to hurt me. Then she stopped being noble, but now I'm freaking exhausted when I spend more than a short amount of time with her. All of this on top of how I feel if I even touch the woman, which I keep doing because I can't help myself."

Vanessa sat up, then glared at Evelyn, placing both hands on her hips as she complained. "Do you know how awful it is? To feel amazing with someone, but the moment they walk away realize they've aged you? It's the worst thing, ever, but if it's the only way we can be together I'll probably continue to do it until it kills me."

Evelyn looked at Vanessa with dark brown eyes warm with compassion. Her dark, springy, chin-length curls bounced when she nodded.

"I know it's hard for you. Just so you know, you're not alone in your suffering; Emma Jane has lived with isolation her whole life, but this is the worst it's ever been for her. There was no one else around before to highlight how painful it would be for her to have the power that she does. When all your loved ones are dead, except for your old teacher who wasn't much of a hugger to begin with, it's not such a big deal if you can suck the life and power out of people with a touch." Evelyn sighed, shaking her head as she pursed her lips. "But with you, this is the most pain she's ever felt, excluding the loss of her family."

Vanessa felt even worse when Evelyn laid everything out so plainly. She was a selfish jerk, complaining about not being able to touch her almost-girlfriend when Emma Jane was suffering with that level of pain. Maybe she didn't deserve her after all.

"So, what do we do then?" Vanessa finally said. "How can we make it so that this isn't so painful for her? So that we have a chance at actually being together?" Vanessa stared at Evelyn, beseeching her, praying that she had an answer.

"Luckily, I may know something. But I'm going to warn you in advance, it's not an easy thing to accomplish. It'll take some serious effort on your part and on hers as well."

"Anything. I'll do absolutely anything to be with her. Whatever it takes, I'll do it."

Evelyn looked satisfied. "Perfect. That's what I hoped you'd say."

VANESSA WAITED IMPATIENTLY for Emma Jane and Cat to return from the university. She'd let Cat know where Emma Jane was spending the day and knew they'd planned to meet up at the school and then take the bus home together. Vanessa had texted her sister immediately after speaking to Evelyn, but it had taken Cat and Emma Jane another hour to get home, as Cat had still been in classes when she'd gotten the message. During that time, Vanessa had talked with Evelyn about her life and business, although she'd stubbornly refused to elaborate about the possible fix to the physical barrier in Vanessa's relationship until Emma Jane was also present.

Vanessa understood why, but her frustration caused her to pounce on Cat and Emma Jane the minute they came through the door. She practically dragged them into the living room, then had to wait impatiently for Cat and Evelyn to hug before they'd sit down. Emma Jane nodded a polite hello as they all sat on the couch, eager to hear what Evelyn had to say. To Vanessa's relief, Cat put the conversation on track immediately.

"I'm glad you made it. I know how busy things are for you now. I wish you could come by more often to just hang out, but I get it. So, what did you find out? Is there a solution?" Cat leaned forward intently.

Evelyn nodded solemnly. "There is a way, yes, but it's super dangerous, because you know that's how stuff always seems to go for us."

Vanessa nodded, acknowledging the truth of her words but wishing she'd just get on with the details already and stop trying to build tension. "Danger's cool. I eat danger for breakfast. What do I have to do? Because I'm ready to do it."

Evelyn shook her head. "It's not that simple. It's going to be a massive undertaking. From what I've seen in my dreams, you guys are going to have to head to the Rockies and hike some crazy, dangerous paths before you can even find where the item is hiding. That's without any added excitement, which I'm certain will interrupt your journey at a few points."

Emma Jane spoke quietly. "Is it guarded?"

Evelyn looked at her approvingly. "Yes, it's guarded by the spirit of Big Bear. He was a fierce warrior known to have strong integrity. You'll only be able to reach your goal if he finds you worthy."

Emma Jane nodded, a small smile playing across her face upon hearing the name. "I look forward to the challenge. I've heard of him before, but only in passing. He signed some treaties with the Canadian government and was said to be a very shrewd chief. He was called Mistahi-maskwa, which means 'much bear'. He was responsible for improving some of the conditions of his people, the Cree, and he held out until the early 1880s before finally signing Treaty 6, which gave his people rights in exchange for the Crown taking their lands. I can only hope I'm up to the very high standards he set for wisdom and bravery."

"So maybe he'll be a nice bear, like Winnie the Pooh?" Vanessa asked hopefully, but Emma Jane just blinked at her in response.

"Unlikely, with our luck," she said, somewhat morosely.

Vanessa looked at Emma Jane, then at Cat as a serious concern popped into her head. "Cat, you won't be able to come this time, will you?"

Cat grimaced. "I could probably try. Maybe I can take a leave or something?"

Vanessa shook her head, trying to smile and reassure her sister, even as her heart sank at the reality of the situation.

"No, I'm thinking this is probably part of the quest. We need to be able to do it together without help from anyone else. Now that I think about it more, it would be like we're cheating. Bringing someone with us doesn't feel right."

Cat nodded slowly as Evelyn smiled.

"I believe you're right, Vanessa," agreed Evelyn. "Part of the quest for you to be together is for you to make it through adversity without help from me, your sister, or anyone else. That will make it much, much harder though, especially for you, Vanessa. You'll run the risk of getting very sick, or even worse."

Emma Jane regarded Vanessa with stoic sadness, before she spoke. "I'll understand if you don't want to do this. It's very risky, spending long periods of time together, especially without Cat's assistance to heal you from my presence. Even with Cat nearby, we've had problems when we've forgotten ourselves."

Vanessa raised her chin, clenching it stubbornly as she looked at each of the girls. Her gaze came back to rest on Emma Jane when she answered. "It's something I have to do. It's time for me to show some of the restraint you've had to have your entire life. Evelyn, do you know the exact location where we're supposed to go to start this hike to find this magical amulet thingy?"

Evelyn shook her head. "I don't, I'm sorry. All I can tell you is that you'll have to go to the Canadian Rockies. I'll write down all the details I can remember from my dreams. The rest is up to you two; you'll have to read the signs and follow where they lead." She sighed, lifting a hand helplessly, then letting it fall again. "I wish I could give you a road map, but I'm pretty sure this is another part of your quest."

Vanessa nodded, then stood up. She felt motivated to do something outside of her own small universe for the first time in what felt like forever. She knew she could be dramatic and impulsive, which made this quest seem as though it was designed specifically to test her strength of character. While she was sure the trip would also be difficult on Emma Jane, Vanessa believed that her love had more character at baseline and so far, this journey sounded more like a personal challenge for her own particular flaws. Yet, as a McLean sister, nothing was guaranteed to get her stubborn side up and working faster than a personal challenge.

"Well, I think I'll go and pack some warm clothing. I'm guessing the mountains in Canada in November can get pretty cold. I'll see what I have, but I'm positive we'll have to go shopping for hiking gear." She looked at Emma Jane, in her trusty uniform of jeans and dark t-shirt and nodded. "Yup. With Emma Jane's limited wardrobe, we're definitely going to need a trip to the store."

Emma Jane looked at her clothes. "What's wrong with what I'm wearing?"

Evelyn and Cat started to laugh and Emma Jane groaned with the realization of what she was up against. "Oh, yeah. I should have remembered. Canada plus mountains plus November. First on the list I guess is the need to buy some layers."

BIG BEAR
CHAPTER 2

As she exited the plane, Vanessa stepped into the arrivals gate at airport, feeling as though her true life was about to begin. She'd finally received clearance from the police to leave the city, since there was no logical way they could blame her for all the decomposing or suddenly senescent dead people. The camera guy's death had been a little dicier, but since he'd attacked Vanessa from inside her own home, with witnesses attesting to the fact that he'd fallen down the stairs without her even touching him, the police had closed that file, deeming it a self-inflicted accidental death, or something that sounded similar. She hadn't understood everything the police officer had told her, just that she was allowed to go.

Time off work had been easier to wrangle than she'd anticipated. It had been plausible for her to cite stress and a serious need for an isolated vacation in the mountains to relax, but when she'd spoken to the director, she'd ended up worried about him. She wondered if he was on the verge of a nervous breakdown, even though he'd seemed okay on her first day back. Her impression was that the stress had continued to pile up from a variety of sources during the week before Vanessa and Emma Jane had departed, as he'd continued to struggle with both the producers and backers. Hoping she still had a show to go back to, Vanessa put thoughts of work aside as looked around for the exit sign and their luggage. Spotting an arrow pointing to the right, she turned to Emma Jane, becoming concerned when she saw her paler-than-usual face.

"Are you okay, Emma Jane?"

Emma Jane was slowly walking down the gangway behind her. Surprisingly, even though Emma Jane was an older and more experienced traveler than she was, it seemed she didn't do well with heights and hardly ever flew if it was avoidable. It was possible their trip to the mountains would end up being just as hard on Emma Jane after all, but for an entirely different reason than Vanessa had anticipated.

"I'm okay," Emma Jane whispered, holding onto the railing a little too tightly for someone who was actually okay.

Vanessa wanted to hold her arm or her hand, to do something to help her out, but she was working hard on being as hands-off as possible. They'd made a deal with each other, and with Cat, that unless one of them was falling off the side of a cliff, they wouldn't touch, *at all,* until after they'd found the item that could protect Vanessa from accidentally being drained of life. At first, it had seemed unfairly harsh to Vanessa, but Cat had pointed out that without anyone around to provide healing, Vanessa wouldn't last more than a day if she touched Emma Jane as often as she wanted to. Grudgingly, Vanessa had bowed to reason, but she didn't have to like it, especially now, as she watched Emma Jane suffer from the aftereffects of her fear of flying.

She sighed while watching Emma Jane make her own way. "Well, at least we don't have to fly again until we go back. Hopefully I'll be able to hold you and keep you safe on the next flight." Vanessa tried to reassure Emma Jane, but also said the words out-loud as part of a fervent prayer.

God, I want this trip to be a success, just so that I can hold her without limits.

"That would be nice," replied Emma Jane, forcing a weak smile. "Which way are we supposed to head?"

"The bags and exit are to the right. Once we get our luggage we can catch the commuter bus to Banff. It's probably the most popular destination in the Canadian Rockies, so it's easy to get there. After that, all bets are off."

Vanessa had just a vague outline of a plan, since Evelyn had only had a vision of the mountains they needed to be in but not the specific location where they'd need to hike. Vanessa had researched the areas she thought sounded most likely to be successful, based on a combination of the geography that Evelyn remembered from her vision, local legends, and pictures she'd seen online. So, she had place to start, although no idea whether or not she was on the right track. Banff had seemed ideal though, being so accessible and nestled in the center of everything. Vanessa had heard about it before, and since she'd always wanted to see the beauty of the mountains, she'd booked them there instead of somewhere else because it seemed like the quintessential tourist destination.

Emma Jane nodded, opening her cane up. While she didn't need the cane to get around, Vanessa had already discovered how useful it was for Emma Jane to carry one. No one questioned why she kept her sunglasses on or expected her to move fast. The flight attendants had been extremely attentive and helpful in response to her perceived disability. That had been an unexpected bonus which led to extra snacks, which Vanessa had enjoyed immensely.

The path to the baggage area involved several escalators which made Vanessa nervous, although Emma Jane smoothly navigated each one without issue. Their bags were waiting when they arrived at the luggage carousel and they caught the shuttle with plenty of time to spare. The bus was half empty, as it was technically the shoulder season in the mountains. To be on the safe side and avoid accidental contact with each other, they sat apart and in their own seats. Vanessa thought about napping, but the scenery as they approached the Rockies took her breath away, instantly removing any thought of sleep.

"Have you ever been to the mountains before, Emma Jane?" Vanessa felt her spirits rising in response to the beauty outside. She knew she was going to have a cold and miserable trek up at least one mountainside over the next several days, but from the inside of the bus, it was so beautiful she couldn't care less about the potential future discomfort.

"Yes, I've been here to the mountains once before, when I hunted a witiko."

Vanessa looked confused, so Emma Jane explained.

"You may have also have heard it called a wendigo, but it has many names depending on who tells the tales. They are lost souls full of evil that are being punished for something they did during their lives."

"Like what?"

Vanessa felt herself settling into her seat, anticipating another one of Emma Jane's stories coming to life, but Emma Jane just shrugged.

"Oh, you know, the usual things, like selfishness, or cannibalism."

"That's a big spread in sin level."

Emma Jane nodded. "Maybe, but when you're dependent on a small group of people to survive, the worst sins are those against a group, like keeping valuable commodities to yourself, or breaking cultural taboos. Every society has a set of rules that its members are expected to follow. In the case of the wendigo, it's seen as a punishment to end up as one, not a reward. No one wants to have this power."

Vanessa tilted her head curiously. "What power do they have?"

Emma Jane looked off into the distance.

"It's said that they have superhuman strength, speed, vision, and hearing. They have physical skills beyond the understanding of any human."

She then looked at Vanessa seriously. "But in exchange for their new abilities, they lose their humanity and are fated to roam hungry and greedy forever, with each life they take never satisfying them but merely increasing the hunger that burns inside. They are horrible, man-eating ice beasts, hence why I was here the last time hunting one. The only way to kill one is to melt their heart."

She smiled mischievously. "Or in my case, by absorbing its powers and burning its heart over a campfire.

Vanessa shuddered. "Ugh. I don't think I want to hear any more about ice monsters while we're driving. I won't be able to sleep. Maybe when we get to the bed and breakfast you can tell me the full story, if I feel a bit braver. On second thought, maybe after we're done hiking in the isolated mountains, where we could be killed and eaten by a wendigo."

Emma Jane inclined her head. "Of course. Have you ever been to the mountains before?"

"No. We moved around a lot growing up, but never traveled just to visit places. I've seen a lot of North America, but pretty much none of the exciting parts."

Vanessa looked at the peaks now surrounding them with appreciation and their conversation lapsed into companionable silence. They passed a picturesque lake on the side of the road which was nestled between two high rocky ranges and Vanessa felt as if they were entering a different land, one where giants could walk freely and birds could coast on the air. Her spirits continued to rise. *That's right. I don't need to walk, necessarily. I can fly.* Smiling, she sat back and enjoyed the rest of the ride.

BIG BEAR
CHAPTER 3

Emma Jane looked out the window with trepidation. The plane ride had almost killed her. She hadn't expected to be so anxious, but she'd been unable to stop thinking about being helpless if the plane went down. She wasn't used to being out of control. She'd always been independent and done her own thing, but planes weren't on her good list for travel anymore. Oh sure, everyone had been wonderful to her, but that didn't help when she felt like a trapped rat.

The only thing that would have made it better was to have Vanessa sitting beside her, to hold and reassure her, but they'd deliberately picked their seats across the aisle from each other so that they wouldn't be able to touch. All Vanessa had been able to do was promise that the flight was going well and would be over soon, but it hadn't helped in the slightest. When they'd landed on solid ground, Emma Jane had almost thrown up from relief. A nice shuttle bus, where she could at least feel the ground beneath them and watch some of the scenery go by, was a huge improvement.

Her nerves somewhat more settled, she was left with thoughts and worries about their quest. If she'd understood Evelyn correctly, her dream had shown them hiking up the side of a snow-covered mountain to a small pool of water that didn't freeze, or at least wasn't frozen. She hadn't been clear on that, so Vanessa had researched all the known lakes in the Rockies located at the middle or end of a trail. They knew for sure the trail they needed was in the Rocky Mountains, but looking around as the shuttle bus continued along the highway, Emma Jane knew that wasn't helpful at all.

The range ran more than 3000 miles across North America, which was a lot of potential ground to search. Evelyn had been adamant it was on the Canadian side of the border, which cut down on at least half of the search area. Vanessa planned to start in Banff, as she wanted to check out the hot springs and there were several decent hiking areas accessible nearby. The only concern was that many of the paths might be closed to hikers due to the time of year.

Emma Jane sighed. She knew it wasn't going to be easy, but at that moment it seemed almost impossible- like looking for a needle in a haystack. Yet she wasn't as worried about herself as she was about Vanessa. Emma Jane looked over, seeing the enchantment on Vanessa's face as she witnessed the Rockies for the first time. Being close for more than a few days, even if they didn't touch, was dangerous for Vanessa. The worst part was that Emma Jane didn't even know how dangerous it would be; she'd never been in anyone's company for more than a few hours at a time since coming into her powers in her teens.

Vanessa looked up at the sound of her sigh. "Is everything okay?"

Emma Jane smiled, deflecting Vanessa from her troubled thoughts.

"Just thinking about tomorrow. You've got Johnstone Canyon on the list first, don't you?"

Vanessa nodded as she looked back out the window. "Mmm-hmm. It's super popular, which you'd think would rule it out as the location for our quest, but it also has pools of water that apparently never freeze. And it's an easier hike than most of the other trails at this time of year. I feel like we could get our feet wet there when it comes to our search, so to speak."

Emma Jane nodded. It made sense. She knew the most challenging part of the quest would be their internal struggles, so she wasn't sure that the physical part necessarily had to be difficult. At least that's what she hoped. Although, if the powers-that-be had seen her terror on the flight over, she'd already earned her reward.

THEY ARRIVED AT THE bed and breakfast in Banff and discovered it was only a short drive to the hot springs, which was enough to make Vanessa happy. She'd booked two rooms, going with the bed and breakfast option for cost as well as coziness. It would have been crazy expensive at a hotel and they couldn't take a chance with Vanessa's health by sharing a room, not until they'd found whatever it was they were looking for, if it even existed.

"I was thinking we should go to bed early tonight," said Vanessa, systematically laying out a stack of pamphlets on the table in her room.

"That way, we'll be rested for the hike in the morning. Sunrise is around eight, so there's no point going anywhere before that. The trails aren't lit and will likely have snow covered sections, so we should try to explore them during broad daylight if we want to stay on the path. We can eat a big breakfast, then make sure we pack lots of food and water and dress in layers." Vanessa looked at Emma Jane and the excitement sparkling in her eyes made her laugh.

"You're enjoying this immensely, aren't you?" Emma Jane asked, amused by the childish glee she saw Vanessa displaying.

Vanessa shrugged, giving her a sheepish look. "I've never travelled before, unless you count Scotland, but my travel arrangements were sort of made by magic that time. This is the first trip I've ever planned anywhere. I've never been hiking in a place where I haven't lived and it seems like so much fun, especially with the beautiful scenery all around us. Then of course, having you with me for the first time adds another level of enjoyment for me." Vanessa smiled at Emma Jane.

Emma Jane gave her a slightly pitying look. "Well, I hope you enjoy tomorrow. I'm not expecting to like much about it, since I dislike being cold in general, but I'm as eager as you are to find the pot of gold at the end of the rainbow. But yes, I'm happy that I'll get to do this with you as well."

Vanessa looked at Emma Jane fondly, letting her gaze roam over her hair, her face, her hands, before finally making eye contact, her eyes shining with promise. "I can't wait to be able to hold you. Even if I hate every minute of the next few days hiking, it will be worth it. A pot of gold is nothing compared to the potential for happiness for us at the end of this quest."

Emma Jane closed her eyes at the words, leaning forward before catching herself, quickly drawing back just before reaching to touch Vanessa. Her words, and the way Vanessa was looking at her, stirred the now familiar, intense longing inside her heart and Emma Jane knew it was time to go.

"Good night, Vanessa. I think I should leave before one of us starts something you'll regret. Sleep well."

Emma Jane went to the door, then paused with one hand on the doorknob and glanced back at Vanessa over her shoulder. "I'll dream of you tonight."

With a final smoldering look, she pulled her gaze away and left Vanessa standing at the table alone, holding a stack of papers with the same look of longing reflected on her face.

Emma Jane closed the door behind her, wondering how she'd reached this place in life. Just as she'd mostly made peace with the long days of travel and solitude that were her destiny, a routine hunt had brought Vanessa into her life. The turmoil created by such a simple change still astounded her. One woman caused her to dream about things she'd never dreamed of before. In her entire life, not one person had caused such strong emotions of hope, happiness, and frustration. She could only pray to the Great Spirit that she'd be found worthy to have the talisman, because a life without Vanessa suddenly seemed to be one that wasn't worth living. As she climbed into bed, Emma Jane sent out her thoughts and prayed for answers.

THAT NIGHT, EMMA JANE travelled to the forest of spirits again. She could always tell when she was there. The sound of children's laughter filled her heart with both joy and pain. She could still recall running around in the woods with her brothers and the sadness of knowing she'd never do that again pierced her like a knife, as it did every time she dwelled on the past. She also knew that when she heard the laughter, her mom wouldn't be far behind and she eagerly looked around for her. It almost felt as if she was there with her at those times; her appearance and words always seemed so solid and real. Sometimes, when fortune smiled on her, she could even feel the warmth of her mom's hug before she vanished again, to the place where spirits go to wait for their loved ones.

However, this time as Emma Jane walked through the trees she couldn't find her. The sound of her brothers playing still echoed around her, reassuring her that she was in the right place. She looked down at her feet sadly, examining the bare, exposed toes. She entered the dreams in whatever she'd been wearing to bed, so that night her feet were bare and her hair was long and loose down the back of a simple t-shirt, reaching to brush the top of her shorts. Her vision became what it had been before the spirits had worked their magic on her. *Maybe mom is upset with me, or unhappy that I've fallen in love with a woman?* Emma Jane felt the familiar hot prickle of tears begin to sting her eyes and turned away.

"Why are you crying, my child?"

Emma Jane whirled at the familiar contralto, a voice she now realized sounded almost the same as hers. She was close to the age her mom had been at the time of her death and each time Emma Jane saw her now, she felt a sense of pride that she looked and sounded so much like the woman she'd loved more than anyone else in her entire life. Until now.

"Mom. I didn't think you were going to come. I thought, maybe, that you were..."

"Disappointed?"

Her mom stepped out of the trees toward Emma Jane, a look of compassion and love wreathing her face with an ethereal glow. "The only way I would ever be upset with you, my girl, is if you lived a life devoid of honor and self-respect. I see nothing in your heart or mind to suggest you have fallen from the path of light," she paused. "But I do see someone new in there. Tell me about her."

Her mom stood beside her and held out her hands, which Emma Jane took with gratitude. She'd been too young to even think about discussing love and life with her mom until after she'd died. Emma Jane hadn't counted on her dreams however, or having the aid of the ancestors either. Yet since her mom had died, Emma Jane had been blessed with many discussions she'd never expected to have.

"She's the sun after the rain, Mom. She has such fire in her soul. Sometimes she speaks without thinking, but her intentions are good. Her anger can boil over like a pot on the stove, but just as quickly she'll calm down and apologize. But the best part is that she loves me back. Even though I'm a danger to her, even though I could kill her with a touch, she wants to stay with me and find an answer to our challenge."

Emma Jane shook her head in wonder as she continued. "I don't understand it, but I've never felt so much joy, or pain, because of one person."

Her mom nodded, a small smile crossing her face. "I know that feeling all too well. It sounds like you have a bad case of love, my girl."

Emma Jane looked at her ruefully. "Yeah, it kind of does, doesn't it?"

Her mom smiled, squeezing her daughter's hands. "Enjoy it as long as you can, my dear. I loved your father so much. If I hadn't had you four children in my life when he died, I think I would have died from heartbreak then as well."

She looked at Emma Jane, searching her eyes as she appeared to consider something before she nodded, setting her jaw as though what she was about to say would be unpleasant. Emma Jane braced herself. "You don't remember all that your father was, do you?"

Emma Jane shook her head, not sure where her mom was going with her question. "He died when I was only eight. I remember him holding me, giving pony rides, and once, putting a bandage on my knee when I'd fallen off my bike. But my memories are faded and he's been gone even longer than you and the boys. Even my memories of our time together have grown threadbare," said Emma Jane, her heart swelling with guilt and apology.

Her mom nodded, looking sad. "Your dad had powerful medicine, my girl. You don't get your gifts from me, but from him. Just as your kokum took you to Samuel to be trained, your father was trained by him when he was a child."

Emma Jane was taken aback. "Why didn't Samuel ever tell me this? How did I not know?"

Her mom patted her hand, a single tear falling down her cheek. "I didn't wish to have my children know about the danger their beloved dada put himself into. I was always proud of him, never think otherwise, but the life of a hunter of dark creatures is one of fighting and is usually brief. I wanted my kids to grow up with a dad that went away to work, like many dads do; I wanted to protect you from the fear that he may never return home."

Emma Jane nodded. Shadowy memories from her childhood suddenly became more clear. "The fire?"

This time, her mom looked away, pausing before turning back to meet her eyes.

"I can't say for sure. I always worried one of my children would take after him and be called by the Great Spirit to fight the never-ending battle between good and evil. After he died though, things mostly went back to normal. No more blood to wash out of clothing, no more injuries to tend, other than those that four active children will naturally accumulate. I'd almost forgotten the worry I lived under every day while he'd been alive, even as my heart remained broken for the one true love of my life. But did this somehow cause the evil to find us, long after he was dead?" She shook her head, her soft brown eyes full of pain. "I don't know. Maybe, or maybe the darkness sensed that one more force for light was about to rise in the world. Was it luck? Or was it just coincidence that caused me to let you go for a sleepover that day?"

Emma Jane nodded. "Or was it the Great Spirit?"

Her mom pulled her into her embrace, holding her tight with warm, strong arms that belied the fact she was only a spirit and no longer flesh and blood. Solemnly, she repeated her daughter's words. "Or was it the Great Spirit."

BIG BEAR
CHAPTER 4

Vanessa woke up early the next morning feeling invigo-
rated. She'd been so wound up after Emma Jane left the
night before that she'd taken a chance on being seen and
transformed into her raven form. The familiar tingle of
warmth as her skin became covered in shiny black feathers,
the not completely unpleasant sensation of her bones and
body rearranging into that of a bird of approximately the
same size as her human form was now a simple matter for
her, one that never failed to exhilarate and restore.

Under the cover of darkness, she'd gone for a flight as a
raven in the cool mountain night. She'd been completely at
peace as she'd glided over the peaceful range in the dark. Although she knew it was below freezing, she didn't feel the
cold nearly as sharply as when she was a human and had
flown for hours. Her flight had also given her a chance to
scout out the area. Her vision was better in the dark as a
raven and she'd been able to mark several possible locations
that fit the description of what Evelyn had seen in her
dreams. Two in particular called to Vanessa, but she couldn't
be sure if they were important or if something shiny had
caught her attention. She was a raven, after all. As she
stretched, thinking about the sheer enjoyment of the night

before, she felt more awake and alive than she had for several days.

She got out of bed, putting on the housecoat that came with the room then grabbed her toiletry bag and towel. Her magic and energy were always replenished after time spent in her other form. She remembered Mai explaining once that her dragon form was her true one, while being human was just the costume she dressed in between transformations. Vanessa had only recently discovered she was able to transform, so she often forgot about the energy boost that accompanied being a raven. Well, not for this trip. She resolved to transform daily, especially without Cat around to recharge her batteries the way she'd grown accustomed to since meeting Emma Jane.

Vanessa washed up quickly, electing to skip a shower until after their hike, as she didn't want her wet hair to freeze, as she knew it would after being outside for ten minutes. She'd save the warm shower for the end of her long hiking day instead. She put her things back in her bedroom then went across the hall to knock on Emma Jane's door. After less than a minute, the door opened and Emma Jane emerged fully dressed.

"Good morning," Vanessa said, surprised to see her love ready for the day. "Have you been up long?"

Emma Jane nodded. "I woke up around six. I dressed, then spent some time mediating. I thought if I was able to focus my power, I could ensure I had my barriers up before I spent all day hiking with you. I'm hoping to stay centered and keep myself from accidentally siphoning your energy."

Vanessa smiled, still proud of herself and eager to share her own bolt of inspiration.

"That's a good idea. Also, guess what? Last night I went out to get an 'as the raven flies' lay of the land, if you know what I mean." Vanessa looked furtively around the hallway, but no one was around them to hear her cryptic statement except Emma Jane, who fortunately understood.

"And? Did you see something interesting?"

"Let's get some food and talk while we eat. I'm famished. I'm always hungrier the day after a flight. I still don't completely understand that one."

Emma Jane rolled her eyes. "Could it possibly be because you totally destroyed the laws of physics and aerodynamics? I'm sure changing forms to become another creature takes a fair amount of energy."

"True, but I actually always feel energized rather than drained after a transformation. Sure, I'm starving, but I also feel way more alive. I think I'm going to do it every night while we're traveling. It'll help keep my energy up during the day, in case you *are* siphoning from me just by being nearby."

Vanessa wondered if they could try an experiment, but Emma Jane must have read her speculative expression and she stopped her before Vanessa suggested what she was thinking. At the same time, she took a half-step back.

"Oh, no you don't! I'm not taking a chance on your raven helping you regenerate from touching me. We're going to take this seriously and not look for short cuts."

Vanessa exhaled, then pouted playfully. "Party pooper."

Emma Jane laughed, shaking her head. "Let's get you something else to focus on. I've heard this place makes a fantastic breakfast."

AN HOUR LATER, FULL of bacon, pancakes, and eggs, Vanessa patted her stomach.

"That's what I'm talking about."

Vanessa practically purred with satisfaction, smiling contentedly at Emma Jane, who'd eaten a more modest, human-sized breakfast.

"Are you up for a nice, cold hike?" Emma Jane asked.

Vanessa wondered how many layers she should wear then remembered what she'd wanted to tell Emma Jane.

"Oh, yeah. What I was going to say is that when I was out flying last night, two places called to me. I'd initially planned for us to hike the Johnstone Canyon trail today, but last night I thought I also saw something down in Sundance Canyon." She looked at the clock on the wall, nodding when she saw the time. "Sundance is closer to town, so I thought we could check it out first, then tomorrow we can head to Johnstone Canyon. The ink pots at the end of that trail are where we need to get to, based on what Evelyn said and what I saw last night, but I think we'll need to get an earlier start to reach them before dark. I don't think we can make it all the way up today, based on what time it is already.

"What are the ink pots?" Emma Jane asked, raising an eyebrow while she waited for Vanessa to explain.

"They are basically pools at the end of the trail that are supposed to be pretty, but also, they apparently never freeze."

Emma Jane nodded absently at her explanation, looking out the window into the bright daylight. Vanessa followed her gaze, watching as the sun sent shards of fire through Emma Jane's mahogany hair. The sun pouring into the room made it feel like summer, although the thermometer on the bird feeder outside read +2 Celsius, which Vanessa knew meant that it was freezing cold.

"I'm open to starting wherever you think we should, but we should get going now," Emma Jane said. "Daylight never lasts long at this time of year and I'd like to be back to shelter before nightfall. I'm assuming the natural terrain of the mountains themselves is harsh, but if there are any creatures out there, supernatural or otherwise, night is when they'll be the most active."

Vanessa stood up and took a deep breath. As she changed positions, her pants felt uncomfortably tight and she wondered if she'd made a mistake eating so much. "I'll get my long johns on and meet you in the lobby. The guide book recommended three light layers for this kind of weather, or long johns and a pair of heavier pants."

Emma Jane rolled up her pant leg, revealing her already insulated leg. She flashed Vanessa a sideways look.

"Okay, so you're already set, obviously," said Vanessa. "I'll be back in just a minute."

She rushed to add another layer, once again feeling unprepared and flighty in comparison to the quiet and competent Emma Jane.

Maybe some of her talent for preparation will rub off on me. That would be nice.

This time, Vanessa moved quickly and made it back in the lobby in under two minutes, where Emma Jane waited patiently for her. Before announcing her presence, Vanessa took the opportunity to watch the stunning woman, marveling again at her quiet, strong beauty before.

"I'm back. Give me a moment and I'll ask the front desk if they can call a cab."

Emma Jane smiled. "Sure. I'll wait here."

Vanessa shook her head at the calm that always seemed to radiate from her girlfriend then went over to the desk where she was able to secure a taxi and a driver that was willing to take them the short distance to the trailhead.

Less than twenty minutes later, they were staring at an empty parking lot with small snow banks lining both sides of the path, as the taxi disappeared into the distance. Vanessa looked at Emma Jane, who was biting her lip.

"Are you ready?" Vanessa asked. What was making Emma Jane look so apprehensive? Surely, she'd had worse experiences during her years of tracking than what the path in front of them seemed to promise.

"Umm, are you sure the trail's open?" Emma Jane asked, frowning as she looked around suspiciously. "What about bears?"

Vanessa glanced up the trail. It seemed innocent enough. She didn't see anyone else ahead of them, but it was a sunny day and the path at least appeared to have been cleared at the entrance.

"It's a quest, right? I'm thinking if we run into a bear, it's part of the gig. Plus, don't they hibernate at this time of the year anyway?"

She shot a questioning look at Emma Jane, but she ignored it and threw her backpack on resolutely.

"Okay, let's see what's up ahead then," Emma Jane said, not turning to wait for Vanessa's reply.

Vanessa nodded anyway, putting on her backpack as well and praying she'd dressed warmly enough. The path was easy enough at the beginning, as she'd expected, and relatively flat and wide. It was just off Cave Street, a short distance from the main town of Banff. It seemed strange to discover that hiking in the mountains could be as flat as this trail was, but then she realized the hike was all about the views, which this one had aplenty. As the trail meandered along the river, providing vistas each more gorgeous than the last, Vanessa stopped frequently to take pictures. She was completely unable to resist the tourist's eternal struggle of attempting to capture a small measure of the beauty around her.

Each time she stopped, Emma Jane waited patiently, indulging Vanessa as she gushed about the river and the mountains, but not contributing much. After a while, Vanessa remembered that Emma Jane wasn't having the same experience, as she was unable to see the non-living scenery and was horrified that she'd been so inadvertently insensitive.

"I'm so sorry, I forgot. And I'm holding us up," said Vanessa, putting her phone away with a grimace.

Emma Jane shook her head, holding a hand out to stop her from apologizing. "No, don't stop. I'm enjoying your happiness. Please, don't feel bad for trying to share your excitement with me. Just because I don't see the world in the same way as you doesn't mean that I can't appreciate its beauty. Pictures aren't something I find useful, as they can't capture the spirit of the land around me. I can't look back at these wonderful moments later the way you or others can."

Vanessa was relieved Emma Jane wasn't bored by her tourist glee, but simultaneously saddened that she wouldn't be able to look at the pictures with her afterward and enjoy them in the same fashion. She'd forgotten once again about Emma Jane's limitations, as they were so rarely a hindrance and invisible the majority of the time.

Changing subjects, Emma Jane pointed down the path. "You said you'd seen something that captured your attention last night? Do you know what it was?"

Vanessa shook her head. "Not really. I mean, it wasn't like I saw a pot of gold or anything. It was more a feeling that there was something there. Something different than what I should have seen. You know what I mean?"

Emma Jane pursed her lips, thoughtfully turning her head from side to side while appearing to listen to the forest around them before she nodded. "I think I feel what you're talking about. I can see the silent fires of the trees, asleep for the winter until the sap begins to run again. I can see the small creatures moving under the snow, or sleeping in their small winter nests. But I can also feel another presence. Something larger hides in these woods."

Vanessa stood closer to Emma Jane, spooked by the hushed quality of her words. She wondered if they needed to be quiet to avoid the creature Emma Jane had sensed.

"Should we go? What do you think it is? Are we in danger?"

Emma Jane tilted her head again, then shook it slowly. "I'm not clear on that. I don't think I've ever sensed whatever this being is; it has an unfamiliar energy. It doesn't feel clearly dangerous, although I still think we need to be cautious. Whatever it is though, I can feel it ahead, only a short distance away."

Emma Jane looked back at Vanessa, who felt her body hum with a sudden shot of adrenaline. "I felt like we needed to come here for some reason. Maybe I was distracted by something shiny, or maybe whatever's ahead is a challenge we need to encounter as part of our quest. I'll go with what you think is the best plan."

Emma Jane shot Vanessa a look that passed for a smile, barely quirking the corner of her lips before she pointed her chin at the path once more.

"Let's see what lies beyond. This whole journey is a quest to find our way together. I agree, maybe this is part of the larger goal."

Vanessa took a breath, then led Emma Jane further up the trail. The trees began to thicken as they approached the hot springs Vanessa had looked forward to seeing. As they neared the water, their surroundings acquired a surreal quality. The trees hung thick with frost where as the steam from the springs coated everything above and beside them. When they crossed a bridge encrusted with ice, Vanessa ruefully wished she had crampons on her boots to assist with keeping her balance. As she didn't, she instead called a small gust of wind to levitate her, allowing her to float just above the ice and gracefully maintain her balance. Emma Jane raised an eyebrow at this magical cheating, but didn't say anything. Her own steps were as smooth as those of any wildcat and Vanessa fell a little more in love with her as she watched Emma Jane move along the trail with her natural abilities on full, impressive display.

The crack of a nearby branch a few feet to the right made Vanessa's head snap up as her eyes moved in the direction from which the sound had originated. Yet Emma Jane was already gone. To Vanessa's ordinary eyes, she was hardly more than a blur of long, dark hair swirling beneath her red, wool hat as she almost flew across the icy ground. Vanessa's mouth dropped open when Emma Jane effortlessly scaled a tree and swung silently into the branches. Vanessa looked around, then realizing that Emma Jane was almost out of sight, hurried to catch up. Spotting the trail looping around behind the tree, she used the air to move her closer. She didn't change yet in case what they were hearing was something human or natural. She could pass off her use of air magic as an optical illusion, but not an entire transformation into a large, black bird.

However, when she arrived on the other side of the tree, nothing was there, including Emma Jane. Terrified that something had happened to her, Vanessa squinted as she peered through the dense forest. She wanted to shout out, but didn't want to call attention to herself in case there actually was something to be wary of. Setting her jaw, she dropped her backpack on the trail and changed. The familiar warm tingle of transformation spread through every nerve ending and when it was over, Vanessa stretched out her wings to their full six-foot span and felt alive in a way she never did as a human. With her sharp, avian eyes, she looked again into the trees, this time spotting a solitary splash of red in the branches of a tree ahead of her. She flew over, pecking at it and holding it up with a claw. It was a piece of yarn from Emma Jane's hat. A caw of anger left her as frustration and worry burst through her attempt to remain silent.

Spreading her wings again, Vanessa lifted off from the branch. She flew in slow circles above the trees and the trail they'd been on a moment earlier. About a hundred feet away, she spotted another piece of fabric, this time black yarn from Emma Jane's scarf. Vanessa wondered if she was leaving her a trail, or if she'd become completely absorbed in the hunt and forgotten Vanessa was with her. Either way, Vanessa was going to have a bone to pick when she finally found her.

She continued to search the air, following the sporadic trail of yarn that she found in the trees, spaced out every fifty to one hundred feet. Soon, she saw something glittering in the deep woods, far from the well-marked trail they'd been walking on. Vanessa flew over, landing on a tree a few feet from the spot where the flash of light had caught her attention. Was this what she'd seen the night before? Even with her extra powerful vision, she couldn't be sure. The forest was now silent. All noise had ceased. There was nothing that suggested Emma Jane was in danger, but nothing to say that she wasn't, either. The woods had an eerie stillness that didn't feel right. With apprehension in her stomach, Vanessa spread her wings and glided closer.

There, almost completely hidden by several thick and ancient pine trees, was the small opening to a cave. It was tall enough for an average adult male to enter, but narrow, almost as though the mountain had cracked open at one point in time and then slightly fallen apart. A glimmer of light briefly flickered from inside the hole before vanishing once again. Vanessa knew without a doubt that this was what had caught her attention the previous night. She also knew she'd find Emma Jane inside, but had no idea what condition she'd be in or what danger lurked within the cave.

BIG BEAR
CHAPTER 5

Vanessa flew down, reluctantly transforming back to her human form, as the entrance looked too narrow for her to enter as a raven. The width of her wings alone made her larger as a bird than she was as a woman. She was grateful that part of her magic involved her clothes transforming with her, as the thought of being naked in subzero temperatures wasn't appealing. Still, she was unhappy that she couldn't remain in her raven form, where she knew she'd be stronger. Sadly, raven claws and wings were only effective as part of an aerial attack, which likely wouldn't be an option inside a small cave.

Moving as silently as she could, she winced at the faint sound of a leaf crunching underfoot. Hoping against hope that nothing had heard her, Vanessa belatedly used the air to provide a cushion against the ground and any other hidden noisemakers under the snow, then floated through the crack into the cave.

At first, she couldn't see anything in the darkness. Then a faint glow became noticeable from the narrow path. Cautiously, she moved toward the light. Peering around an unexpected corner into a surprisingly large chamber, she was shocked to see the interior was at least twenty feet high in the middle and as large in diameter as the average living room. When she examined the walls more closely, she could tell that they had been roughly carved into their current shape by an unnatural force. Marks resembling those made by a chisel were visible in several places and she knew that someone, or something, had created this space through painstakingly hard work.

As her gaze traveled around the dim interior, she saw Emma Jane. She was sitting calmly in front of the only light source, a small fire, with her legs crossed as if she was mediating. Vanessa's mouth dropped open, then she began to fume.

What the heck? Why did she leave me alone to hang out while she chills in a hidden cave?

Vanessa was ready to storm over and give Emma Jane a piece of her mind when she noticed that something was off about Emma Jane's relaxed pose. She was sitting with her back toward Vanessa, so she couldn't see Emma Jane's face, but the way her hair had fallen in front of her was wrong. Normally when Emma Jane mediated, her hair hung straight down her back with her face pointed up toward the Great Spirit. This time, her head was down as though she was asleep or perhaps looking at something on the floor. Consequently, her hair cascaded over her shoulders in a way Vanessa knew the usually fastidious Emma Jane detested.

Vanessa paused with her foot poised to step inside the main cave. She pulled back to rethink her first impulse, which was to barge in and start shouting in anger and relief. Something odd was happening, after all. She took a longer, more precise look at the area, searching for anything that might be important. She'd already noticed the walls, but as she looked at them again she could now make out several old paintings. They were similar to those she'd seen depicted in an old National Geographic magazine article on cave men. These could have been mirror images based on the colors and shapes she saw flickering in the firelight in front of her.

She noticed a small indent in the cave wall just below the drawings, in which there was a collection of metal objects. They appeared to be everyday metal tools, like hammers and chisels, and were stacked neatly together, as though placed there for ease of use. She couldn't make out what they all were from where she was standing, but one stood out in a particularly unpleasant way. It looked dangerous, with an edge that caused her to swallow hard. She recalled the time she'd encountered cannibals in the cave in Scotland. Praying this wouldn't be a repeat of that awful and disgusting experience, she forced her gaze elsewhere.

A faint noise from the other side of the chamber startled her and she drew back, barely allowing herself to peer into the gloom within the cave, not wanting to be caught if something or someone had brought Emma Jane there. Vanessa spotted another passageway she hadn't initially noticed. The opening lay across from Emma Jane and was where the faint sound was coming from. At first, Vanessa wasn't sure what she was seeing in the semi-darkness and retreated further to rub her eyes. Positive her mind was playing tricks on her, she turned to look again. Nope, she'd seen it correctly the first time.

Standing in the passageway was an imposing figure. While at first glance, Vanessa thought it was wearing a fur coat, when she looked again it was crystal clear that, with the exception of the face, the creature was completely covered in real fur. Whatever it was, it most certainly was not human. The creature's face had a blue tinge, while the fur was mostly white, except for a few dark patches marred by grime. Its hands were dark brown and featured large claws, resembling those of a bear. Within the grasp of these enormous hands was a strangely modern appearing blue bucket containing snow and ice. Vanessa couldn't see any ears, but the hair on the creature's head was long and shaggy and could have easily obscured them.

Damn it!

Vanessa pulled back all the way and leaned on the rock wall. Where was Cat when she needed her? Or her other friends? Growling inwardly with frustration, Vanessa wished she had her whole team with her to deal with the threat. But as she didn't, she knew she had to come up with a plan.

The first problem was that Emma Jane seemed to be out of the picture completely. Whatever this creature was, it had been able to incapacitate her somehow. That meant it was most likely dangerous, because there was no way Emma Jane would be sitting with her hair on her face while something resembling Harry, from *Harry and the Henderson's,* walked around. Either Emma Jane was unconscious or under some kind of mind control. Both options were frightening, since Emma Jane was the one who had all the experience with fighting and hunting.

Mentally running through her own list of abilities, Vanessa tried to determine the best plan of attack. She could control air, which meant she could extinguish the fire or make it larger, or even cause a small tornado inside the chamber. But all of those things could potentially hurt Emma Jane in addition to the creature. Vanessa could turn into a raven, but not until she was in the center of the cave near the fire where the ceiling was higher. That option could trap her without an exit, however, as the hallway already felt tight when she was in her human form. Vanessa spiraled into doubt and fear, then shook her head.

Nope, not going down that path. I've faced worse and that's my woman in there. I'm going to go in, personality blazing, and wing it. Figuratively and literally, if need be.

Her plan made, such as it was, Vanessa stepped into the chamber and waited. It didn't take long for the creature to notice her. It lifted its head and looked directly at her. Vanessa approached slowly, keeping the fire between herself and the creature while simultaneously inching closer to Emma Jane. Maybe she'd be able to wake her up so she could help get them out of here, but Vanessa wanted to make sure that Emma Jane was still breathing first. The thought had crossed her mind and once there, it was almost all she could think about.

To her relief, when she was finally in position in front of Emma Jane, she saw her breathing deeply, as though she was sleeping. No blood or obvious injuries were visible, so after a quick scan of Emma Jane's body, Vanessa turned her attention back to the creature on the other side of the fire.

The fur-clad beast tilted its head, seeming confused by the presence of a stranger in its home, but then its mouth curled into a snarl and Vanessa's initial suspicions were confirmed. Not a welcoming and friendly host, that's for sure. She took a nervous half-step backward, but was unprepared by the speed with which the creature lunged at her. Vanessa flew up, using the air to move a few feet away from the beast, grateful she'd recently recharged in her raven form before entering the cave.

Yellow teeth bared, resembling those of a sabre tooth tiger, the creature growled. The sound reverberated through the cave and fear shot through Vanessa like shards of ice, piercing her and leaving her weaker. Shaking her head, Vanessa refocused, realizing during the few seconds of weakness that she'd dropped much lower than she'd intended. A flash of understanding about the cause of Emma Jane's stillness in the middle of a developing battle field struck her, so Vanessa did the only thing that made sense to her. She plugged her ears.

The instant she did so, she felt stronger again. Something in the noise emitted by the beast affected her ability to concentrate and she was positive that was why Emma Jane was under the monster's spell. Vanessa looked around, remaining out of reach of the creature while keeping her ears plugged and floating as high as she could within the confines of the cave's environment. She didn't transform, since her hearing was better as a raven and that would only help strengthen the creature's ability to control her through sound. Instead, she searched for a way to wake Emma Jane. As soon as Vanessa had covered her ears she'd regained control, so if she could rouse Emma Jane and tell her to cover her ears, maybe they'd be able to get out in one piece.

Vanessa spotted the bucket the creature had dropped on the chamber floor when he'd first seen her. She flew through the air, narrowly avoiding another lunge from the creature and threw it right in Emma Jane's face. Her plan worked immediately. Emma Jane leapt to her feet with a gasp, hyperventilating for a second before she recovered a full awareness of her surroundings.

"Cover your ears!" Vanessa shouted, as the beast opened its mouth again.

Emma Jane quickly plugged her ears without question and the creature howled. The noise echoed around the chamber, although not completely without effect as Vanessa had hoped. To her horror, Vanessa felt herself once again losing control of her element, feeling almost as drained as when she'd first kissed Emma Jane. She knew then that plugging her ears wasn't going to work for long. Luckily, Emma Jane was now awake and pissed off. Vanessa had never seen her so angry, even when Emma Jane had been attacked in the bathroom at a nightclub, which had been the first time Vanessa had seen her in action. Conserving her energy, Vanessa floated down to stand with Emma Jane.

"Now what?" asked Vanessa.

She shouted as she kept her ears plugged and the furry giant in view. It looked angry, but was watching them for their next move.

"Now I must defeat him," Emma Jane replied. "He tried to trap me here, destroying any potential for me to allow him to go free. I saw him from the trail and followed him at first. I've heard varying tales through the years of the sásq'ets, so I wasn't sure if it was a creature for good or evil. The legends differ, depending on which story you hear and which group tells them. It's been described as everything from a peaceful creature that eats plants to a man-eating demon."

Vanessa raised an eyebrow. "So which is it? I mean, so far we're both alive, but why were you sitting there in a trance?"

Emma Jane's face took on a cold, hard look, one Vanessa had seen before during a hunt. "At first, I wasn't sure. But now that we're here and my mind is clear, the spirit I saw within the fur of the animal is one that's become twisted and dark. This creature is every bit as evil as any wendigo. I must kill it before we leave here, otherwise people will begin to go missing in the canyon and surrounding area."

Vanessa nodded, deferring to Emma Jane's skill at gauging evil, but wondered why the creature wasn't attacking yet. Then she noticed its hands. At first, she'd thought it was clenching and unclenching them, but as she watched, she realized the creature appeared to be drawing small patterns in the air. She felt ripples of power spread around the cave, creating a disturbance. The feeling of bad magic moving though the air prickled against her skin.

"Emma Jane, you need to move, now. He's doing something to the air that's not normal. It's making my skin feel tight."

Emma Jane nodded and approached the beast, pulling out a silver knife Vanessa had never seen her use before. She began to dance around the creature. It stopped moving its hands and Vanessa felt the pressure on her body ease, but watched with trepidation as the creature instead began to mirror Emma Jane's movements.

Vanessa had never seen two animals square off before, but couldn't help but think how much Emma Jane resembled a fierce and beautiful panther as she danced around the beast. They moved in sync, as though they were performing capoeira or a tango in which they were trying to kill each other. When Vanessa and Emma Jane had taken on the witch together only a few weeks earlier, Vanessa had felt like she was watching Emma Jane dominate an MMA fight, with kicks, lunges, and punches. This fight, in the cold, shadowy cave, was more sinuous and so smooth that Vanessa nearly missed the moment when Emma Jane spotted an opening. Like lightening, the hunter dove toward the center of the beast, which towered almost two feet above her small but muscular figure. The creature reached out its large arms, attempting to scoop Emma Jane into its grip, but instead Emma Jane slipped through, coming up underneath and into its guard.

Vanessa caught her breath, filled with dread that Emma Jane had made a deadly mistake. She watched with surprise as Emma Jane began to glow, becoming so bright that Vanessa had to squint and put a hand up to cover her eyes. Just as quickly, the light faded away and she watched as Emma Jane stepped back from the now motionless creature. Her knife was raised and the blade was covered with dark blood that dripped down her arm. Vanessa paused in her celebration at the victory as the look on Emma Jane's face caused her to worry about the shape of her girlfriend's soul.

BIG BEAR
CHAPTER 6

E mma Jane breathed deeply, containing the rush of energy that roared through her every time she took a life, like whitewater flowing through the mountains. It was overwhelming. Power flooded her body, lighting up each nerve ending with the familiar, intoxicating hit that she received whenever she absorbed the magic and life force of a defeated foe. She worked to contain it, feeling the familiar call of darkness as she struggled to balance the evil with the good.

It called to her, promising her miracles and life everlasting; power beyond that of all others in the universe. She alone could rule the world and have everything she ever desired, if only she came over to the dark. But its promises were lies. She knew that and yet still it beckoned to her. Every time this happened, ever since the first fight over twenty years earlier when she'd absorbed the power of the wendigo, she forcibly reminded herself of the words Samuel had spoken to her.

"Remember, every time you kill, you become that which you hunt. You must always guard against the darkness, as you will walk the line between light and dark out of necessity in order to hunt. Do not be tempted by the power you find in these creatures; it is tainted and will bring you no lasting joy.

Remember to always center yourself and pray to the ancestors that you do not lose your way. Remember your loved ones."

This time, Emma Jane felt calm return more quickly than usual. She knew exactly why when she looked up from where she'd knelt beside the beast, into the worried face of the beautiful woman beside her, who stood just far enough away to prevent Emma Jane from accidentally touching her. Vanessa. She was the new, and most important, reason Emma Jane had ever found to continue to fight on the side of the light, no matter how much she became tempted to turn to the darkness.

"Emma Jane?"

Vanessa was hesitant, holding a hand out as if offering to help, but avoiding direct contact. Emma Jane took a deep breath, allowing the excess energy to leave in a rush of air. She visualized it dissipating into the world like dandelion seeds in the wind. She didn't know why, but that particular image always seemed to help. She then stood up and smiled weakly.

"Hey, thanks for coming to find me. So...how good are you at building a bonfire?"

Vanessa exhaled, shaking her head as she looked down at Emma Jane with relief.

"You scared the crap out of me, you know that? I didn't know what the hell had happened to you. Then I found this minuscule hole in the wall, literally, and see you sitting all zoned-out in front of this tiny fire in a monster's mansion. What happened?"

Emma Jane could tell by the edge in Vanessa's voice that along with relief she was also feeling a fair amount of anger. Emma Jane did the only thing she knew how to do. She told the truth.

"I don't know. Really. Like I told you, at first, I followed him, it, to see what it was and if it had good or bad intentions. Just because something's big and unfamiliar doesn't necessarily mean it's evil." She shrugged then wrinkled her nose. "Obviously in this case, it did turn out to be bad. One minute I was in the trees and the next you were here. I've got no idea what happened in between."

Vanessa nodded and Emma Jane watched as her hands tightened and relaxed, knowing without a doubt that Vanessa wanted to touch her. She wanted that more than anything else at that moment as well but couldn't chance hurting her, especially after absorbing such a huge rush of energy. Emma Jane was wide open and could accidentally drain Vanessa in seconds if she gave in to her own desires.

"I think it was through the air, or maybe through sound waves, I'm not sure," said Vanessa. "But when it growled, I felt myself lose strength. Then when you were about to fight him, I saw him do something with his hand that made the air tighten around me. Have you heard anything about that? Do these creatures have magic of some kind?"

Emma Jane shook her head. "I've got nothing. The sásq'ets are a myth, even among my people and the many storytellers I've encountered. It's like a unicorn. Everyone's heard of one, but no one actually believes they're real. We need to document this encounter for the future, in case of further attacks or sightings." Emma Jane gave Vanessa a smile, trying to show her how proud she was without touching her. "You did really well today. I don't know what would have happened to me if you hadn't been here. I believe you've also discovered something important that could help other hunters in the future. I only wish Samuel was still able to hunt, because he'd be proud of you too."

Vanessa blushed, waving away her praise while simultaneously looking pleased with herself. "Well, we're here on a quest, after all. I guess it only makes sense that we get to find a mythological creature that everyone on *Legend Hunters* is searching for." She shrugged, still trying to look modest, but failing. She burst into laughter when Emma Jane raised an eyebrow in response. "Okay, maybe this isn't exactly the quest we're supposed to be on, but it's nice to know we make a good team. I must have seen this during my flight last night, but I guess it wasn't related after all."

Emma Jane shrugged. "Maybe, maybe not. It's hard to say. Either way, we came, we saw, we overcame. Now we have to clean up. If we want to make it back to the bed and breakfast in time for supper, we should get a move on. Something this big will take time to burn."

Vanessa groaned, but nodded and began to search for wood outside the cave. They worked together, building up the fire as high as they could. They both appreciated the natural chimney effect of the cave, which Vanessa discovered had a hole directly above the fire when she got closer. It allowed the open sky to supervise as they burned every last scrap of the beast they could. The majority of the smoke danced straight up to the heavens instead of choking them, although the stench of burning hair was so intense that they waited outside for most of the process. They buried the rest of the creature in the soft ground inside the cave, using the creature's own tools both to bury and dismember it, which Vanessa found somewhat ironic. Hiding all evidence of what had happened that day, they knew that someone might find the bones years later, but they'd never guess what they had belonged to.

By the time they'd finished, the moon was up and the walk back was silent, cold, and beautiful. Emma Jane took in a deep breath of the crisp winter air, feeling more alive than she'd felt in years. The evil had been beaten back with her love by her side and the hope that they could eventually be together was only a day away along another road. Nothing could be better than that.

BIG BEAR
CHAPTER 7

That night, Vanessa slept deeply, hardly even moving in her bed as the hours passed. Then she began to dream. To her surprise, she opened her eyes inside the familiar glade where she'd always encountered Robin. She hadn't seen him since...wait, was it in Scotland? That had been so long ago. She walked around the glade, watching as tiny fairies floated in the breeze like seeds. She joined them, drifting above the glade's carpet of emerald grass with a lightness of heart that had been missing for a long time. She whirled in the air, her magic allowing her to play with them, and she only stopped when she heard the sound of someone laughing below.

Vanessa touched down, giving the man watching her a big smile before she ran to greet him. She knew that Cat treated him with what their dad considered an appropriate amount of deference, given he was technically the earth god of their ancestors, but Vanessa wasn't big on formality. Luckily, neither was Robin, at least as far as she'd seen with Evelyn and herself.

"Robin! I'm so glad to see you here! Wait, why *am* I here? Is this a dream?"

Suddenly remembering that she hadn't gone to a gate in order to find him and had been on the verge of falling asleep the last time she'd been aware of anything, Vanessa pulled back, looking at him with a puzzled expression.

Robin laughed, then twirled her around a few times before letting her go. His skin was still a heathy nut-brown and his curly-hair and mischievous look were unchanged, but he was no longer the cheerful eight-year-old boy she'd first met. Ever since he'd come clean to Evelyn about their shared past, he'd always appeared as a handsome young man whenever he visited. It was possible that this was his true form, or maybe he thought it would be more appealing to Evelyn, but either way since Scotland, no one had seen the little boy version of Robin. Vanessa was a little sad about the change, as he'd been such a cutie then, but had to admit that his grown-up look wasn't hard on the eyes. He stood about six feet tall now, with well-muscled arms and a chiseled jaw, and could have appeared on the cover of any magazine in the world had he wished to.

"I wanted a quick word with you before you wake up."

Vanessa wondered if she was in trouble. After all, the creature Emma Jane had just killed was technically of the earth.

As if reading her mind, Robin smiled before he answered. "No, my child, it's not that. You were right to find your love and protect her, and she was merely doing her job, balancing the forces of good and evil. Neither of you are prone to violence for its own sake. That is not why I'm here."

Vanessa exhaled, relieved he wasn't banishing her to the naughty corner. What would that even look like? She'd no idea if having Robin Goodfellow mad at her would count as a death sentence, but she was pretty sure it wouldn't be great for her health.

"Why am I here then? I mean, I'm glad you aren't mad at me and I always like to see you, but generally you're too busy just to say hi."

Robin smiled, then did a quick somersault, rolling over to a tree before hopping gracefully onto a branch and dangling upside down. Vanessa shook her head. Ever since she'd met him he'd always done stuff like this, but it looked totally different as an adult than it had when he'd appeared to be a child. Now he resembled a circus performance instead of a kid playing around.

"I wanted to let you know that the first part of your challenge has been successfully navigated. You were correct that you were meant to face the sásq'ets as a team. But as you suspected, it was only half of your quest to be together. Tomorrow, you will reach the summit of your journey."

"Really? That's so exciting! You've got no idea how much this means to me." Vanessa could have hugged him, until she saw his expression.

Robin smiled, but looked troubled as he reached out a hand to touch her face, still regarding her from his upside-down position.

"Oh, but you would be mistaken if you assume your remaining tasks are simple. That's why I'm here. You will be tested, brought to a place you think you cannot handle, but you will be able to persevere if only you can remember what is at stake. Your love for each other shines so brightly I can see it from Summerland. Is it necessary for me to be here? No, probably not. But I know that Evelyn and Cat are concerned about you and Emma Jane being so far from their help. I can now let them know you are well and on your way to success. Remember when you awake that you will succeed, but only if you are able to hold the course."

Vanessa felt his warm hand against her cheek and heard his words. Then, with a flash of light, he was gone. She was alone in the glade with only the memory of his presence and the words he'd spoken ringing in her ears.

THE NEXT MORNING WHEN Vanessa rolled out of bed, she was eager to see if her planned hiking trail would be the right one. She couldn't help but wonder if their last adventure had merely been a decoy, a fork in the road meant to slow them down in achieving their goal, or worse, to prevent it entirely. Yet, Robin had implied it had been a necessary part of their journey. If Emma Jane or Vanessa had been alone, neither of them would have made it out alive. She shuddered to think how many other hikers had met a grisly fate in the small home they'd found hidden deep within the mountain. She wondered how many memories had been altered over the years, if someone as strong and gifted as Emma Jane could be hypnotized so easily and not recall how she'd arrived at the cave.

Vanessa dressed quickly for what she hoped would be the day she could finally, physically be with Emma Jane, then paused. Had she actually spoken with Robin last night? Her memory was foggy, but she had the vague recollection that she'd been in Summerland at some point during her sleep. She struggled to remember what they'd discussed, but could only recall the hazy feel of him touching her cheek while giving her a cryptic pep talk. Try as she might, she couldn't remember anything else from her dream. Instead of forcing the memory she grabbed her purse and headed across the hall to Emma Jane's room.

Vanessa knocked on the door, taking a surprised step back when it opened a split second later.

"Good morning. Are you ready to get some breakfast? I have a good feeling about today." Vanessa beamed, practically chirping with excitement, although she had no reason to feel elated other than the hope Robin may or may not have left her with.

Emma Jane smiled, tilting her head. "What are you so happy about?"

Vanessa shrugged. "Beats the heck out of me. I think I had a visit from Robin last night, but if not, I had a great sleep and I'm in a super mood. A delicious breakfast with my girl is the only thing that could possibly make me feel better right now."

Emma Jane let out a short bark of laughter. "Okay, if that's what a visit from Robin can do, sign me up. I've never met the guy, but I've heard enough about him from you and Cat that I'm looking forward to it. Let's feed you then hit the trail. I want to check out the hike you've got on your mind for today. Hopefully, it's a little bit less dangerous than yesterday's."

Vanessa nodded, but a cloud cast a shadow fell over her jubilation. If this truly was the last part of their quest, it was almost certainly going to be every bit as dangerous as the previous one, if not more so.

AFTER DISCUSSING THE details of the trail over a much earlier breakfast than they'd enjoyed the previous day, they had a taxi take them to the trailhead again. Johnstone Canyon trail was one of the most popular hikes in the area and easy for tourists without any hiking experience, which meant it remained open and relatively busy year-round. The pictures Vanessa had seen online would have convinced her to make the hike even if she'd no reason to believe it would lead them to their goal. However, in this case, the online write-ups had also boasted of pools of water that never froze, which she very clearly remembered Evelyn saying would be where their quest ended. Not only was the trail going to be scenic, it seemed to fit the bill as door number one for the location of the talisman.

As Vanessa exited the taxi and looked up the trailhead, which looped between majestic pines, she closed her eyes and sent out a quick prayer. Had she really spoken with Robin last night? If so, she wished she could remember the specifics of what he'd said. Looking at Emma Jane standing beside her, listening to the sounds of nature with her eyes closed and sunglasses off, Vanessa knew she'd do whatever it took to reach their goal.

They headed up the trail single file, even though it was wide enough to walk beside each other in some places. In the snowier areas, they'd be forced to either move to single file or risk touching so to keep it easy, Vanessa went first. She instantly loved everything she saw around her. The sun, the cold air, and the sounds of birds chirping high in the pines filled her with joy. The smell of the air was so invigorating she felt as though she'd never need any other kind of sustenance. They passed a waterfall that emptied into a slowly trickling stream, leaving an intricate ice sheet along the canyon wall. They continued higher and every step they took lead to more breathtaking views.

Vanessa was seriously wondering if she could somehow move to Canada. Maybe when they found the talisman, they could get married and move to Banff. Emma Jane was Canadian, after all. By the time they passed the second waterfall, Vanessa was all warmed up and beginning to sweat. "I'm going to take off a layer. How are you doing?"

Vanessa glanced over her shoulder at Emma Jane, who'd been quietly soldiering along behind her. She didn't have the same look of joy Vanessa was sure was plastered on her own face, but she seemed at peace with hiking, which made Vanessa happy.

"I'm good, thanks. I think the ink pots are about twenty minutes ahead. Are you okay to keep going?"

"Of course," replied Vanessa, as she practically sang the words.

She was dying to see them, with or without the quest. When she'd read about them she hadn't understood why they were called the ink pots from merely looking at the pictures. It had appeared to be a mineral spring area in a meadow, picturesque with the mountains rising around them, but not exactly looking like a place where ink would come from. As she'd read more however, she'd discovered the name was due to the different colors of the water in the ponds, and she'd been intrigued to see them in person.

"This is the most fun I've had in *forever*. I'd love to go hiking every week with you. Hey, when we get back, do you want to go hiking with me? I used to go all the time with Mai and Jake in San Francisco, but Cat would rather go for a run, which isn't my thing, so I haven't had a chance lately."

Vanessa was sure she sounded manic, but she didn't care. It was a perfect day. Or at least it was until a low rumbling sound penetrated her happiness. "Umm, what was that?"

Vanessa turned around as Emma Jane's face drained of color, becoming deathly pale. There, about one hundred feet above them on the trail, was a large, brown bear.

BIG BEAR
CHAPTER 8

"Is that a grizzly?"

Emma Jane's question was hardly louder than a whisper and Vanessa nodded slowly, her mouth still open in surprise.

"It seems to be. I thought they were supposed to be hibernating?" Vanessa's voice trembled slightly.

"Apparently, this one isn't ready for bed yet."

Emma Jane started to turn back down the hill, when a similar sound came from behind her. "You've got to be kidding me!"

Vanessa's knees felt weak as she looked past Emma Jane to see another, darker colored bear behind her, standing about the same distance away.

"That looks like a black bear. Emma Jane, I'm not a zoologist, but I didn't think different species of bear ever traveled together."

Emma Jane's expression changed from scared to certain. "They don't. This must be part of the test. It's obviously meant to scare us away."

Vanessa's eyes were open as large as she could get them as she swiveled her neck to try to keep both bears in sight. "Well, it's totally working on me. I'm terrified! Now what are we supposed to do?"

"Hmm, well, if it were two normal bears, I'd say we were screwed and recommend trying to run or climb a tree, especially if that actually is a grizzly. I'm not sure we're not screwed now, but if this is part of a supernatural challenge, we stand a better chance of not dying as quickly. Vanessa, are you able to transform into a raven right now?"

Emma Jane looked at Vanessa, who she nodded, feeling the calm on Emma Jane's face dampen the fire of her own fear.

"Yes, why?" Although Vanessa might be terrified, she had no intention of transforming and leaving Emma Jane to deal with the bears alone.

Emma Jane considered the grizzly behind Vanessa before throwing another brief glance at the slightly smaller black bear behind her. "You said you have more power and energy in that form, so I'd like you to get behind the bear and head for the ink pots. Don't worry about me. I'm going to keep walking along the path as though they aren't a problem and treat them like another hiker we've met along the way."

Vanessa looked at her with horror. "Emma Jane, there are two bears within running and killing distance. What the hell are you thinking?"

Emma Jane smiled and Vanessa recognized it as her usual cool and confident hunting smile. She looked nervously at the bears, which were standing still on their hind legs, just watching the girls, not making any move. Vanessa wondered if they were waiting for them to make a break for it.

"If they get too close, I'll just have to slow them down. Now, go!"

Emma Jane spit the last word out as an order, so Vanessa didn't argue further. Instead, she let the comforting tingle run over her as she transformed into a massive black bird. She then flew straight up into the air while the two bears followed her with their gazes before looking back at Emma Jane, who now stood alone on the path. True to her word, she began walking toward the grizzly, completely ignoring the black bear and stopping when she was only a few feet away. Vanessa hadn't continued to the ink pots as Emma Jane had directed because she'd been unable to leave her. What if she needed help?

Maybe I should fly back down?

Vanessa watched, torn with indecision as the scene below unfolded in a way that clearly highlighted Emma Jane's nerves of steel, the fact that she had a plan, and that this most definitely wasn't a natural encounter.

Emma Jane bowed to the grizzly, showing the back of her neck without flinching.

"I greet you in peace, Mother Grizzly. I am here with my mate to seek your wisdom and blessing in our journey. We have travelled far to bring you gifts and ask for your help, should you find us worthy."

Emma Jane bowed even lower, holding out a handful of sweetgrass and sage she'd brought with her on the off chance that an offering would be needed. Vanessa had thought she was crazy when she'd seen her packing actual grass earlier, but when Emma Jane had explained its significance to the ancestors, Vanessa agreed they needed all the help they could get, even if she didn't understand or believe in the same things as Emma Jane. After all, with all the crazy stuff she'd seen over the previous few years, she was a lot more open-minded than she'd been in high school, before she knew magic was real.

Vanessa returned, cautiously settling in the branches of a nearby pine tree where she could hear Emma Jane better, as well as provide back up if necessary. She almost fell off the branch when she heard the bear speak, its voice a deep but understandable rumble, not unlike the sound of a large truck going by on a gravel road.

"Greetings, my child. You have shown yourself to be wise and courageous by your very presence here. You have fought the sásq'ets and lived to tell the tale of the ghost of the mountain, with your spirit and heart intact. You have been found worthy to continue with your quest. At the top of the trail you will find that which you seek with all the fire of hope in your heart. You will face one more challenge before you can succeed, however. Be prepared and be humble, lest it slip out of your grasp forever."

As Vanessa watched, waiting to see what would happen next, both the black bear and the grizzly faded into mist. Their previously solid forms vanished without a trace. Even the sweet grass Emma Jane had placed on the ground in front of the bear had disappeared, as though it had never been there in the first place.

Vanessa changed back, using the air to glide down and came to stand beside Emma Jane. Awestruck, she shook her head. "That was amazing! How did you know what to do? How did you know it wasn't a real bear?

Emma Jane smiled, shrugging one shoulder. "It was a real bear. Well, the essence of one anyway. I didn't know, not for sure. But like you said, two bears that don't travel together in nature blocking our path in such a deliberate way wasn't likely to be an accident or a coincidence, unless it was part of something bigger," she said, then smiled. "As to how I knew what to say, I grew up listening to the stories Samuel taught me, remember? You must always be polite and bring gifts. There's never a guarantee the spirits won't be offended, but good manners can save the day in many different situations, even when nothing supernatural is at play."

Vanessa tilted her head. "True. Sounds pretty much the same as the fairy tales I grew up listening to at bedtime. Don't piss off the little people if you want to continue to have a good life, or something along those lines."

Vanessa looked up the trail, suddenly tired at the idea of more hiking and the possibility of what else lay ahead of them. Her earlier hopefulness faded to a bare remnant of what it had been. "Should we continue? It seems like this is the right place after all, if we're meeting spirit animals. What do you think the next task will be?"

Emma Jane shook her head, following Vanessa's gaze up the snow-covered path.

"I've no clue, but I'm sure it'll be more difficult than this one was. We just got lucky."

"That's kind of what I was afraid of." Vanessa groaned, turning to continue up the mountain while hoping they weren't marching to their deaths.

IT TOOK ANOTHER TWENTY minutes before they reached the end of the path. The narrow trail widened to reveal beautiful emerald green pools of free-flowing water, which glistened in the sun in varying shades of green, blue, and hints of yellow. Vanessa leaned over to touch the water, finding that while it was cold, it was quite a bit warmer than the surrounding air. Vanessa smiled back at Emma Jane, who'd stopped to watch her by the pond. Vanessa was struck with awe, as Emma Jane's smile caused the corners of her eyes to crinkle into a smile.

She stopped, breathless from the sight of the soaring mountains behind Emma Jane. The smile on Emma Jane's face, however, eclipsed even nature's beauty. She looked timelessly elegant and Vanessa couldn't imagine anything more precious.

"You're so beautiful," she whispered.

Suddenly, Vanessa felt herself being pulled toward Emma Jane by a strange and overwhelming force, desperately needing to touch her more than she'd ever needed to touch anyone before.

Emma Jane's expression changed to one of confusion as she began to back away. "Vanessa, what are you doing? You know we can't, especially not now. Vanessa!"

She spoke sharply, almost yelling as she continued to move away from Vanessa, who was advancing with complete disregard of Emma Jane's words.

But Vanessa could hardly hear the concern in her love's voice, trapped in something she couldn't control. She felt compelled by an external force that threatened to crush her chest with its power. She couldn't stop; she needed to touch Emma Jane so badly that it felt like a hot poker was being pushed through her heart.

"Emma Jane...I need you...please..."

Vanessa tripped and fell, slowing her progress, but when she looked up to see Emma Jane's horrified face she knew that something wasn't right and that her feelings weren't entirely her own.

"Emma Jane, I'm so sorry. You have to go, please. Don't touch me. Something's wrong. I can't... I can't stop myself. Leave now, before I get to you. Please..."

Vanessa's words trailed off in a whisper, as she got up and began to move toward Emma Jane again, fully aware it wasn't a good idea, but unable to stop herself from continuing.

BIG BEAR
CHAPTER 9

E mma Jane looked around, searching for the cause for Vanessa's behavior. Her gaze fell to the water and she remembered Vanessa had touched it mere seconds before she'd started to act strangely. It was lucky it hadn't been Emma Jane who'd touched it first or Vanessa would have been in even more trouble. Emma Jane couldn't think of anything that might counteract whatever magic was driving Vanessa's involuntary movements. Then suddenly, she was struck by one idea. Emma Jane turned to look at Vanessa.

The raven-haired beauty had managed to get up from where she'd tripped. She was now just a few feet away. Emma Jane stepped back down the trail further, moving away from Vanessa's grasping hands.

"Vanessa, you need to focus. I want you to transform again. You're stronger as a raven. Maybe it will be enough to throw off whatever power you're under. I know you can do it, you're stronger than the spell that's making you act this way."

She watched helplessly as Vanessa struggled against the invisible compulsion. Soon, however, her shoulders relaxed as Vanessa shimmered into the large black bird she'd been only a few minutes earlier. Vanessa flew up, resting on a nearby tree. Shaking her head, her feathers ruffled as she moved.

"It's still strong, Emma Jane. I need to get even further away from you. I can still feel the longing and it's almost overpowering me, even in this form. Will you be okay if I leave for a while? I don't want to go, but I don't know how much of this feeling is me and how much is a spell."

Emma Jane shooed her away. "Go on, I'll be fine. Come back as soon as you feel the compulsion has faded enough so that it's safe for you to be near me."

Emma Jane watched sadly as Vanessa took off, flying high into the sky and circling around before heading down the trail toward the parking lot. Looking around, Emma Jane realized how very isolated she was and how lonely it was in the mountains, away from everyone and anything familiar.

A wave of despair crashed over her. She was so lonely. She would always be alone. Tears rose up to choke her. She tried to force them back as she looked for a place to rest and think. Spying a bench near one of the pools, Emma Jane collapsed onto it, the tears now streaming down her face. She sat like that for several minutes, before a thought crossed her mind.

Maybe these aren't my true emotions, either. Maybe whatever caused Vanessa to act the way she did is also affecting me.

She found herself latching onto that thought as though it were a lifejacket, remembering the way Vanessa had looked at her, seemingly compelled to move against her will. She'd been almost zombie-like, saying she had to touch her. Maybe this was the same thing. Maybe whatever force was here brought out their deepest, darkest needs. For Vanessa, it was her need to be physically close to Emma Jane, but Emma Jane's need was deeper. Having been alone most of her life, the feelings of loneliness due to her isolation were what over-whelmed her.

Emma Jane straightened up on the bench, looking out across the beautiful ink pots with eyes that were now bone dry. Yes, she'd been alone for as long as she could remember. Yet one day, even if she and Vanessa couldn't be together, she'd still see her family in the afterlife. She was never completely alone, even if it sometimes felt that way. Emma Jane closed her eyes and focused on finding her center then began to meditate. She controlled her breathing while she sat motionless on the bench, breathing in and out until the sadness returned to its usual, more bearable levels. Once she felt she'd achieved control, she opened her eyes to see Vanessa walking toward her in her human form. Emma Jane tensed.

Vanessa held her hands up in front of her palms up, stopping several feet away. "It's okay, Emma Jane, I'm okay now. That was bizarre. I know I love being close to you, but that was like, a thousand times stronger and so, so *painful*!" She shook her head, examining Emma Jane with concern. "Are *you* alright? You look like you've been crying. I hope I didn't make you..."

Emma Jane shook her head. "It wasn't you, don't worry. I think that whatever power made you feel the way you did also caused me to have a similar issue, only mine was extreme loneliness instead of the need to touch you. I've never felt that depth of isolation before and it was horrible."

Emma Jane shuddered as she recalled the crushing anguish that had gripped her. It wasn't a feeling she ever wanted to experience again.

Vanessa looked around the peaceful clearing. "Well, here we are, I guess. It sounds like the feeling has passed for both of us now, but what are we supposed to see here? Is this it? I mean, it's pretty, but I don't see anything that looks like a talisman."

Emma Jane followed Vanessa's gaze as she examined their surroundings, but her vision once again was limited to viewing the faint glow of the animals and plants that were sleeping nearby. "I'm not sure. Evelyn hinted we'd find an amulet or talisman, but didn't tell us where to search or what it even looked like. Maybe we should look for a cave or hiding place of some sort. Why don't we split up? We can start here and go in opposite directions and meet in the middle." Emma Jane looked around the clearing again and nodded. "It's not that big, so we'll still be able to see each other. I'll go clockwise and you can go counterclockwise."

"Sounds good. Be careful and don't touch anything at all, okay? We'll just look, then call the other one over if we find something that seems out of place," Vanessa replied.

They parted to walk around the snowy clearing, moving slowly through the pillowy snow. It wasn't very deep, and was more of a nuisance than an obstruction, but the crunch of the snow echoed like gunshots in the quiet clearing. They searched fruitlessly, finding nothing that seemed out of place or caught their eye.

"It's not going to happen," said Vanessa, when they returned to their starting position. "Whatever it is we're looking for, I don't think we're going to find it like this."

Emma Jane exhaled, her frustration bubbling over. "So now what? This has got to be the place. We've encountered two bears and we've been emotionally devastated. Is there a third thing that we have to do?"

Emma Jane looked around the clearing with full-blown irritation, beyond seeing the beauty of the location, even had she been able to fully appreciate it.

"Not to mention all the work it was just to get to this far," Vanessa added.

Emma Jane sighed and looked at Vanessa. "Maybe I was hoping for too much from today. We should go back."

Vanessa stared at her with shock, her eyebrows shooting up underneath her wool hat. "What? No way! After all that? Absolutely not. I'm going to sit my butt right down on this bench and stay until something else mystical happens. I can't believe you'd be willing to give up, after everything we've already been through."

As she spoke, she moved to sit on the bench and unzipped her jacket. Emma Jane sat beside her, but left enough space so that she didn't accidentally brush against her.

"What if we aren't worthy and that's why they haven't appeared? The spirit of Big Bear was supposed to be here..." Emma Jane trailed off sadly, adding, "it's all my fault. I wasn't strong enough."

Vanessa looked at her, eyes wide as she shook her head. "Seriously? *You're* going to say that? The girl who's been alone since she was twelve, hunting witches, demons, and all things dark in the night? The girl who ran away in fear that she'd hurt me, then came back, when trying is the scariest thing in the world?" she said, conviction ringing in her voice. "The same girl I watched go toe-to-toe with a human-shaped rug-monster yesterday? No, you aren't lacking strength, but maybe you have the same problem that I do, after all."

"What problem do you mean?" Emma Jane saw the belief behind Vanessa's words and what she'd said rang true to her hopeful ears.

"I've always leapt before I looked, " said Vanessa, "wanting everything to happen immediately, impatient for the next great thing to occur. I've been particularly guilty of that with you, Emma Jane." Vanessa flashed a rueful smile, shrugging before she continued. "I've wanted to be close to you so much, to touch you, to just hold you, that sometimes I've felt everything was unfair and I'd get angry, feeling I *deserved* to be allowed and able to touch you. But maybe that's just my pride and not what I need to focus on. Maybe I need to accept this is just how my life is, at least for now. Maybe one day it will change. Maybe we'll find this amulet, but maybe we won't. I feel blessed right now just to have had this amazing day with you and to have met you in the first place. Maybe this Bear guy will show up today, maybe we'll never see him, but either way I got to hike in beautiful winter woods, in a breathtaking mountain range, with the most amazing person I've ever met. I have an entire week to spend with you alone, away from work and reality, and that's all the beauty I'll ever need."

Emma Jane felt tears build behind her eyes. The pressure gathered force as Vanessa spoke. She was right. They'd been so focused on each other and on getting to the goal that she'd lost sight of the reason why they were there in the first place. Why did everything have to be right now? Sure, it was hard not moving their relationship further, but how many couples kept chaste, hardly touching or sharing physical love until they were married years later, and still had amazing relationships?

"Thanks, Vanessa. I needed to hear that. You're right, I can wait. Being with you like this is the best experience I've had in a long time. It's enough for me too."

As she said the words, a sense of peace wrapped around her. It felt as though she'd reached the end of a long journey and was returning home for the first time in ages.

A sudden chill caused her to shiver as the bright winter sun passed behind a cloud. Curious, she squinted at the emerald pool and noticed an odd shimmer on the surface. The disturbance became larger, expanding outward in a fine, glowing mist.

"Do you see that, Vanessa?" she whispered.

Complete silence descended on the clearing, as though cotton had covered her ears. The birds stopped singing, highlighting her sense of altered reality. Vanessa nodded slowly, not taking her eyes away from the eerie glow.

"Yeah, I do. What do you think it is?"

Emma Jane shook her head as she watched the shimmer hover above the shifting liquid of the pool, before coalescing into the semi-solid form of a man. It became more defined as it moved away from the water, coming to rest on the ground in front of the pool. In front of them was a man, dressed simply in traditional leggings with a buffalo robe and moccasins. His face was solid and chiseled, as though he'd emerged from the mountain itself.

Emma Jane got up from the bench and approached, stopping a few feet away from the man. She bowed her head respectfully and spoke while avoiding eye contact, keeping her head lowered as Samuel had always insisted upon when speaking with an elder.

"Greetings, Mistahi-maskwa. We are here to learn from you, if you wish to share your wisdom with us, though we be unworthy to receive it. I have brought sweetgrass and tobacco in thanks for honoring us with your presence."

Vanessa stood up, moving to stand behind Emma Jane.

"Am I supposed to say something? I don't know what to say," she murmured.

Emma Jane shook her head almost imperceptibly, but Vanessa understood and fell silent. They waited, watching as the spirit of Big Bear moved closer then stopped. He stood and watched them with an unreadable expression for several minutes while the sun stayed hidden. The shadows created an eerie atmosphere, which surrounded him like a cloak.

"You have come seeking a treasure."

Emma Jane looked up briefly then bowed again in acknowledgment. "Yes, we have, *kihtehayah*, but we have discovered the treasure was with us this whole time. We hope we haven't disturbed you from your rest, or bothered you by our presence in your mountains."

Big Bear nodded in approval. "I am pleased. Your journey of discovery has indeed been fruitful. You have shown respect to the grizzly spirit and learned to harness your own emotions, a difficult task many people never accomplish. You have rid the mountain of an evil spirit which has dwelled within the rocks for centuries. As a reward for your service and your bravery, you will find a pebble beside the green pool that is different from the others. You will know it at once.

Place it on a rawhide string for the raven to wear. It will provide great protection and can only be removed by her hand. You both have much to accomplish to balance the world and this stone shall help you on your path. While your way will be rocky you will travel it together, as long as the raven keeps the talisman close to her heart."

"Thank you..." Emma Jane started, but at that moment the sun broke through the clouds and temporarily obscured her spirit vision in a way she'd never experienced. When she opened her eyes, Big Bear was gone. She turned to Vanessa and they shared a moment of silence while they processed what had happened.

"He came after all. That's cool," said Vanessa, starting for the pool. "Let's look for the pebble!"

Emma Jane shrugged. "That's our target, and our reward, if he wasn't just a shared hallucination."

Vanessa laughed, as they hurried to the green pool from which Big Bear had just materialized.

"I'm pretty sure that happened. Shared hallucinations usually involve some peyote or LSD and it hasn't been that sort of quest so far." Vanessa raised an eyebrow. "You don't have any peyote on you, do you?"

Emma Jane gave her a look. "Really? We went through customs. You think I'm crazy enough to chance that going through security?"

Vanessa laughed and shook her head, waving away Emma Jane's indignant tone. Her mood had returned to the same hopeful one she'd almost flown up the mountain with that morning. They spent several minutes looking diligently under every piece of dried grass and each of the snowy chunks surrounding the pool until Vanessa spotted a glimmer of a dark green, sitting just inside the water.

She looked at Emma Jane with trepidation, biting her lip. "I think that's what we want, but is it safe to touch the water again?"

Emma Jane wrinkled her nose. "I think so. The last time was about testing us, not because of the water itself. I'm almost certain. After all, tourists come here by the score and no one has reported any mass delusions or weird events before or there'd be warning signs up beside the water. Go ahead, pick it up."

BIG BEAR
CHAPTER 10

Vanessa leaned over, feeling nervous as the cool water covered her hand. It wasn't cold enough to be painful, but it was cold enough to encourage her to move quickly. She grasped the dark spring green stone on the bottom of the pool, bringing it out and holding it up to her face to examine it more closely. It was smooth, shaped like a tear drop but with the unexpected feature of a hole at the narrow end, like it was created to be worn. She held it up for Emma Jane to see.

"It's not very exciting. It's pretty though."

She rolled it around in her hand, feeling the cool stone calm her at the mere sensation in her palm. She wondered exactly what this rock was supposed to do to keep her safe from Emma Jane. She looked at the beautiful woman next to her. Curiosity and need urged Vanessa to try it to see if it worked.

"Should we test it? See if it protects me?"

Vanessa watched Emma Jane, sure that her emotions were written on her face, and was relieved to see the same emotion, albeit tempered with caution, reflected back.

"Yes, but not here. You don't see anything else that could be the right stone?"

Vanessa shook her head. "No, this one feels right to me. I don't see anything else remotely close to being 'special' and Big Bear said we'd know it on sight."

Emma Jane nodded. "Okay, in that case, let's go back to the bed and breakfast. If it doesn't work, I don't want to chance accidentally draining you at the top of a mountain. At least if we're somewhere populated, we're closer to getting help if..." Emma Jane trailed off, hope warring with her practical nature that was more used to disappointment than happiness.

Vanessa quashed her own excitement, telling herself there was no need for impatience at this stage. If it worked, it was only a little while longer. And if it didn't, Emma Jane's logic would be much appreciated.

"Okay, let's go back now then. I want to see if it works as soon as possible. Like, yesterday. Do you have any rawhide?"

Vanessa wondered where they could get a piece, so that the stone would be exactly the same as what the spirit told them it needed to be. Maybe it needed a cord to fully activate the magic, in which case they should probably get it first.

"There's a bunch of shops on Main Street, isn't there? We can get the rawhide before we try it out," said Emma Jane. "Just in case."

Vanessa agreed. "My thoughts exactly. Follow me. It's a long walk back and its getting dark."

BIG BEAR
CHAPTER 11

M ain Street in Banff during shoulder season wasn't all
that bustling, although because it was a weekend
there were still a fair number of people walking up and down
the sidewalks. Vanessa noticed the Christmas decorations
for the first time, surprised to realize it was almost December. She didn't know where the time had gone. It felt like
everything had piled together into a single week and now the
year was pretty much over. She looked at Emma Jane beside
her, grinning at her stunned expression.

"Are you okay?" Vanessa asked.

Emma Jane startled at the question. "What? Oh, yeah,
I'm fine. I was just looking at everything. I don't go shopping
much so I may not be the best judge of this, but damn, is this
place touristy. Even with my vision being the way it is this
place is bright. Look over there."

Emma Jane pointed to a window display with various animals wearing clothing saying they'd been to Banff, or Canada, or Alberta, or some mutant combination of all three. It
was garishly loud to Vanessa. She wondered what it looked
like to Emma Jane to have captured her attention so intensely
when she couldn't see inanimate objects very well.

"Yeah, the wharf is like that in San Francisco as well, but I didn't take you to those areas. Most really scenic locations seem to have stores whose sole purpose is to capture the tourist dollar in some way. But that isn't the store we need. I'm hoping this one here will be able to provide us with a rawhide cord."

Vanessa pointed out a jewelry store across the street advertising fossils. They used the crosswalk, entering the store just as the clerk was preparing to close the doors. She was an older woman with white hair in a bun, wearing an atrociously ugly Christmas sweater. She wore a name tag that said 'Flo', and gave them a sour look as she paused, blocking their entrance.

"We close in five minutes. Can I help you with something?"

The tone of her voice didn't suggest helpfulness, but Vanessa gave her a sparkling smile anyway. She found it was easier to take people at face value when they were being snarky than to comment on it.

"Why, thank you so much! That would be great. I'm looking for a rawhide cord that I can use to hang this stone from."

Vanessa displayed the green stone with the small hole for the woman to see and she huffed, but nodded.

Flo huffed, but nodded. "Over here. I was hoping to not have to use the register again tonight," she grumbled under her breath to no one in particular.

Vanessa looked at the small selection, picking up a creamy strip of tanned leather that felt soft but strong and held it up, sliding the end through the hole. It fit perfectly, with just enough room for the stone to move easily while remaining secure.

Emma Jane nodded. "That's perfect. I can tie it up for you, if you'd like."

Emma Jane's face was a swirling mix of hope, fear, and attraction which drew Vanessa closer, until the sound of the woman's strident voice behind them brought her back to her surroundings.

"Is that the right one? How would you like to pay?" Flo's demanding voice broke the moment and Vanessa nodded, answering Emma Jane as she walked toward the register where the woman stood waiting for her impatiently.

"As soon as we pay. Let's put it on outside. We don't want to keep Flo waiting, after all."

She winked at Emma Jane before focusing her attention back on the transaction. The second the purchase was complete they were whisked out of the store. As they regrouped on the sidewalk, they heard the click of the lock as the closed sign flipped over.

Vanessa held out the cord for Emma Jane. "Well, she was lovely," Vanessa quipped, rolling her eyes. "Anyway, here it is."

The foggy spring green stone became infinitely more elegant once it was on the rawhide cord.

As Emma Jane took it from Vanessa, her hands were shaking. "Let's see if this works. It doesn't look like much, but sometimes the most powerful things don't."

She placed the cord around Vanessa's neck from behind while Vanessa scooped her hair out of the way. Emma Jane's hands continued to tremble as she tied a knot, then doubled it for strength. To Vanessa, the warmth of her fingers touching her neck felt marvelous. While it had only been a few days, it seemed like years since the last time they'd touched. They'd even avoided small contact, such as a holding hands or brushing against each other accidentally in a hallway. Now that they had the stone, it was supposed to be safe and they should be able to touch like regular people- if Vanessa understood correctly how the stone worked. But the only way for them to find out was to take a chance.

Standing on a street corner in Banff, Canada, outside a shop run by a cranky old lady, Vanessa turned to face the object of her affection, lightly touching the stone that seemed familiar and alive around her neck.

"Now what? If Big Bear and Evelyn are correct, this should allow you to be near me without taking my powers. It should actually make it so that no one is able to take my powers, which is cool, but it's you that matters most. How shall we test it?"

Emma Jane looked at her with the magical swirling eyes that Vanessa loved so much. She took one step closer, then another. Vanessa's heart rate increased. She was unable to take a breath as she anticipated her approach. Then Emma Jane wrapped her arms around Vanessa and leaned toward her, tilting her face up. Vanessa leaned down to meet Emma Jane's lips as they kissed for the first time in days.

The cold air vanished as a warm blanket of feelings wrapped them together tightly. Vanessa felt the same intense need and attraction she'd had every time they'd kissed, but this time it was without the pulling sensation that simultaneously drugged her and dragged her down. This kiss was simply intoxicating. She sank deeper into the moment. She could have stayed in the warm waters of love forever had it not been for the rude intrusion of a car honk which pulled her back to reality.

Startled, she looked around, realizing the car had been honking at someone who hadn't used the pedestrian crosswalk appropriately. Even though not directed at them, the noise had lifted her from the embrace long enough to realize that they were still standing outside in the middle of a street in Banff, on a cold November night.

"Maybe we should go back to the bed and breakfast." Vanessa smiled at Emma Jane, incredibly happy and hopeful about the future that lay ahead.

"I think we should," Emma Jane agreed, a corresponding smile lighting her face. "How do you feel?"

She sounded so sweet and nervous that Vanessa couldn't resist leaning over to give her another quick kiss. "I feel like a million dollars. Let's go talk in private."

They smiled at each other, excitement at the possibilities for their relationship adding a giddiness to their love-struck grins.

BIG BEAR
CHAPTER 12

They caught the next taxi to pass them on the street. After a short ride back to the bed and breakfast, they paid the driver and raced upstairs without encountering anyone in the hallway. By mutual agreement, they went to Vanessa's room first. Looking around the room, Vanessa saw her stuff was scattered everywhere again, and a flush of embarrassment colored her cheeks.

"Give me a minute to tidy in here and freshen up. We've been outside all day and I'd love a quick shower. Then we can order room service and...hang out."

Vanessa blushed as she stuttered over the last two words. She didn't want to push anything, but at the same time, she wanted to be with Emma Jane in whatever capacity she was ready for. Emma Jane smiled back, appearing every bit as anxious to spend time together as Vanessa was.

"That sounds good. I'll do the same and come back when I'm clean. Did you want to order food first, or wait until...later?" Emma Jane paused, stumbling over the last word as well. She blushed and shook her head as rueful laughter bubbled out.

"Just come back. We can order from here. Together."

"Together." Emma Jane repeated the word, savoring it.

Vanessa shivered at the warm, deep throatiness of the promise she heard hidden in Emma Jane's voice before she left the room.

As soon as the door was closed, Vanessa went into overdrive. She rushed around the room, shoving clothes back into her suitcase and clearing the counters. The room had a nice sitting area, but she'd somehow managed to occupy every square inch of it with her stuff, so the process took several minutes. She jumped into the shower once she was done, washing away the sweat and the smell of the outdoors and replacing it with the scent of a fruity body wash instead.

The hot water relaxed her while also heating her blood, making her anticipation of spending the night with Emma Jane even more intense. She'd never wanted to spend the night with anyone so much, had never felt such a strong yearning, even with Dave in high school, when she'd been a hormonal teenager in love for the first time. The fierceness of her need shook her. After so many years of existing in a gray world of disinterest when it came to romantic feelings, she was suddenly living in Technicolor.

She stepped out of the shower, quickly drying off and putting on a comfortable pair of pajamas. They weren't overtly sexy, but she loved the way the soft fabric made her feel. She brushed out her hair, removing most of the wetness by towel drying and had just put on tinted lip gloss when a knock on the door interrupted her racing thoughts. As she went to answer it, she felt as nervous as if she was on a first date with a big-name movie star.

"Hey."

Emma Jane's rich voice set Vanessa's nerve endings on fire, causing a blush to creep up her neck to her face as she stepped back from the door, allowing her to enter.

"Hey, yourself. Come in. Did you want to order something to eat first, or just...hang out?" Vanessa gulped, finding her mouth suddenly dry with a mixture of anticipation, nerves, and hope.

Emma Jane shook her head. "Let's talk first. We can order later, when we get hungry."

Vanessa followed Emma Jane to the cute love seat that had a place of honor beside the window. It was a cozy sitting area, meant for cold nights with hot cocoa and was the perfect place for a couple to snuggle, if they could touch each other normally, of course. Vanessa had spent the first two nights at their lodgings longing for the chance to do just that and now she could finally try it out.

They sat on the couch awkwardly until Emma Jane reached out and touched the stone without warning. The rawhide strip was soft against Vanessa's skin and the stone was smooth, but strangely warm. It seemed to give off a gentle pulse of energy, which Vanessa chalked up to it being a mystical object. She didn't feel any different wearing it and she knew by the look on Emma Jane's face that she, too, was still skeptical regarding whether it would actually work.

"What are you thinking?" Vanessa asked softly, as Emma Jane silently examined the stone.

"I'm just wondering how such a small, ordinary looking object can keep you safe from me. Wondering if it's even safe for me to be here now. Wanting to find out but scared to be disappointed and terrified that I'll hurt you."

Vanessa fell into her swirling eyes for the hundredth time, feeling the same worries as Emma Jane, but as impatient as always. She knew that even if it didn't work or couldn't help, she'd risk it a hundred times anyway. She might be willing to live life on the periphery of Emma Jane's touch, but by God, if she didn't have to, she wasn't going to.

"There's only one way to find out."

Vanessa felt the words leave on the barest whisper of breath as she fell into the orbit of Emma Jane. First her head, then her entire body followed cautiously, but inexorably. As she slid closer, her heart sang with a repeating refrain of joy that this was actually happening, that Emma Jane was actually touching her.

Throwing caution to the wind, Vanessa leaned in for a kiss. Fire bloomed, hotter than hot chocolate, more comfortable than her pajamas. Vanessa wrapped her arms around Emma Jane, drawing her closer against her heart. Her warm body finally, wonderfully, pressed against Vanessa's, their kiss evolved into hands, arms, and legs, touches and embraces, and became a never-ending discovery of delight. Vanessa sank into the intoxicating, mild-altering drug of love, feeling her soul fly free of her body, before coming back down to earth exhausted but whole for the first time in her life.

As her breathing settled, she gave Emma Jane one more kiss, feeling the same urgency almost overwhelm her again. She pushed it down for later in order to say the important thing that tugged at her mind and to ask the most important question of all.

"I love you, Emma Jane."

Vanessa cradled the warm woman in her arms, resting her head against Emma Jane's. She breathed in the special fragrance of earth, clean air, and something completely unique to Emma Jane. She'd recognize her by that smell alone and knew she would follow her anywhere she went.

"I love you, Vanessa. I can't...I..."

Emma Jane's words stuck in her throat and Vanessa watched as tears flooded her eyes, rolling down the high cheekbones she loved so much. She tenderly kissed each one before looking into her eyes.

"What are you crying about? I feel amazing, better than I've ever felt. I could climb that mountain outside, I could run a marathon," Vanessa said, smiling, then added, "and I can do all of it while being right beside you." She touched the green stone with reverence. "It works, you know. I mean, we can check with Cat or Evelyn to know for sure, but I don't feel tired and I don't feel drained. I feel whole. And happier than I've ever been. So why are you so sad? Did I...." Vanessa trailed off, wondering if she'd done something in her awkwardness and the newness of the experience.

"I'm not used to..." Emma Jane shook her head before kissing her, leaning her forehead against Vanessa's. "No. You were wonderful. It, you, everything, was amazing."

Emma Jane leaned back to look at her again and Vanessa watched as a blush crept over her face now as well. "I'm just so happy right now. I don't think I've ever been happy, but now I'm worried that because I know what it feels like, I'll never be able to live without you. I don't think I can be that strong again. I don't know how I'll ever leave you, even to do the work I have to do. And if anything ever happened to you, I know I couldn't go on."

Vanessa held on to Emma Jane as tightly as she could, knowing she'd hold her forever if that was within her power.

"You don't have to leave me. Ever. We can work around things. My career has some built-in flexibility and we can figure the rest out as we go. I don't want to be apart from you either." Vanessa reluctantly pulled away from the hug to look at Emma Jane's face again, memorizing every feature before her words escaped with a mind of their own. "This is forever. We're two halves of a whole."

Emma Jane's face crumpled again, but this time Vanessa knew it was happiness creating the tears that fell. Their mouths met again, tears adding a special richness that was soon engulfed by another wave of love which overwhelmed them and carried them away into the night.

THE MORNING SUN ROSE over the mountains, sending bright rays of gold into the bedroom through the checkered curtains. Vanessa thought they looked quaint and rustic in the dawn's light as she stretched luxuriously in bed. She bumped into someone's arm and reality returned with a rush of happy disbelief. Rolling over she smiled, biting her lip at the sight before her.

Emma Jane was still sleeping soundly, her hair in disarray around her upper arms and shoulders, hiding most of what wasn't covered by the sheets under its dark, velvety weight.

Instead of getting up, Vanessa curled into bed around her love, spooning her while she slept and watching as the sun outside her window began its daily climb into the heavens.

Was it only a few weeks since she'd been devastated when this amazing woman had tried to run away, out of the very real fear that she'd accidentally hurt or kill her? Right from the beginning, they'd been so drawn to each other it had been difficult to resist the attraction. It had seemed impossible, but after everything that happened they'd magically found the answer to their prayers. Vanessa fingered the warm green stone nestled between her breasts close to her heart, closing her eyes with wonder as she sent out a prayer.

Thank you. Thank you for everything.

Vanessa wasn't sure who she was thanking, whether it was God, Big Bear, Evelyn, Robin, or the universe, but it didn't matter. She was in the one place she'd never known she wanted to be and now never wanted to leave. She was with her other half. She caressed Emma Jane's shoulder, softly brushing her hair away. Vanessa sighed with contentment. Everything was perfect.

Except one small thing, but it was a crazy thought. Vanessa looked down at Emma Jane's sweet, strong face. Would she agree? Vanessa leaned closer, kissing her neck to wake her in a way she knew would delight. Emma Jane made a small purr of approval, moving against Vanessa sleepily before slowly turning to look at the source of her awakening, eyes still cloudy and soft from sleep.

"Good morning, love," said Emma Jane, yawning as she rubbed her eyes clear of the sleep that blanketed them.

Vanessa drew her closer, holding onto her as if she was a fragile ornament that would break if she let go. "Good morning."

Vanessa kissed her softly, falling under Emma Jane's spell once more. When they were finally ready to get up, it was much later and they only moved then because they were starving and needed food. They showered separately to avoid distraction, then got dressed.

"Let's eat out," said Vanessa. "I want a change of scenery, in case we end up spending the rest of the week in the room."

Vanessa gave Emma Jane an impish smile which made her laugh.

"You are a bad girl," said Emma Jane, then she smirked. "Bring it on. I'll raise you a week in here for the rest of your life."

Vanessa stopped, turning back from opening the door to face Emma Jane with a serious look on her face as her love uttered the words she'd been unable to find.

"If you're asking, I accept."

Emma Jane stopped, eyes wide. "Do you mean..."

Vanessa nodded, moving to stand across from her, then grasping Emma Jane's hands and bringing them up to her heart. "I want to be with you forever. If you're serious about the rest of my life, I'd love to add a ring or two to this necklace."

She watched as emotions flew across Emma Jane's face like a fast-moving prairie storm, overjoyed to see the moment when they coalesced into a decision.

"Let's do it. You already own my heart. I'd promise a thousand forevers to have the rest of you."

It was Vanessa's turn to shed tears of joy. Her life changed, becoming perfect in that instant. They embraced passionately, the excitement of a promise of forever carrying them away again

BIG BEAR
CHAPTER 13

Vanessa smiled as Emma Jane walked down the airport gangway independently. She'd offered to hold her hand for support, but Emma Jane was way too proud for that. Instead, while she'd been a little shaky in the knees and paler than usual, she'd walked proudly off the plane into the airport, promptly bee-lining it to the nearby Starbucks.

"Was the flight better this time?" Vanessa watched as Emma Jane carefully sipped hot chocolate, then looked at her.

"No, not really," said Emma Jane, giving her a rueful smile. "I mean, it was nice to have you next to me on the plane, but I don't think flying is something I'll get used to anytime soon. If we were meant to fly, we'd have wings."

Vanessa raised an eyebrow, causing Emma Jane to laugh.

"Well, okay, you already have wings. It's completely different. That did help a little, actually. It crossed my mind more than once that if the plane crashed, you might be able to fly us to safety. Unless you were dead, in which case I wouldn't want to live anyway."

She spoke matter-of-factly, and Vanessa knew she was telling the truth, as morbid as it sounded to her. "Yikes. I'm not sure what to say to that. Thank you? Or that's incredibly disturbing?"

Emma Jane shrugged. "It is what it is."

Vanessa rolled her eyes as they headed for baggage claim. Emma Jane had her cane out again since they were in public, but otherwise the two girls were completely indistinguishable from any of the other travelers streaming in all directions through the airport. A glint of light sparkling from Emma Jane's left hand caught her eye, causing joy to warm her chest for the thousandth time.

It wasn't much, but it had been what Emma Jane had wanted. They'd spent a week in Banff playing tourist and had gone to the hot springs as Vanessa had initially planned. They'd also had one very special moment at the top of the mountain, which was witnessed by employees from the company they'd booked for the ceremony.

It had taken most of the remainder of the week to arrange everything they'd needed, including the paperwork, licenses, and venue. Vanessa had been surprised how much she enjoyed the details of what she'd normally have found to be frustratingly slow and tedious administrative details. Yet for some reason, the knowledge that everything she was doing was to tie them together forever had lifted her spirits and she'd loved every minute of it. They'd gone to every jewelry store in the small tourist town, the sheer number of which they hadn't been prepared for. Vanessa had chosen an emerald stone to complement the necklace as her symbol of love, but Emma Jane had selected a deep blue sapphire that matched the color of Vanessa's eyes. She'd also chosen it because of the stone's association with wisdom, love, and commitment.

Vanessa remembered the day with crystal clarity and knew that every moment was now locked forever in her mind. They'd gone to the Fairmont Banff Springs Hotel for the actual ceremony, cancelling their reservation at the bed and breakfast for the final few days they were in Banff. While it was more expensive to stay at the old hotel, first built by the Canadian Pacific Railway in 1887, the place was magnificent. Vanessa's romantic side felt that it was the next best thing to getting married in a Scottish castle.

The weather had been beautiful, as though the spirit of Big Bear was blessing their day. The sun, always so elusive in San Francisco, had shone brightly over the crisp white snow, while the mountains outside the elegant room in which they made their promises to each other rose up as solid and eternal as their vows. With the presence of only the required witnesses, Vanessa and Emma Jane stood together with all of creation smiling down on them. They promised to love and cherish each other, gave each other rings to symbolize their commitment and promises for life, and finally sealed their vows with a sweet kiss.

And now as they returned home, to their home, Vanessa smiled and looked at her finger. They hadn't called anyone to tell them about what they'd done in Banff. Vanessa hadn't wanted to be interrogated about what she knew would be seen as a crazy caper. Not only was it sudden and unpredicted, but her parents hadn't even met Emma Jane yet. Vanessa hoped they'd be okay with it, but realized it was more likely that they'd be upset they hadn't been at the ceremony.

Vanessa had known all the possible repercussions, deciding to go ahead anyway because she'd wanted it to be only the two of them when it happened. She still remembered the craziness of Mai and Jake's wedding day far too clearly and never wanted anything like that for herself or Emma Jane. Marriage was two people vowing to be together forever. The idea of everyone she knew being there, at such a private and special time, made her feel constrained. She didn't want to get married because of other people's expectations. She'd wanted to do it just for Emma Jane, to show her exactly how much she meant to her.

"What do you think Cat will say?" Emma Jane sounded nervous, which brought Vanessa back to the present.

"Hmm? What? Oh, Cat?" Vanessa smiled at the small emerald on her left hand again. "She's going to be mad we didn't call her. Otherwise, I think she'll be happy for us."

Vanessa grabbed Emma Jane's suitcase off the carousel, but Emma Jane didn't appear convinced when she stood up. "Okay. Did she say she'd come pick us up?"

Vanessa shook her head. "No, I told her we'd cab it. I thought it would give us time to get home and relax prior to getting bombarded by questions." She bit her lip. "I also kind of booked the return flight for when I knew she'd be in school and maybe kind of didn't tell her exactly when it got in so that she didn't try to surprise us."

Emma Jane raised her eyebrows and Vanessa grimaced.

"Okay, maybe I'm nervous too. I want to have you in my room at home and just hold you for a while longer before we have to get back to reality."

Emma Jane's expression changed from judging to loving and she leaned over to give Vanessa a quick peck on the lips. "You're funny. Let's hit the taxi stand then, because I can't wait to cross the threshold with my wife for the first time."

BIG BEAR
CHAPTER 14

An hour later, Vanessa unlocked the door to her apartment and was bombarded by the familiar sights and smells. She closed her eyes and inhaled deeply, exhaling with satisfaction at the air that almost seemed to be welcoming her back. She knew she'd have to call her parents, followed by her work to find out her schedule, but for now she wanted to rejoice in the moment. They'd packed light for their trip, so they each only had one suitcase to bring into the bedroom. It was strange, unpacking their clothes together. For the first time ever, they'd be sharing Vanessa's room. The bed was a queen size, so space wasn't a problem. However, when Emma Jane had stayed at the apartment before the trip, Vanessa had slept in the spare bed in Cat's room. Not only would Vanessa be getting her bed back, it now also came complete with a wife.

"Come here," Vanessa said, holding out her hand for Emma Jane.

Once she accepted it, Vanessa drew her into an embrace. As they stood together holding each other, Vanessa could feel Emma Jane's heartbeat against her and the same familiar melting sensation came from within.

"I love you, Emma Jane."

Emma Jane pressed herself more tightly against Vanessa, entwining herself as completely as she could. "I love you too, Vanessa."

They stood silently, holding each other while Vanessa thought about how completely at home she was now. She didn't think it was possible for her heart to have any more room for happiness. As the warmth spread lower, she reached down to kiss her friend, her lover, her wife. Sinking into her forever home, she gave thanks to all the gods above and below and for all the circumstances that had brought them together.

A voice from the kitchen abruptly returned them to the present. "Hello? Vanessa? Emma Jane? Are you guys home? I can see your shoes in the kitchen."

The sound of Cat calling for them elicited a groan of frustration from Vanessa. She rested her forehead against Emma Jane's and whispered, "there isn't enough time to do what I'd like to do to welcome you home. I'll have to make up for it later." She leered, causing Emma Jane to swat her on the arm.

"Of course you will. I'm holding you to that."

The searing look Emma Jane gave her caused Vanessa to reconsider answering her sister, but she knew that Cat was relentless and would keep knocking on the door until she answered, which would completely destroy her mood. She gave Emma Jane a scorching look in return, then answered her sister's call.

"Hey, Cat, we're in here, unpacking."

Cat burst into the room, launching herself at Vanessa with an attack hug, before holding her out at arm's length to look at her. Delight lit her face. "You did it! Your aura looks amazing! I don't even have to give it a touch up. And Emma Jane, you look amazing too!"

Cat let go of Vanessa to grab Emma Jane in a tight hug, spinning her around before putting her down.

"Tell me all about the trip! You were so vague and frustrating while you were away. I was pretty close to coming to find you because of the lack of details you were feeding me."

Vanessa shrugged, giving her a half smile before responding airily. "It wasn't any of your business, little one. I was perfectly capable, as was Emma Jane, of keeping us safe."

Cat gave her an incredulous look.

"Okay, fine, fine. I know, I was vague on purpose. I didn't want you to worry," said Vanessa then paused, biting her lip. "Umm. I also...well, there's something else..." She hedged, looking to Emma Jane to see if she was going to hop in, but her new wife merely shook her head with amusement while she watched Vanessa fumble her words.

Cat looked at Vanessa suspiciously, then her eyes went wide and darted first to her hand, then to Emma Jane's hand, coming back to rest on her sister's face.

"What? No way!" Cat squealed, giving them both another hug before her expression changed. "Wait a minute. Is that an engagement ring or...?"

Vanessa looked at the ground and when she didn't answer, Cat hit her gently on the top of the head.

"Oh, you're going to be in so much trouble when Mom and Dad find out. Getting married without family present? What were you thinking?"

"I just wanted it to be the two of us. It was private and special and Emma Jane doesn't have any family, so it didn't feel right for me to have all you guys there if she didn't have anyone. We can have another ceremony as a celebration, but this one was about our promises to each other."

Cat rolled her eyes, but Vanessa was relieved to see her irritation had already faded. Cat usually had a slower fuse, so when it did go off, it could sometimes be days until she calmed down again.

"Fine. An acceptable response. But we're definitely having a party to celebrate. I'm not planning on getting married anytime soon, maybe never, so this could be it for Mom and Dad. You know that Dad needs his rituals and Mom needs to have her 'say yes to the dress' moment with at least one of us. Congratulations, you guys."

Cat smiled, taking both of their hands and inspecting the rings with a low whistle.

"These are really pretty. We have to call Mai and Zahara to let them know. They'll be so happy for you."

"What about Evelyn? Shouldn't we call her too?" Vanessa asked, confused why Cat hadn't mentioned her.

"No, she's still around. She's been in and out of the apartment all week."

"What? Why?" Vanessa asked, surprised.

She couldn't remember the last time Evelyn had hung out like that. Not since Scotland, when they'd first met Zahara and spent time at her parent's place watching movies.

Cat shook her head. "I don't know. She said she had some things to do, but I think it's because she's been having more bad dreams lately and it helps her to be near me."

Cat spoke seriously and Vanessa knew that she was worried. Evelyn's dreams had taken on a whole new quality since discovering she was the goddess of dreams, so bad dreams for her had an intensity other people would never experience.

"I'll call the others soon. Do you have plans for tonight? I was thinking we could go out to celebrate, maybe have sushi? Unless you'd rather do takeout?" asked Vanessa, surprised when Emma Jane shook her head.

"Let's do takeout, if that's okay. I need some time to decompress from everything and I'd love a quiet night in."

"Of course. We'll likely have more than a few celebratory dinners coming up in the future with friends and family."

Vanessa looked at Cat, who nodded her head emphatically. "We can totally do takeout tonight. I want all the details."

NIGHT FELL IN THEIR cozy apartment, with laughter and Chinese takeout adding spice to the evening. Cat and Vanessa laughed at stories of Emma Jane's past bloopers, while Cat embarrassed Vanessa with tales from their childhood in which she didn't come out looking like the strong and capable woman she currently was. They'd just finished eating when Evelyn came over, looking drawn and worried. Cat got up, while Vanessa and Emma Jane watched from the couch with concern.

"Are you okay?" Cat moved closer, resting her hand on Evelyn's shoulder while Vanessa watched, almost positive that Cat was sending healing energy into their tired friend.

Evelyn shook her head then sighed, as she looked at Cat with worry. "It's not me, I'm fine. It's Zahara. I've been seeing her in my dreams for the last few nights and I think she's in danger. I need to go and see what's happening in real life." Evelyn shook her head again, a scared look in her eyes. "I think something's coming after her, but everything's blurry, so I can't see what it is. Maybe if I can talk to her in person, I can figure out what's going to happen."

Cat gave Evelyn a hug before letting go. "How bad?"

Evelyn exhaled shakily. "I'm not sure. But I know it's big. I'm leaving for Scotland through Summerland tomorrow morning and I don't know when I'll be back."

Cat looked at Vanessa, who could tell that her sister was conflicted, but wasn't sure why.

"What is it?" Vanessa asked, curious what was going through her sister's mind.

"My last exam was yesterday. We don't start again until after winter break is over. I wanted to go with you to see Mom and Dad, to see their faces when you tell them the news, but..." Cat trailed off.

Vanessa knew exactly what she was thinking. "It's fine, Cat. I still have a few weeks of shooting left before I can take any more time off. I shouldn't have had time for a vacation right now, but with all the murders and stuff, shooting was off schedule and the director was overwhelmed. Be back for Christmas, if you can? Maybe we can have another small wedding celebration then."

Cat smiled gratefully before turning to Evelyn. "I'm coming with you."

Evelyn appeared taken aback. "What? No, I can't ask you to take time off school like that."

Cat shook her head, firming her jaw. "I just said I'm done for a few weeks. I can always come back before you, but I don't like the look on your face. I have a feeling my power may be useful for that reason alone. Zahara's my friend too. I can't let you go over to Scotland on your own. You'll need someone to watch your back," said Cat. She gave Evelyn a stern look, before adding more playfully, "besides, Mrs. Khan makes some truly delicious pakoras. I've missed them ever since we left. Give me an hour to pack my stuff and I'll be ready to go."

Evelyn smiled, shaking her head with amusement at Cat's reply. "I'd love to have you with me, so I won't say no. It'll be just like old times."

"Well, sort of," said Vanessa.

She got up from the couch to stand beside Cat and showed Evelyn her ring.

Evelyn took her hand, admiring the emerald. "Congratulations! I'm so happy everything worked out for you lovebirds. I'm sorry I couldn't say more before." Evelyn gave an apologetic shrug.

Vanessa wrinkled her nose. "I get it. You can't give away all the details or the outcome could change. Man, I prefer my powers to what you two got saddled with. I can fly and use the air as my toy, but have no pesky extra knowledge, which I much prefer."

Evelyn raised an eyebrow then looked at Emma Jane who was sitting on the couch watching them quietly.

"How are you making out, being surrounded by such a loud group?"

Emma Jane looked at her, calm radiating out from her. "I've never felt happier or more at home then I feel here. I'm so grateful for your help and can never repay you for what you've done for me."

Evelyn waved her thanks away. "Pshaw. Go on with you now. This was your destiny, you just didn't know it. I barely even told you where to look. You and Vanessa were the ones who came through all the obstacles and earned your happy ending."

Emma Jane dipped her head in acknowledgment. "Still, thank you a million times over. If you ever need help, I'll always be there for you."

"I'll remember that," Evelyn replied. "Still, you'll be busy on your own battlefront in the future, so we'll touch base when needed. For now, it's all good," she said, smiling.

"Most likely you're right. Evil never rests, unfortunately." Emma Jane looked wistful.

Vanessa crossed her arms firmly. "Well, I don't care what evil is doing. It's going to give Emma Jane the next few weeks off to enjoy married life before it comes knocking on our door. And that's an order."

Vanessa punctuated her sentence with a firm nod, causing Evelyn to shake her head and laugh.

"Well, of course! I'm sure things will conspire to give you a few day's rest. I'm going to go pack my things and head to bed early tonight. It's an eight-hour time difference from here to Edinburgh and I'm hoping if we leave first thing, we can be at the Khan's by supper tomorrow."

"Good idea," Cat agreed. "I'll pack my stuff too. Sorry I can't stay longer guys, but I think a few days, or weeks, of me being away will be a nice chance for you two to settle into married life. Send me a text if you need anything, okay?"

Vanessa and Emma Jane assured Cat they would, then said goodbye to Evelyn and goodnight to Cat, heading to bed themselves. They lay in the moonlight, holding each other while they both marveled over the fork in the road that had turned into their relationship. Neither of them had seen it coming, but it had arrived at a point when Vanessa had been lonelier than she'd ever been and when Emma Jane had completely given up on the thought of happily ever after. And now they lay together in complete contentment as the moon tracked over the clear and starry sky. They didn't know what tomorrow or the next day would bring, but tonight they were together.

Life was perfect.

THE WEDDING
CHAPTER 1

E mma Jane was nervous. She'd struggled to recognize the odd sensation at first. She was rarely anxious, but when she was, it was usually due to the possibility of a brutal, bloody sudden death, not a public event where people would merely be watching her speak. As she sat quietly and listened to the people milling around her, she couldn't help but wonder what exactly she'd gotten herself into.

"Absolutely not! If we're going to do this, we're going to do it right!"

Vanessa's firm tones intruded onto Emma Jane's silent reflection, causing her to smile despite the fact that she was on the verge of running away with her tail between her legs. You'd think after everything they'd already been through together that arranging a reception for Vanessa's family and friends to celebrate their elopement shouldn't be that big a deal. After all, they'd fought a witch and a yeti, spoken with the spirit of a powerful medicine man, and had already taken the leap into marriage without any hesitation.

Intellectually, Emma Jane knew that nothing was going to happen at the ceremony to change their union and told herself that everything would be fine. But, the knowledge she'd be surrounded by what seemed like every person Vanessa had ever met in less than twenty-four hours filled her with an unexpected amount of trepidation.

Perhaps it's because I've spent so much time alone, or maybe, it's because every time I've been near a large group of people something bad has happened.

"Emma Jane? What do you think?"

Emma Jane startled, turning her head to see Vanessa looking at her from across the room; her fists balled on her hips as she tapped the toe of her right foot.

Emma Jane groaned inwardly. While she hadn't been with Vanessa very long, she already knew that look far too well. That was the look of Vanessa on the verge of losing her patience. With an average bride, that might have meant a tantrum. With Vanessa however, it could mean an indoor tornado. Literally.

Emma Jane stood and quickly moved to stand at Vanessa's side, looping her right arm through Vanessa's left and giving her a quick side hug.

"I'm sorry, Vanessa. I was distracted by all the noise. What did you ask me?"

Emma Jane turned her cloudy eyes toward Vanessa, grateful to see the edge of irritation smooth out as Vanessa looked down. Her shoulders relaxed as she gave Emma Jane an apologetic half-smile, then rubbed her face with her other hand.

"Oh my God, Emma Jane. I don't know if I'm going to make it through tomorrow. What was I thinking? This is making me crazy!"

Emma Jane tried to give her a reassuring smile, but couldn't help that her thoughts closely mirrored Vanessa's.

"You were thinking that your mom and dad were disappointed they weren't there for the original wedding. You wanted to give them a more traditional service, so that they could celebrate our happiness with us, and you also wanted a pretty dress and a party with all your friends."

Emma Jane spoke the words by rote, having already had this discussion what felt like a thousand times over the last week, each time Vanessa began to panic about the big day. For someone who was an extrovert, loving crowds and all the attention that came with being an actress, Vanessa had surprised Emma Jane by being a complete bundle of nerves during the entire planning process. Apparently being extroverted did not correlate to enjoyment of the planning portion of the party.

Luckily for Emma Jane's sanity, and for the world at large remaining in one piece, they were going to have a simple service at their favorite local dim sum restaurant. The place held importance for the group of girls and their friendship, so when Cat initially suggested it as a possible location, Vanessa had leapt at the idea. It was the same restaurant where Vanessa's best friend had been proposed to by her husband, as well as a place where the girls had eaten many times after a long day of work or school. As their established gathering place for camaraderie and comfort food, the restaurant was seen as ideal for the occasion.

"IT'S PERFECT! I'LL see if Mai, Jake and the kids can come, and Zahara and... what did you say his name was?"

"Omar," Cat had answered helpfully.

Vanessa nodded. "Omar. Evelyn? Do you think Robin would come if you asked? He's been super important to me over the years, well, to all of us of course."

Evelyn shrugged noncommittally.

"I can ask him. But I know that *I* wouldn't miss it for the world. Something tells me it's going to be one hell of a reception."

Vanessa nodded eagerly. "Absolutely! Just think how cozy the ceremony will be if we move all the tables out of the way in the main room and put an aisle in the middle. We can have red and white poinsettias for flowers at the entrance and the front. It will be gorgeous!"

Evelyn had smiled mysteriously, but at the time, Emma Jane hadn't thought anything about it. But now, as Emma Jane watched Vanessa panic about the service that was only hours away, Emma Jane wondered if Evelyn's innocent smile had, in fact, been more cryptic than she'd appreciated. After all, Evelyn was known for having prophetic dreams which always came true. The only problem was that she didn't always share all the details with her friends, citing concern that she didn't want to compromise the end outcome of events.

Emma Jane glanced over to where Cat and Evelyn were standing with Mr. and Mrs. McLean. She narrowed her eyes as she considered her new friend, and sometime goddess, Evelyn. Due to Emma Jane's unique way of seeing the world, she was normally met with lights and darks, blacks and grays around normal people. Their energy was often a pale and unremarkable glow, hardly distinguishable from the plants and animals she viewed with her spirit vision. Since she'd met her new friends though, the world had exploded in colors and beauty. She still couldn't understand how she'd spent so long hunting by herself and then somehow ended up being so fortunate. To have fallen into such a warm and welcoming group would have been one thing, but to be surrounded by other women who also had serious power of their own and understood how hard life could be, had been a blessing from the Great Spirit himself.

The most important person of all, of course, being the enchanting woman who was standing right beside her, holding onto her waist as she bit her lip absently and regarded the decorations with a look of skepticism.

"I don't know, Emma Jane. It still doesn't look right to me."

Emma Jane gave her another squeeze, but was unable to help.

"Vanessa, I'm sure whatever you've done will be absolutely perfect. I wish I could help more, but you know, eyes." Emma Jane gestured at her cloudy, white eyes and Vanessa slumped against her.

"I'm sorry, Emma Jane. I don't know why I'm getting so unhinged about tomorrow. I guess I just want everything to be perfect. I want everyone in the whole world to know how much I love you."

Emma Jane gazed into Vanessa's deep blue eyes, then shook her head as she calmly reassured her.

"If this day is important to you, it's important to me. But Vanessa, I know how much you love me. I don't care what other people think. We're already married. This is just a big celebration so your friends and family can be a part of everything. We don't even have to do it. We could cancel everything and walk away."

Vanessa's head snapped back. Without warning, her eyes became dark and a little wild. "What do you mean? Are you crazy? Of course we have to do it! Everything's already paid for and half of the people I've invited have already arrived in the city. We can't turn back now!"

Emma Jane burst into laughter, shaking her head at Vanessa's surprised look.

"I'm sorry, but you make it sound like a life or death mission. It's hardly that, Vanessa. Think about how much we've already been through. Tomorrow will be a breeze."

Vanessa sighed, laying her head on Emma Jane's shoulder. "I know, you're right. It's not even like there's going to be that many people. I think only about," Vanessa paused, "two hundred or so? That isn't even everybody I work with."

She gave Emma Jane a brighter smile, not noticing the paleness of her face at the mention of how many people were expected. "Thanks for talking me down, Emma Jane. You're right. Everything will be absolutely fine. Once tomorrow's out of the way, we can finally relax."

Emma Jane smiled weakly, feeling as if she'd just started the fear-sweat she sometimes had before meeting a large opponent. "Exactly. Now, I think we should probably go home and try to get some sleep before our big day."

Vanessa nodded, dropping a light kiss on Emma Jane's forehead and pulling away from her arm link. "Sure, just let me speak with the head chef one more time, then we can leave. Why don't you go talk with my mom and dad for a few minutes? I'll be right back."

Emma Jane nodded, smiling as Vanessa headed back to the kitchen, then looked back toward where Peter and Mindy McLean were standing. Yesterday had been the first time she'd met them in person. They'd arrived the night before, and to Emma Jane's great relief, they'd rented the same apartment they'd stayed at the last time they'd visited Vanessa. It wasn't that Emma Jane didn't like them; they seemed like nice people, and she knew that because they were Vanessa and Cat's parents, they'd understand about the more special qualities Emma Jane possessed. But at the same time, she felt awkward and uncomfortable around them, mostly because she wasn't sure how they would react to the fact Vanessa and Emma Jane had eloped without speaking to anyone. When she'd actually met them, she'd felt even worse about eloping. While they'd been completely gracious and welcoming, Emma Jane knew Mindy in particular had been disappointed. She could tell Vanessa's mom had been hoping for a big wedding where she could pull out all the stops and Vanessa had been the daughter most likely to provide it for her. That is, until she'd chosen to elope with someone they'd never met.

Emma Jane took a deep breath for courage as she reluctantly sauntered over to the group. Peter was the first to notice her, greeting her with a warm smile.

"Hey, Emma Jane. How are you doing? Holding up okay?"

Emma Jane attempted to match his cherry greeting and wondered if it was entirely possible, as Peter was clearly happy about tomorrow. He had a light that shone brighter than most of the people she'd met, although not nearly as bright as those of her friends. It allowed her to see his blue eyes and features well enough to see where Vanessa got her striking good looks from.

"Yes, so far. Vanessa's anxious about tomorrow, but I'm sure that everything will be fine. I'm not much for socializing, so it's a little out of my wheelhouse."

Peter chuckled. "Oh, I know exactly how you feel." He gestured at his wife and then at Vanessa, giving Emma Jane a commiserating look. "I've been surrounded by women who enjoy a good party for quite a number of years now. Luckily, I have Cat." Peter winked at his more introverted child who smiled, but didn't interrupt. "Between the two of us, we've managed to find places to hide at nearly every party we've ever been subjected to."

Emma Jane laughed, suddenly picturing Cat and her father hiding at one of Mindy's art shows in a storage room.

"That sounds about right. Come to think of it, the first time I went to the bar with Cat she was quick to inform me where the best place to hide was."

Cat looked sheepish, but Peter threw back his head and laughed along with Emma Jane.

"It's a wonder we ever survived with our two happy extroverts to keep up with. Mindy and Vanessa are a lot alike that way." He shrugged. "But isn't that what they say? Opposites attract?"

Emma Jane nodded, feeling a comfortable sense of rapport developing with Peter just as Mindy protested.

"Hey! It hasn't been that bad. I mean, it's not like we're total party animals."

Peter grimaced at his wife's frown, hastening to add the qualifiers she obviously needed to smooth her ruffled feathers.

"Of course not, honey. But you know, both Cat and I would be happier locked in a room with a good book than to ever go to another party."

Mindy rolled her eyes as she turned to Emma Jane but grudgingly agreed.

"He's not wrong. Which makes tomorrow even more important."

Mindy took Emma Jane's hand, causing her to stiffen with surprise and concern. She'd already spoken to both Peter and Mindy about the fact that she sometimes inadvertently siphoned energy from others. She wasn't used to having people touch her without getting hurt, with the exception of Vanessa, and possibly Cat, who had her own built-in protection from Emma Jane's power. But before she could attempt to pull away, Mindy trapped her hand and squeezed firmly.

"I want you to know how honored I am to be here, to see you two together like this. I've never seen Vanessa so happy. I was worried about her when you first came into her life, especially when she called me so brokenhearted."

Emma Jane remembered that phone call and how it had changed everything for them. That had been the moment she'd decided to throw caution to the wind and try for a relationship with Vanessa.

"But you guys are absolutely perfect for each other."

Mindy gave Emma Jane a teary smile, and to her surprise, Emma Jane felt her own eyes sting from unshed emotion.

"Thank you for saying so, but-"

Emma Jane's words were cut off when Mindy shook her head quickly and squeezed her hand once more, adding emphasis to her words.

"No buts. I understand what a difficult decision it must've been for you." Mindy smiled nervously before abruptly changing topics. "Vanessa has told me you don't have any family of your own left. I know it's a bit quick but I'd like you to consider calling us Mom and Dad. I already think of you as another daughter, and I'm proud of who Vanessa has picked to spend her life with. If you ever need anything, give us a call anytime, day or night."

Emma Jane nodded. The lump in her throat made it impossible for her to speak as Peter added his affirmations.

"That goes double for me."

Cat smiled, looking at her mom's hands which still held Emma Jane's, then she winked at her new sister-in-law and put her arm around her mom to give her a hug. Emma Jane knew she was giving her a surreptitious burst of healing and was grateful. The main reason she didn't usually let people touch her was fear for their safety and now for the first time she could remember, she was getting more physical affection from people than she'd had since before her mom died. Having a sister-in-law like Cat to reverse the downside to her power was almost as amazing as finding Vanessa in the first place.

"Thanks, both of you. It may take me a little time to get used to calling you Mom and Dad." Emma Jane smiled, grateful to have been offered the option. "But I promise, I'll try. Is it okay if I call you Peter and Mindy though?"

Mindy laughed, retrieving her hand and waving it in the air. "Of course. We're trying to get the other girls to call us that too, but so far, it hasn't been going well."

Emma Jane chuckled. That explained why Evelyn kept calling them Mr. and Mrs. McLean, which felt oddly formal to Emma Jane, especially with how confident and forthright Evelyn was with everyone else.

Emma Jane looked around the room again and her attention caught at the sight of the familiar grey, shadowy outline of objects interspersed with the dazzling spirit energy of the people surrounding her. Everyone in her life was breathtaking in both their human and supernatural qualities. She knew, with a sudden clarity in the midst of the din of preparations, how incredibly blessed she was they'd all be here tomorrow to witness as she promised once again to love and honor Vanessa.

Life simply couldn't get any better.

THE WEDDING
CHAPTER 2

Vanessa wiped her palms along the sides of the white dress. When she realized what she'd done, she groaned and carefully examined the area for damage. Thankfully, the creamy white satin didn't show the evidence of her nervous perspiration. She turned from side to side, inspecting her appearance in the mirror again, and frowned. If she wasn't careful, she'd have to go on a diet. The last few weeks with Emma Jane, especially since their friends had arrived in town, had turned into a wild food-fest. It was funny how every time she got together with her girlfriends it seemed to involve dinner or drinks, or other high-calorie items. She sucked in her stomach as she contemplated the damage.

"Hey, how are you feeling? Ready for your big day?"

Vanessa turned to see Cat standing in the doorway of her bedroom, looking slightly uncomfortable in the dress Vanessa had picked out for her to wear. If this was as close to a real wedding day as she'd ever get, Vanessa insisted on doing it properly. That meant she got a white dress and all her friends had to get dolled up as well. Evelyn and Zahara had jumped at the chance, eager to have something pretty to wear, and Mai had accepted with quiet amusement. Cat, on the other hand, had put up a stronger protest. When she'd found out that Emma Jane wasn't planning to wear a wedding dress herself, she'd almost refused outright.

"How's that fair?" Cat had whined.

Vanessa shrugged. "It's her wedding ceremony, too. If she doesn't want to wear a white dress, she doesn't have to. However, that same liberty does not extend to my sister. You get to wear a dress because I say so, case closed."

Now, as Vanessa examined her sister, she couldn't help but think how beautiful she was. She was so used to seeing Cat dressed in jeans and a sweatshirt that Vanessa sometimes forgot her baby sister was gorgeous in her own right.

She'd never tell her so, but ever since they'd been kids Vanessa had been jealous of Cat's long red hair. More than half the world had black hair, but red hair really made a person stand out, something Vanessa would have appreciated far more than Cat ever had. It was ironic, really.

While Vanessa had been anxious, and probably verging on being a bridezilla over the previous few weeks, the one place she knew she'd done a great job was picking what her bridesmaids would wear. Along with her mother's artistic eye as a second opinion, the girls had all gone shopping at a bridal store which had come highly recommended by one of Vanessa's friends from work. Not only had the selection been outstanding, but they'd also done a stunning job with the alterations, all at a great price.

As it was a winter wedding, Vanessa had stuck with more muted colors for her theme. For Mai and Cat with their paler skin, she'd chosen a navy blue which highlighted their fairness and figures, and for Zahara and Evelyn, she'd gone with a ruby red which made their darker complexions pop.

She couldn't wait to see what they looked like in their dresses, but seeing Cat in hers confirmed her initial impressions from the bridal shop, and she knew the wedding pictures would be stunning.

"You look beautiful, Cat. But what did you do to your hair?"

Cat glanced down at her loose hair before looking back at Vanessa with confusion. "What? It's clean and not in a ponytail. Those were your only requirements."

Vanessa raised her eyebrows. "Must you be so literal? Okay, fine. Come over here."

She pointed at the bed and Cat stomped over, her gait belying the graceful lines bestowed upon her by the dress. Still, she knew better to object aloud to the direct order, especially on today of all days. Vanessa quickly brushed her sister's hair, then twisted it into a messy bun, allowing a few tendrils to escape, as if by magic.

"There, that's better," she pronounced, with satisfaction.

Cat stood up, peering into the full-length mirror with a look of shy astonishment. She touched her hair with surprise before looking at Vanessa. "I look really nice. Maybe I should wear my hair like this more often. It looks easy enough to do."

Vanessa smiled patiently at her self-effacing sister, wondering if she'd ever convince her to get out and meet people. "It is easy. And let's face it, the ponytail's getting old."

Cat rolled her eyes, reverting back to being a bratty little sister once more. "All right, I'll try to switch it up a bit more. I'm assuming you want me to put makeup on as well?"

Vanessa smiled, pointing back to the bed. "You guessed right."

Cat sat down again and Vanessa quickly applied a light layer of makeup, just enough to highlight her sister's eyes and unblemished fair skin. When she was finished, Cat looked the best she'd ever looked. Vanessa's heart warmed as she took in her sister's wide-eyed expression in the mirror.

"I wish you knew how beautiful you truly are."

Cat blushed, looking down at her hands before gazing back at Vanessa with a hopeful look on her face which surprised her. "Do you really think so? I mean, you're not just saying that, right?"

Vanessa shook her head, pulling her sister in for a quick hug. When she drew back, her eyes brimmed with tears.

"No, I'm not just saying that. I could get you a job acting in a heartbeat if you wanted one, but I'm so proud you're doing well in university."

While Vanessa had never been interested in continuing school after finishing grade twelve, she'd been impressed with her sister's dedication over the past three years. Especially with all the extracurricular activities she'd had to deal with in addition to studying, like battling witches and evil jinns. Vanessa didn't think she would've been able to handle everything with the same grace that Cat had.

But while still as poised as ever, Vanessa was suspicious that something was up with Cat. She spent more time at school than Vanessa thought was strictly necessary, but she'd never known her to date or hang out with friends outside of their little circle of gifted girls. Cat had been quieter over the past few months as well, more wistful, especially after she'd returned from her impromptu winter vacation with Evelyn and Zahara. Vanessa had been waiting for Cat to tell her what had been bothering her and was wondering if there was someone special Cat was crushing on. It was possible her sister had a secret romance and Vanessa was desperately curious to root out all the details. She knew her sister and something was definitely up, but the trick was to find out what.

Cat blushed. Vanessa knew she wasn't comfortable with compliments, and as Vanessa hardly gave them, she imagined her sister was a little surprised.

"Umm, thank you?"

Vanessa smiled, knowing today was going to be a tough one for her own makeup if getting her sister ready for the ceremony was causing her to tear up. So, she did what she did best. Deflected.

"Tell me about this guy at school." Vanessa figured she'd jump right in and see if she could shock Cat into revealing any details.

Cat looked startled, then began to stutter. "What guy? There's no guy."

Vanessa laughed, the expression on Cat's face alone making her glad she'd asked, even if she didn't get any information. "Methinks the lady doth protest too much."

Cat groaned, dropping her head back as she looked at the ceiling for strength. "Not Shakespeare again!"

It was an old joke between the sisters. After moving to their last of a long line of new towns, their favorite mutual high school English teacher had been obsessed with Shakespeare. That meant whenever anyone quoted one of his plays, the students who'd had Mr. Grayson tended to groan in memory of all the fun group activities. But it was a good memory and now a running joke.

"Hey, you're the one who said there was no guy, like, three times just now. What do you call that if not protesting too much?"

Cat's cheeks flushed even brighter, if that was even possible. Vanessa watched her with amusement as she started to say something, then stopped and glared at her. Finally, she answered with a scowl. "It's none of your business."

Vanessa raised her eyebrows. "Okay, I won't press. But, I can see I've hit a nerve. Whenever you want to share, I'm more than ready to hear all the details."

Cat looked as though she was going to protest again, so Vanessa gave an airy wave of her hand.

"Anyway. Now that you're ready, you can send Emma Jane in." At Cat's surprised look, Vanessa mock-pouted. "What? You think you're the only one being subjected to a hair and face makeover? No way. We're getting pictures and they are going to be good. I'll make certain of it."

Cat laughed, her cheeks now only a faint pink. "That actually makes me feel better. I'll go get her now. Good luck."

Vanessa smiled, then once again turned back to the mirror with a sense of unease. She'd already done her own hair and makeup and knew she looked great, but she still had the same strange pit of anxiety in her stomach that had made her skip breakfast. It was weird, because she'd never been anxious during plays in front of a whole town, or even when she'd first auditioned to act in San Francisco, so she was positive it wasn't the idea of speaking in front of a crowd. Maybe she was having the unexpected case of the jitters because this time, she'd be in front of everyone she knew.

As she searched her worried expression in the mirror, the door reopened and a vision in a slim-cut dress walked in. Vanessa had fibbed when she'd told Cat that Emma Jean wasn't going to be wearing a wedding dress. She was, sort of. It was just she hadn't been sure if Samuel would be able to find the one she wanted and she'd had no interest in wearing a modern, frilly one.

Vanessa had never seen anything like it. It was a cream-colored dress made out of the softest leather, with beading intricately placed along the shoulders and a fringe along the chest and arms. Under the tunic, she wore a close-fitting pair of pants in the same color which closely resembled leggings.

Emma Jane came to a stop behind Vanessa, but in the mirror, they appeared to be standing side by side. Her swirling white eyes were a slightly darker shade than normal, resembling clouds on an overcast day. Her hair was down, allowing the mahogany silk to cascade like a waterfall ending just above her hips. Her cheekbones always made Vanessa jealous, and her mouth was cherry-red and delicious, but it was the look of adoration on Emma Jane's face that made Vanessa melt. All of her anxiety faded away against the strength of the love she saw shining out from Emma Jane.

She turned around, holding her hands out, palms-up. "How are you holding up?"

Emma Jane took her hands and Vanessa pulled her in for a hug. She took a quick nibble from her luscious lips then drew back slightly as she waited for her to answer.

Emma Jane let out a quick exhale, her lips curving into a smile. "Much better now. Your parents are lovely, and I've had a wonderful week with all of your friends." Emma Jane shook her head with an expression of bemusement. "I'm still having a hard time wrapping my mind around the fact that I went from alone and lonely for the better part of my adult life, to the reality of being surrounded by so many wonderful people."

Vanessa leaned down to give Emma Jane a quick peck on the nose. "You're welcome," she said, then wrinkled her nose as she admitted her own concerns. "Don't tell anyone, but I'm pretty nervous about today. I don't know why. It's not like I've never been in front of a crowd before."

Emma Jane gave her a meaningful look. "Yes, but it's because of who the audience is and because of what today means. You're basically telling everyone that I'm the one you want to be with forever. That's fairly momentous, even for an extrovert."

Vanessa chuckled dryly, then leaned down to rest her head on Emma Jane's shoulder. "Maybe you're right. But at the same time, I really can't wait to tell everyone. So I'm not sure why I'd be so nervous."

Emma Jane stroked Vanessa's back, her hands sending small tingles of excitement wherever they touched bare skin. "You just are. Now, speaking of nervous, I'm here as ordered for makeup. Please, be gentle."

Vanessa rolled her eyes, reluctantly standing up straight again. She gestured for Emma Jane to sit in the place Cat had recently vacated. In only a few moments, Vanessa had transformed Emma Jane's naturally beautiful face into one that was strikingly, more exotically beautiful. She knew Emma Jane wouldn't be wearing her sunglasses for once, as a special gift to Vanessa, so she'd taken extra care with her eyeshadow. By the time she was done, Emma Jane could have graced any magazine cover in the world.

"Damn. I don't know how I got so lucky. You're the most beautiful woman I've ever seen."

Emma Jane blushed, but Vanessa was pleased to see she didn't actually protest, for once. Maybe Emma Jane was starting to believe Vanessa when she gave her compliments, but since they were true, Vanessa felt she deserved to hear them as often as possible.

"Thanks. Is there anything else we should do before we head over?"

Vanessa bit her lip, thinking for a moment, then shook her head. "Not that I know of. Cat's already dressed and made up. You have on makeup and look amazing in what you're wearing. I'm sorry I forgot to say that the second I saw you, but I was too dazzled by your beauty to get the words out."

Emma Jane smoothed the dress she was wearing, smiling shyly down at it as she did so. "It was my grandmother's. She wore it to her own wedding, many years ago."

Vanessa saw the sadness and pride on Emma Jane's face and nodded, swallowing the lump that suddenly appeared in her throat. *I'm going to have to get that checked out. I'm swallowing a lot of lumps lately. Maybe it's my thyroid, not because I'm getting soft.*

"It's beautiful. Whoever made it was incredibly gifted. I'm so pleased that you're able to have a piece of your family with us today."

"Thanks, Vanessa. Me too. But Samuel will be there; I consider him family. He's been a constant in my life from the moment I lost my regular vision and he was the reason I was able to develop my spirit vision. I wasn't sure he'd be able to make it, but now that he has, everything seems that much more special."

Vanessa hadn't met Samuel yet. While Emma Jane had been in contact with him by phone, he'd elected to stay elsewhere, citing his age and need for rest and comfort as the reason he hadn't attended any of the pre-wedding events. Vanessa couldn't help but wonder what he was like and what Emma Jane would be like around him. She'd found that people often acted differently depending on who they were with and knew that people from different parts of your life could cause you act in unexpected ways, depending on which part of life you'd been with them.

Suddenly realizing they were still standing in front of the mirror, holding onto each other, Vanessa shook her head and smiled down at Emma Jane's more diminutive frame. "We should leave. The service starts in an hour. I'm sure there'll be a few last-minute hiccups to finagle when we arrive."

"Sure. Are you driving, or were we going to go with your family?"

Vanessa wiggled her eyebrows. "Even better. As it's our wedding day, I rented a limo. Everybody else can get there on their own. In fact," Vanessa looked down at the delicate silver watch she'd put on to match the dress, then batted her eyelashes at Emma Jane with a playful grin. "I believe the limo should be here by now."

They left the bedroom together and Vanessa took one last glance at the room. It was strange, leaving the house with her wife, on their way to another wedding ceremony to repeat vows they'd already spoken, but at the same time, it felt as if another chapter of their lives was about to begin.

Although she was ecstatic about committing herself to Emma Jane in front of her loved ones, Vanessa couldn't keep her anxiety from rebounding. The nagging thought that she was forgetting something surfaced once more.

THE WEDDING
CHAPTER 3

E mma Jane had never ridden in a limo before. Now that she had, she wasn't sure what the fuss was all about. To someone without the ability to tell the difference between objects that weren't alive, it felt exactly the same as any other vehicle she'd ever been in. Maybe if she could see the way everyone else could, she'd have been more impressed, but the only thing the limo had going for it, in her opinion, was the fact Vanessa was able to sit beside her for change. Normally when they went anywhere, Vanessa was driving and both of her hands were busy.

For the first time, Emma Jane was able to appreciate Vanessa's soft and silky presence sitting close beside her in a vehicle. They didn't speak much on the way over, as Vanessa was visibly nervous, but they did hold hands. Emma Jane thought it was cute to see her outgoing and talkative wife so nervous about the ceremony. At the same time, she couldn't fault her for it, given her own niggling worry that she wore silently, like a backpack.

Emma Jane had chalked her own nerves up to the simple fact that she'd never been fond of crowds, but she wasn't sure why Vanessa was so wound up. She hoped it wasn't a sign anything was about to go wrong, but Emma Jane thought it was important to prepare for the worst, just in case. Which was why, unbeknownst to Vanessa, Emma Jane had hidden her trusty silver knife in a concealed pocket on her leggings. While not visible to anyone else, her kokum's wedding dress had a slit on the right side, conveniently located in such a way that she was able to carry a small weapon without anyone being the wiser. She patted it lightly, grateful for the reassuring weight on her leg. Silver could kill almost anything, even if the actual knife was small.

Of course, she didn't say anything to Vanessa, knowing she would've been horrified at the idea Emma Jane was going to their wedding armed. Emma Jane figured what Vanessa didn't know couldn't hurt her, and in the case of impending doom, she wanted to be able to protect both herself and her wife. After all, that was her job as a witch hunter.

The car rolled to a stop and Emma Jane leapt to open the door, holding it for Vanessa. She waited as Vanessa arranged her voluminous white dress to avoid stepping on it as she got out.

"I've got it, thanks." Vanessa beamed, holding her skirt out of the way as she stepped delicately out of the limo, raising Emma Jane's suspicion that her wife may be using a touch of air magic to keep her shoes clean from the grit of the road.

Emma Jane raised an eyebrow then took Vanessa's arm as they walked the short distance from the curb to the restaurant. Emma Jane held open the ornate, red door with engraved gold handles and allowed Vanessa to enter, then took a deep breath and followed her wife inside.

They were greeted by the sight of several people already milling around, talking while holding glasses of a ruby-red punch. One of Vanessa's major pet peeves about sitting through wedding services was the fact that if you got thirsty, there was no relief until the service was over. Given that it was her day, she'd insisted on the punch bowl remaining at the back of the room and Emma Jane gave Vanessa an amused smile as she remembered how insistent Vanessa had been that her guests wouldn't suffer from dehydration.

To her relief, Emma Jane spotted Cat and Evelyn already in the thick of things. Vanessa always joked that Evelyn would've made a great CEO, and based on the way Evelyn seemed to be directing several people at once, Emma Jane now understood why. Cat noticed them enter and hurried over, rubbing her hands together.

"I think everything's ready. Vanessa, Emma Jane, would you guys like to go sit in the back room? Everyone should be here shortly. And don't worry, Evelyn's already taking care of everything." Cat smirked, adding, "you know how she is. That girl could direct traffic on the moon."

Emma Jane smiled, looking at Vanessa with a raised eyebrow. "Vanessa? Do you want to hide? I mean, I'm always okay with that plan."

Vanessa's eyes darted around the room, appearing to be unusually tense and uncertain to Emma Jane's concerned eyes. But once her bride's eyes fell on Evelyn, busy speaking with one of the wait staff, Emma Jane saw her wife's shoulders soften.

Vanessa nodded, giving Cat a grateful smile. "Thanks, that sounds good. Where are we supposed to wait until the ceremony begins?"

Cat pointed to the back corner, where Emma Jane could barely see a hallway, half-hidden behind a potted plant. "They're letting us use one of the private function rooms. I've already got it set up with drinks and a lounger. There's even snacks, if you think you can handle eating anything right now."

Vanessa shook her head and Cat reached over to touch her sister's shoulder without saying a word. Emma Jane recognized Cat had given Vanessa a quick pulse of healing when Vanessa's pale and nervous expression became smooth and her aura glowed brighter.

"Thanks, Cat. I don't think I can handle food right now, even with your much appreciated pick-me-up." Vanessa looked around again, narrowing her eyes. "Have you seen Samuel yet?"

Emma Jane surveyed the room as well, but when she didn't see him either, she looked at Cat questioningly.

Cat shook her head. "Not yet, but I'm sure he'll be here."

Emma Jane tilted her head, unfazed. "Samuel has impeccable timing. He won't be early, but I'm not worried about him being late, either. He'll be here when it is the correct time to begin."

Cat nodded, then gestured for them to go in front of her as she walked them to the room.

"All right, you guys try to relax. Evelyn's been here for an hour already, so I think she's got everything as perfect as possible. You can take a load off for a half hour and I'll call you when it's time." Cat bit her lip, then wrinkled her nose as she first looked at Vanessa, then Emma Jane. "How are you guys going to do this? I mean, am I getting you both at the same time to walk down the aisle, or..." Cat trailed off.

Vanessa and Emma Jane looked at each other, then smiled.

"You can get us at the same time. We've already decided that we're going to do this together. After all, we're partners and equals, so I see no reason why we shouldn't," said Vanessa, answering for both of them.

Emma Jane watched as Cat's eyes became shiny, then she blinked and nodded as though nothing had happened.

"That sounds perfect. Okay guys, enjoy the quiet. I'll be back as soon as everything is ready."

"Thanks, Cat," said Emma Jane.

Cat smiled in response, briefly resting her hand on Emma Jane's shoulder before she left the room. The moment the door closed, Emma Jane let out a sigh of relief and looked at Vanessa. Although Cat's touch had temporarily relieved her anxiety, Vanessa was beginning to look tense once more.

Emma Jane raised her eyebrows. "Vanessa, are you sure you're okay? I've never seen you look this nervous about anything."

Vanessa sat on the lounger, leaning forward on her knees as her dress spread out around her in a puddle of white satin. She looked every inch the beautiful bride, but she didn't shine as brightly as usual, and Emma Jane knew she was having a hard time.

"I don't understand it, Emma Jane. I mean, this isn't me. I feel like I'm going to be sick. Maybe this is how everyone feels when they get married?"

Emma Jane shrugged. Sitting beside the strangely skittish version of her wife, she wrapped an arm around Vanessa and pulled her in close.

"Maybe," Emma Jane began, "but we're already married. Usually people are nervous before they say 'I do' because of what the promises mean. Which makes me think your excessive anxiety has more to do with just the wedding service today."

As Emma Jane watched the preparations over the previous few days, seeing what an amazing support system Vanessa truly had, an idea had slowly taken root. She glanced at Vanessa's neck, breathing a sigh of relief when she saw the green stone that still hung safely around her love's neck on its slender rawhide cord. Emma Jane looked down at her dress, surprised to realize the cord on Vanessa's necklace matched the rawhide on it perfectly. *Symmetry in the strangest of places.* She focused on the stone again. With Vanessa safely protected by the stone, Emma Jane knew that Vanessa wasn't having a hard time because Emma Jane was siphoning her energy. The necklace ensured that her powers were safe. But she couldn't help wonder if other forces were at work, which was the main reason why her wedding dress included a silver weapon.

Vanessa looked at Emma Jane, moving her head so that it still rested on her shoulder but so she could also look into Emma Jane's eyes. "I'm not sure I understand what you mean. Although if you know why I'm doing this, it would be awesome if you could share the reason with me. I don't feel at all like myself today."

Emma Jane rubbed her chin as she gave Vanessa a thoughtful look. "Something about today feels a little... off." When Vanessa raised her eyebrows, Emma Jane shook her head. "It isn't just the crowd. I had a feeling when we were here yesterday. It's the same today, except watching you being almost overwhelmed by your anxiety only intensifies my worry. That makes me wonder if there's something going on."

Vanessa narrowed her eyes. "Something? Like what?"

Emma Jane shrugged. "I don't know yet. I haven't seen anyone here who worries me, at least not yet. The only people we're expecting are people that you know well, and Samuel, who's been the only constant in my life since I was twelve. So, I'm not concerned about the guest list. Still, I can't help feeling like maybe we should be expecting something big, or someone unexpected, to attend the celebration today."

Vanessa sat back abruptly, regarding Emma Jane with dawning understanding.

"You mean, like a bad guy?"

Emma Jane inclined her head in agreement. "Perhaps. I'm wondering if some of the anxiety we're experiencing is external, placed on us by an outside force. Sometimes wandering spirits can attach themselves to a person and make them feel like this. Maybe it's something like that."

Vanessa wrinkled her nose. "A ghost? Like a ghost attached to us?" She rubbed both of her bare arms, then smoothed her dress down, as though she was trying to feel if there was a presence on her. She looked up at Emma Jane with a sheepish expression. "You don't mean on me right now, right?"

Emma Jane laughed, feeling her mood lift at Vanessa's literal interpretation of her words. "No, Vanessa. I don't mean actually attached to you. I'm wondering if the anxiety is a portent though."

Emma Jane glanced at the side of her thigh, biting the inside of her cheek as she considered sharing knowledge of her arsenal with Vanessa, but before she could say anything, Vanessa raised an eyebrow, her gaze following Emma Jane's to her thigh.

"You brought your knife, didn't you?"

Emma Jane opened her eyes as wide as she could, trying to look innocent, but relaxed when she saw Vanessa wasn't angry. "Yeah, I did. I just..."

"Felt naked?" said Vanessa.

Emma Jane was relieved to see a look of understanding instead of the irritation or anger she'd feared. She nodded, and Vanessa smiled.

"I understand." Vanessa dropped her hand to her necklace. Emma Jane watched as she fingered the green stone at the end of the cord. "I feel the same about this stone."

She held it up, allowing Emma Jane to get a better look before letting it drop to her chest. "If it makes you feel better to have your knife on you, I'm not going to stop you. Plus," she added, raising her eyebrows. "We may need it. It's not like evil takes a holiday. I'm never shocked when one of our outings ends up in a fight to the death with one creature or another."

Emma Jane pursed her lips, nodding glumly. "Yeah, I'm sorry about that. I really want today to be special for you."

Vanessa smiled, relaxing back into Emma Jane's arms then reciprocating by wrapping her own arms around her as she snuggled closer.

"Don't you know that every day already is special, just because you're here?" Vanessa drew her head back slightly to look at Emma Jane. "The reason I wanted to have this ceremony and party today isn't just because I wanted to have a big party where I got to wear a white dress."

Vanessa shook her head and Emma Jane could feel the love radiating out of her smile.

"It's because I want everyone to know that you belong to me and I belong to you. I know my parents wished we'd been together longer and done this with them present the first time, but I didn't want you to run away. I wanted to tie you to me." She gave Emma Jane a sheepish look, then shrugged. "This is just another layer to bind you to me and my world. I realize that's completely selfish, but I don't care one iota."

Emma Jane smiled, bestowing a brief kiss on Vanessa's lips. "Well, if it's selfish, then I'm selfish too, because that's the only reason I agreed to do this in the first place."

At Vanessa's look of surprise, Emma Jane smiled. "I want everyone to know to know that you belong to me, as well."

She saw the exact moment when the last trace of anxiety departed from Vanessa's eyes. It was the moment she saw the deep, sapphire blue turn into a warm, inviting pool that made her want to sink into the depths and never leave. This time when their lips met, the delicious fire was there. They lost themselves for one perfect moment as they rode the twin waves of love and desire.

A loud rapping on the door harshly interrupted their warm cocoon of love. They pulled back, Emma Jane feeling somewhat bewildered as Cat's voice floated through the closed door.

"Vanessa? Emma Jane? Are you guys in there?"

"Yes, you can come in, Cat."

Vanessa pulled back, her breathing shaky and her hair slightly disheveled from their embrace. Emma Jane felt a twinge of sadness as Vanessa straightened her appearance, but a surge of excitement replaced it as she realized their big moment was almost here.

Cat stood in the doorway, her eyebrows raised as she assessed them. "I'm thinking it's a good thing I knocked first?" Cat wiggled her eyebrows, giving them a mischievous look.

Vanessa rolled her eyes. "Hey, it's your fault if you see something you don't want to. There's a reason why Mom and Dad taught us how to knock on the door from an early age."

Cat shuddered with mock disgust. "Oh my god, Vanessa. It's bad enough watching my sister make out with someone, but please. Do not put thoughts of Mom and Dad in my head. There's way too much going on for me to be able to handle that today as well."

Emma Jane laughed, remembering how the McLean's still looked at each other after a quarter century together. "Well, you'd better make sure that you keep knocking, Cat. If I'm not mistaken, I think that might actually be the reason your parents wanted their own place for the week."

Emma Jane laughed even harder as Vanessa and Cat shuddered in unison.

"Emma Jane! Don't go there," said Vanessa, curling her lip and looking as though she'd bitten into something rotten, then all three of them burst into laughter. Once they'd calmed down, Cat returned to the reason she was there.

"I came to tell you that all the guests are here. Emma Jane," Cat looked directly at her.

"Yes?" asked Emma Jane, wondering what could be so important for Cat to suddenly become so solemn.

Cat wrinkled her nose, hesitating before finally speaking. "I think Samuel is here. And he looked...." Cat pursed her lips, squinting one eye as she searched for the right way to say it. "He looks nervous."

Emma Jane nodded, her suspicions confirmed at that moment. "Can you send him in? Do we have time to talk to him first?"

Cat nodded. "Of course. It's your day, so take as much time as you need. I think everyone who's coming has been seated now, so we're just waiting for you. Everything should be ready to go, but I thought you'd like to know that before..." Cat stopped, giving Emma Jane a look of concern.

"Thanks, Cat. You're right. Send him in. I'd like to talk to him before we proceed."

Although Emma Jane hadn't shared her suspicions with Cat, she could tell by the look on her sister-in-law's face that she had her own. With both Emma Jane and Vanessa feeling so anxious about today, it was no surprise that her perceptive, aura-reading sister-in-law would also be worried that something evil was about to crash the party.

Cat nodded, slipping out of the room to return a minute later with someone Emma Jane hadn't seen in what felt like years, but who hadn't changed at all.

"Samuel."

Emma Jane spoke only his name, but knew by the look on his face he understood everything she was feeling. He was a man of few words and their time together had been one of periods of quiet reflection interspersed with hard training. But when he'd spoken, she'd always felt that he said three times what anyone else could impart in terms of wisdom. It was because of him, and him alone, that Emma Jane had managed to triumph in one way or another against every creature she'd hunted so far. While she may not have always succeeded in killing or even containing her adversary, she'd always escaped to fight another day. All thanks to the man now standing in front of her.

Samuel stood quietly, dressed in a simple black suit, looking traditionally Western until you noticed the snowy white braids which hung down his back, nearly reaching his waist. When she'd first met him, his hair had been steel gray. He'd already been old when she was a child, but he was much older now. She wasn't sure exactly when he'd been born, but knew he was coming up on the hundred-year mark, if he hadn't already passed it. He seemed ancient now but still stood straight-backed and proud, looking as immovable as the mountains themselves. He had a strong nose and chin, with his skin permanently tanned by the suns of many summers.

"My girl. You look happy," He said, giving her a proud smile and nodding once, as though bestowing his blessing on her.

Emma Jane bowed her head, smoothing her dress as she smiled back at him. "Thank you for finding my grandmother's dress. It's more beautiful than I remembered from her pictures and it makes me feel like I have her with me today."

Samuel nodded serenely. "You're welcome."

He turned his gaze upon Vanessa, who'd stood with Emma Jane when she'd gotten up to greet him. He examined her carefully, then a smile broke out on his face as he turned to Emma Jane with an unexpected look of almost childish glee.

"I did not realize."

His voice was quiet, but Emma Jane could hear amazement in his words, and she was surprised. Samuel had never been shocked or amazed by anything he'd encountered that she could recall.

"Did not realize what, sir?"

This time, Samuel beamed. He reached his hands out to Vanessa, who extended her own with a look of confusion as Samuel took them both in his to examine her with wonder.

"I knew you'd found someone with magic to be with, but I did not realize you were married to Raven."

It was Emma's turn to look at Samuel with confusion. "I'm sorry? What do you mean? This is Vanessa. I told you that she can change into a bird and has air magic. Don't you remember?"

For a moment, Emma Jane wondered if senility had caught up to Samuel, but when he gave her a chiding look, she once again felt like a child who had disappointed her teacher.

"You didn't tell me your beloved was Raven. You know who I'm talking about. I've taught you all the old stories."

Emma Jane shook her head, still perplexed, until she realized what Samuel was talking about. Now it was Emma Jane's turn to look at Vanessa with amazement. Her mouth dropped open as she put the pieces together.

"I never even considered that to be real."

She shook her head as the tales of Raven, Coyote, Spider and all of the other traditional Cree legends, along with all the Celtic myths, flooded into her mind.

"Okay, I'm missing something," said Vanessa, looking between Emma Jane and Samuel with suspicion. "Why are you guys calling me Raven?"

Vanessa had succeeded in retrieving her hands from Samuel, who now stood silently watching Vanessa with a bemused smile on his face, so Emma Jane jumped in with answers for her wife's consternation.

"In our culture, there are many tales of animals with supernatural abilities. They are thought to be gods or magical creatures. It is always wise not to anger them, but they are a part of the fabric which makes up our everyday lives. When Samuel says you are Raven, he believes that not only can you turn into a Raven, but you actually are the mythical Raven from our legends."

Vanessa shook her head. "No, that's not possible. I'm not a goddess or god. Not like Evelyn, not even with half as much power as Cat."

Emma Jane shook her head. "Legends are like that. I'm thinking that if you look at your own culture, Vanessa, and talk to your dad, you could find that you might be the present day manifestation of the Morrigan."

Vanessa shook her head, crossing arms. "Nope. I definitely don't have that kind of power."

Emma Jane shrugged. She knew there was no need to belabor the point, but she also knew that legends and myths had a funny way of having a basis in reality.

"Maybe not. But that's why Samuel is looking at you the way he is. He's impressed with your abilities, so I think that means he approves of our relationship."

Vanessa uncrossed her arms and gave Samuel a hesitant smile. "It's nice to finally meet you, Samuel. Emma Jane has told me many wonderful things. It sounds as though you've had an incredible life." She trailed off lamely, giving Emma Jane a slightly panicked look.

Samuel nodded, still smiling at Vanessa. Emma Jane knew that no matter what else happened today, Samuel was happy with who Emma Jane had found for a life partner.

"Yes, I've had a long life, full of many adventures. I have many tales I could tell you, but we need more time for that. I understand you are looking to do an exchange of vows in front of everyone at this time." He looked between Emma Jane and Vanessa, nodding once when they both answered in the affirmative. "And you are both aware of what is coming?"

Samuel looked at Emma Jane after his calm pronouncement with one eyebrow raised. She felt her heart sink, having hoped her feelings were wrong and merely a product of social anxiety.

"We've both been...inappropriately anxious," she replied simply, catching Vanessa's answering nod out of the corner of her eye.

"I'm not a nervous person, Samuel, but I've been finding myself very anxious about this ceremony." Vanessa shook her head irritably to punctuate her statement. "I'm an actress. I make my living in front of strangers. I'm used to acting crazy in front of large crowds. I had no problems saying I do when we did this the first time, so I know it isn't fear of commitment, either. But something about today has been making me act out of character. If I didn't know better, I'd say I had stage fright." Vanessa glowered at the idea. "I do *not* get stage fright."

Samuel nodded, then began to pace the length of the room between the window and the door as the girls observed him in silence. Emma Jane was familiar with Samuel and knew he was thinking, and when he was thinking, it was better to let him move and wait until he was ready to speak again. She glanced at Vanessa, giving a slight shake of the head when she seemed as though she might speak, biting back amusement as Vanessa appeared to be choking on the words she'd been about to say.

A few moments later, Samuel stopped walking and looked out of the window, peering off into the distance. They were only on the first floor, but he seemed to be staring at an object far away, in a place Emma Jane couldn't see.

"Legend tells of a woman with eyes like fire and the body of the snake. The Lakota speak of her as a demon, who will punish any wrong done to her and who will eat everyone in the way of her capricious desires. Her hard scales are hidden underneath a cloak of smoke and fog, and she is said to be able to defeat the strongest of warriors with ease." He turned to Emma Jane, his eyes lowered.

Her eyes widened the moment when remembrance struck. "Uŋȟčéǧila? I thought that we..."

Emma Jane's voice trailed off as Samuel shook his head.

"We fought her, yes, but we did not defeat her. She only went into hiding to regroup. She is known for being vindictive and nothing would give her greater joy than to destroy your child, the way we destroyed hers. But as you do not have children, she has had to wait for love to have her revenge."

Samuel pointed his chin at Vanessa before turning back to Emma Jane with a sympathetic look. "She will attempt to take that which you love the most, instead."

Emma Jane shook her head, her heart almost stopping in her chest as she looked into Vanessa's frightened eyes. "No. We destroyed her. And her children."

Samuel smiled sadly. "No, we didn't. I'd wondered at the time, but now I am certain of it. When we encountered her in the Badlands, we failed in our mission." Samuel looked down, his face crumpling with painful emotion, and Emma Jane was shocked to recognize a look of shame. It passed over his face quickly, then he met her eyes once again. "It is the one time where I know we left a job unfinished. This is all my fault."

At Emma Jane's look of disagreement, he sighed. "When we encountered that nest of vipers, we did succeed in slaying her offspring. But we didn't manage to pierce her with the magic arrow at the correct location. We missed. I didn't say anything at the time because she'd vanished, and we were both injured and unable to give chase to a ghost."

He looked troubled by the memory and Emma Jane nodded. It had been a difficult battle, the nearest she'd ever come to dying while under Samuel's tutelage.

"She was gone. It wasn't as though we could have followed her, even had we been able to," she said, agreeing with Samuel.

Emma Jane hated to see Samuel looking so unsure, and when he raised his hands helplessly, she knew it was a question he'd asked himself many times over the last twenty years.

"Perhaps. But perhaps we should have tried harder. I told myself if we ever heard anything about her, or if she came looking for us, that we'd face her if and when the time came. But, we were younger then, and had much less to lose." Samuel gave Vanessa the same gloomy look he'd given Emma Jane. "Now that I have seen your Raven, I understand just how much you stand to lose. I have nothing of value except for you, my child, and we have both been long reconciled to the lives that we live. I have always understood that one or both of us could die at any time, but have consoled myself with the knowledge we will see each other in the afterlife, in the place where our people meet. But now that I see your happiness with Vanessa, I believe Uŋȟčéǧila is the fear we've been experiencing leading up to this day. She is a dark cloud which spreads panic and disorder and she is coming for you."

"What do we need to do?" Vanessa stepped forward, her jaw set with the same stubborn tilt Emma Jane had seen whenever Vanessa put her mind to something in the past.

Samuel nodded with approval. "The first step is to be ready." He looked at Emma Jane, then raised an eyebrow. "Did you bring it with you?"

Emma Jane knew instantly what he was talking about. Her right hand dropped down to her thigh, pulling the knife out to display the sharp-edged silver dagger he'd given to her when she'd finished her training. He nodded again.

"This is good. While it is no magic arrow, that knife has been blessed and carries great medicine within it. You'll only have a moment, a single instant, in which to succeed. You must place the knife directly through the space above her seventh rib. That is the only way to ensure she will stay dead."

Emma Jane nodded, sliding the knife back into its sheath as Vanessa raised an eyebrow.

"I guess it's a good thing you brought your knife, after all." She turned to look at Samuel. "What can I do?"

Samuel smiled again. This time, Emma Jane caught a look of respect flash across his face.

"You can protect each other. You can make sure everyone else is safe. Uŋȟčéǧila would love nothing more than to destroy everyone and everything where she touches down. She is a pestilence, she is darkness and death. You'll need everyone's help when she shows her hideous face."

Vanessa nodded, looking at Emma Jane with resignation and squaring her shoulders. "I agree that would explain why we've been feeling so strange. Should we let the others know, before the ceremony starts?"

Emma Jane bit her lip, trying to decide if knowledge would be better than not knowing. "I'm not sure, Vanessa. There are a lot of people in the audience who don't have any knowledge of our world. How do we keep them from becoming hysterical?"

Vanessa wrinkled her nose. "That's a good point."

Just then, a knock on the door interrupted them and any chance they had to decide what to do.

"Are you ready?" Cat poked her head in, looking apologetic for the interruption.

When Emma Jane glanced at Vanessa for confirmation, she knew they'd delayed long enough. "Yes, we're ready," Emma Jane began, but when Cat regarded her with a shrewd expression on her face, Emma Jane knew nothing else needed to be said about the danger that was looming.

"I'll let Evelyn know." Cat nodded, giving Emma Jane a calm smile before turning to Samuel. "Sir? If you'll come with me, I'll show you where to stand. Perhaps you could fill me in on the necessary information as we walk."

Cat shyly offered her arm to him and Samuel strode over, giving a small nod as he accepted her elbow.

"I would be honored, my girl. It has been many years since I've heard tell of a phoenix." Samuel's eyes warmed as he examined Cat, who was now blushing at his appraisal.

Emma Jane wondered what story or event Samuel was referencing, as she couldn't recall ever hearing of a phoenix before she'd met Cat. As they exited the room, she thought she overheard him speaking to Cat about something unrelated.

"I once knew a woman whose name was Fiona..."

Emma Jane wondered who Fiona was, but brushed the thought aside, returning to the danger at hand. "I'm sorry my past seems to be rearing its ugly head today. I didn't want to ruin this for you," she said, grimacing.

Vanessa placed her hand on Emma Jane's shoulder and squeezed lightly. "It's hardly your fault, Emma Jane. One thing I've discovered over the last five or so years is that evil kinda doesn't care if you've got better things planned. In fact, it seems to take the greatest pleasure in ruining special moments. Well, mine, anyway. So if it's planning on trying to do that to us today, then I plan on giving it a taste of its own medicine. Or rather, your little silver knife's medicine." Vanessa winked.

Emma Jane laughed. "Well, as long as you're okay with what's about to go down. Let's get this show on the road."

THE WEDDING
CHAPTER 4

Vanessa knew she was close to hyperventilating. She was holding Emma Jane's arm and they were standing at the back of the room, waiting for their cue to walk down the aisle. The entire audience was before them, seated in chairs that had been separated in the middle, creating an aisle just wide enough for them to walk down together. They'd put their friends and family in the first row, with everyone from work and all of Vanessa's other acquaintances behind the handful they held the nearest and dearest. This basically meant that the room was arranged so that everyone with an iota of power was right at the front.

Vanessa wasn't sure if that was good or bad, but as she looked around the room, she prayed that nothing would happen to anyone there. Although she knew it wasn't her fault, she couldn't help but think about all of those she'd seen or known in the past who'd had awful things happen to them because of the evil which seemed to be on a constant collision course with her and those she loved. Also, she had no idea how to pronounce the name of the demon snake-lady who was trying to kill her, which was irritating. Was it uncheckulna? Unugigula? What had Samuel called her? Either way, she wasn't going to let anything ruin today.

"Are you ready?"

Emma Jane's deep contralto whispered over her nerve endings, soothing them in a way that only she could. Even through her nerves, Vanessa was overpowered by the strength of her love for this woman.

She nodded. "I'm always ready to tell the world how much I love you."

Emma Jane blushed, smiling shyly, and Vanessa settled for squeezing Emma Jane's hand, knowing they didn't have enough time for her to show Emma Jane the extent of her affection. She caught Cat's eye as she stood beside Samuel at the front of the room. Once Cat knew Vanessa was ready, she nodded and signaled the organist. As the haunting chords of Pachelbel's Canon filled the air they strolled down the aisle, nodding as they passed familiar faces smiling happily back at them, completely unaware of the anxiety lurking beneath the surface of the happy couple's smiles.

Samuel stood straight and strong at the front of the room, but Vanessa could see the keen awareness in his eyes as he surreptitiously surveyed the room, scanning it in the same way she'd seen Emma Jane do while out on a hunt. He may be old, but Vanessa knew he was still a hunter at heart, regardless of whether or not he'd been active in recent years. Vanessa blinked, realizing with a start that they'd already reached the front and now stood only a few paces from Samuel. He gestured for them to turn and face the crowd, and as Vanessa looked out, she saw her family in the front row. Her mother was smiling through tears while her dad sat up tall, a proud look on his face. Evelyn sat beside them, watching them approach with an odd smile. To Vanessa's surprise, her handsome partner, Robin, sat beside her. He gave Vanessa a cheeky wink, causing her to shake her head with amusement. He was definitely the most attractive man in the room, but she only had eyes for Emma Jane.

Sitting beside Robin was Evelyn's mom, Mary-Jean Baptiste, who calmly smiled at Vanessa with both hands folded in her lap. Evelyn's mother had been part of everything they'd done, right from the beginning. With magic of her own, she'd pushed and prodded her only daughter until she'd finally achieved her destiny. Vanessa shook her head, still in awe of the woman.

The front row on the other side had Zahara with her fiancé, Omar, seated next to her. Vanessa had met him for the first time a few days ago, overjoyed to find him to be an absolutely perfect match for her friend. Not only could he shift into a fox the way Zahara could but he also had ties to her family that went back centuries. Vanessa was touched they'd been able to make the long trip, as she knew Zahara was bound to protect the magic where she lived in the same way that Robin was necessary to protect the earth magic of the British Isles.

Seated beside Omar were Jake and Mai. As Vanessa has suspected would be the case, they'd been unable to leave their children behind, so all three of the triplets were there as well. The tired parents were currently struggling to keep them quiet and almost succeeding. If Vanessa was right, she thought they'd be almost three now. They were as cute as could be and easy to tell apart by the varying shades of dark brown hair as well as their eyes colors; brown, blue, or hazel. But as cute as they were, they were still toddlers, and Mai looked frazzled. The moment she'd seen the children, Vanessa was glad she'd decided against having the girls stand up at the front in the traditional fashion for bridesmaids. If they had, she was certain there would've been children running amok down the narrow aisle. As it was, it looked like the little boy was ready to bolt, but Jake had noticed at the last moment, snagging him by the pants before he could escape. Vanessa almost laughed aloud at the look of frustration on his face, but managed to bite it back before the sound escaped.

All of Vanessa's loved ones were there, and she couldn't help but feel blessed that she had so many, especially in comparison with Emma Jane, who'd asked only Samuel to attend. She planned to spend the rest of her life making sure that Emma Jane was never alone again. All the other faces in the crowd were a pleasant addition to the day, but Vanessa knew that none of them were required for her happiness. She smiled down at Emma Jane, her anxiety temporarily damped down by love.

Samuel cleared his throat and began.

"We are gathered here today, to witness the promises between these two individuals. They have pledged to love and honor each other, through sickness and health, through good times and hard times."

Vanessa's eyes prickled with tears as Samuel's deep voice imparted a marked solemnity to the occasion. She looked out at her friends and family and her sense of rightness multiplied. These vows were important and she knew they would honor them always, knew that their love could handle anything life could throw at them. But even as Vanessa exhaled with a sense of fulfilment, she began to feel cold.

As though someone had just opened the door to the outside and the frigid air of winter was drifting in, the temperature in the room dropped precipitously. She sensed the tension more than actually saw it, but as the temperature dropped, both Emma Jane and Samuel instantly went on the alert; like cougars ready to pounce on their prey.

Vanessa searched the room, but saw nothing. As she knew all too well from past experience, that didn't mean there wasn't anything there. She caught her sister's eye, then Cat turned to Evelyn. Without a word, Evelyn closed her eyes. When she opened them again, they'd changed to a swirling, pearlescent white, similar to Emma Jane's, yet different. Hers glowed as though rainbows had become trapped inside clouds, and as Vanessa watched, the faintest hint of light suffused Evelyn's skin, making her look as though she was being powered by something luminous inside. The faces in the crowd became dreamy, then slack, as fog began to roll in over the ground. At that exact moment, all hell broke loose.

THE WEDDING
CHAPTER 5

Emma Jane's hand went to her right leg to ensure her knife was easily available, but didn't pull it out as her foe hadn't yet presented herself. Remembering the civilian audience in front of her, she noted with satisfaction that Evelyn had already taken care of them. While grateful for her assistance, she knew that meant Evelyn would be occupied and unable to help without risking losing control of their consciousness, given how many people she was controlling.

Quickly, Emma Jane sized up her advantages. Samuel was old but experienced. He had his own gifts and would still be helpful. Jake and Mai would be good as well, with their ability to control water and shift into dragons, but the downside was the room size, as well as their small, vulnerable children, who would need protection. She knew it was unlikely they could help much in their more powerful form or while distracted.

Zahara and Omar would, however, be able to shift within the small space. Their fox forms were smaller than their human shapes, and as they were both powerful earth mages, they'd be able to help with their magic if needed. Emma Jane was less certain about Robin. Other than knowing that he was a powerful god, she also knew from Vanessa that he could be unpredictable. Cat was a phoenix and possessed fire magic, in addition to her extremely useful ability to heal, should it be required. She was concerned about the girls' parents, although she hoped they wouldn't panic. Peter had minor water magic, but to the best of her knowledge, both Marie-Jean and Mindy would be useless against a supernatural force, which meant she needed to get them to safety. The demon would most likely attempt to attack them first because they were important to both Emma Jane and Vanessa.

Emma Jane turned to Vanessa. "Is that fog from Evelyn?"

Vanessa shook her head. "I don't think so. The last time I saw anything like that was in grade twelve. The fog was being used by a soul thief in order to control the audience while his master took their life energy. Is that something your evil lady Uncheckula can do?"

Emma Jane smirked at the gross mispronunciation. "Unc-Cekula," she corrected before she nodded grimly. "I guess she can, although I don't remember much from that particular fight. Samuel mentioned that she hides her body with a cloud of smoke and fog when he spoke with us earlier, but I was hoping this was Evelyn's handiwork. Vanessa, I want you to get your parents and Evelyn's mom to safety. Can you hide them in the bathroom?"

Vanessa nodded, looking determined. "I've got it. The bathroom should be safer and it's only got one way in or out, so we'll be able to protect them better from there."

Emma Jane smiled grimly. "Perfect. You should probably stay with them as well. She's almost certainly going to come for you first."

Vanessa glared, then shook her head sharply. "No way. Not this time."

Emma Jane narrowed her eyes in frustration but didn't argue. While a huge part of her wanted Vanessa to be locked away in a room safe from the demon, she had a feeling they'd be safer together than apart. At least this way, she could keep an eye on her.

"Okay, but hurry back. I need to know where you are or I'll be distracted trying to see if you're safe."

Vanessa nodded, then Emma Jane watched as she moved surprisingly quickly in her long wedding gown toward her parents. Luckily, they'd already realized something was amiss and went with her without question. Emma Jane followed them with her eyes as they escaped to the bathroom, making sure they got there safely. The second Vanessa returned, Emma Jane turned her full attention toward the fog that now rolled toward the front of the room.

The fog was a dense cloud of gray mist which seemed to seep through the feet of everyone seated. Mai, Jake, and the children had moved to the front of the room to stand behind Samuel; Zahara and Omar had taken one look at Vanessa guiding her parents to safety and transformed. Emma Jane wasn't sure where they were at the moment, but was confident they were ready for a fight. Robin, on the other hand, had remained seated next to Evelyn. He had his right leg crossed over his left knee and was swinging his foot as he waited, as though preparing to see a show.

When he caught her incredulous look, he flashed Emma Jane a grin. "Don't worry, Tiger. You've got this."

Robin winked, then wrapped his arm around Evelyn. He inclined his head toward his love, giving her a fond look as she concentrated, oblivious to his actions.

"I'll keep an eye on her, you do what you need to. I think I've met this snaky lady who's put the party in an uproar in the distant past." He wrinkled his nose, raising an eyebrow. "She's kind of nasty. Reminds me a bit of my own personal nemesis, Carman, but our girls took care of her for me a few years ago. You should be fine; you have a lot more firepower this time. Don't worry, I'm here if you need me."

Emma Jane shook her head, and when Vanessa caught her incredulous look, she smirked. "It's not worth trying to figure him out. I've been trying for years. He's never screwed us over, although there's been more than once where I felt that he should've stepped in long before he did."

A voice with a Scottish accent from behind Emma Jane caused her to turn around.

"I'll vouch for him. He's always been there when I've needed him. And he's surprisingly powerful with portals, if that should happen to be required."

A small fox with large ears that reached only as high as Emma Jane's knees stood between her and Samuel. Emma Jane blinked at the creature with surprise as she recognized the voice.

"Zahara?"

The small fox bobbed its head in response, her whiskers twitching. "Yes, time to look sharp. I feel the presence of evil, and whoever they are, they seem right pissed off." She tilted her head, flicking her ears. "What did you do to them anyway? This feels personal."

Emma Jane turned back to watch the fog inching closer. "Samuel said we killed her family, but she didn't die the way we'd thought she had."

The fox bobbed her head. "A blood vendetta then, righty-o. Where would you like us?"

Emma Jane smiled, appreciating the no-nonsense Zahara even more now than she had over the past few days. Of all of Vanessa's powerful friends, Zahara seemed the most like herself in personality; stable, dependable, and stubborn. Looking around the room, Emma Jane decided quickly.

"I'd like you and Omar to keep an eye on the bathroom where Vanessa put her parents. Evelyn and Robin are going to watch the audience and make sure they stay unaware and safe. The demon after me is Uŋȟčéǧila," Emma Jane grimaced, before continuing. "She likes to go for the heart of whomever she's after. So, her main targets will be you guys, the parents, and Vanessa, in ascending order of importance. I'll keep Vanessa with me, but it would be nice to know that everybody else is safe."

She looked at Mai and Jake standing with their three children near the front and bit her lip. The idea of children present while Uŋȟčéǧila was bent on revenge was troubling. As the swirling fog became thicker, Emma Jane worried that they'd become frightened or worse, injured. At that moment, Jake approached, his gaze firmly fixed on the roiling darkness.

"What do you want us to do?"

He was another person Emma Jane felt immediately safe and comfortable with. He may have been a dragon with water magic, but he was solid and quiet, and reminded her more of Samuel than the usual, often flaky, water adepts she'd encountered in the past.

"I'm not sure, but I'm worried about your kids." Emma Jane gave him a nervous smile, but he just laughed.

"I wouldn't be." Jake shook his head, looking at his off-spring, who were currently trying to break free of their mother's firm grip while she whispered words of admonishment through gritted teeth. "We've got a hard enough time keeping up with them on a good day. I think they'll be just fine. My advice?"

Emma Jane nodded when Jake appeared to be waiting for her response.

"Lock the door, then I'll set them loose. Normally, I wouldn't advise it," Jake pointed at the slowly coalescing fog which was beginning to gain form. It no longer hovered over the audience but was now congregating in the center of the aisle. "But the last time I saw something like this, we discovered distractions could be useful. My kids are nothing if not a distraction."

Jake sighed and Emma Jane heard both the parental pride and frustration coming through, loud and clear. She bit her lip and raised her hands in surrender.

"If you're sure. You know them better than I do, but if you could keep an eye out for Samuel, I'd be most grateful." Emma Jane's eyes flicked quickly to her old mentor before moving back to Jake. He nodded, placing his hand briefly on her shoulder, then squeezed it reassuringly.

"I understand. Don't worry, I won't let anything happen to him."

Giving Jake a thankful glance, Emma Jane turned to face something she thought she'd never see again.

Uŋȟčéǧila

It was a good thing the ceilings were ten feet high, she thought, as she looked up to see the large demon almost touching the ceiling, and an even better thing that Evelyn was a goddess who could keep a crowd of average humans under the spell of her mind, or there would have been pandemonium. Emma Jane's eyes narrowed as the fog solidified in front of her. She slowly worked the kinks out of her neck and joints, readying her body for quick movement. She bent her knees slightly, shifting her weight to the balls of her feet as she kept her hands loose by her sides. She didn't reach for her knife yet, hoping to keep it hidden until the last moment so that the demon remained unaware of it, and of her plan to stab her in the one vulnerable area she possessed.

Emma Jane had been barely fifteen the last time she'd seen the demon, but time hadn't diminished the horror of Uŋȟčéǧila's appearance. Her eyes glowed with the same fiery darkness, while the hard scales which formed her sinuous body seemed to absorb the light around her. Most of her appeared serpentine with the exception of her head, which was vaguely dragon-like, but with elements of gnarly troll. Emma Jane realized as she looked at the monster that parts of the demon defied description, almost as though Emma Jane couldn't retain the information from her eyes long enough to process it in her mind. She was, however, able to see what appeared to be writhing tendrils emerging from her torso. Uŋȟčéǧila radiated a malevolence larger than her body which was directed toward Emma Jane and Samuel, as though the audience wasn't even there.

Good. Hopefully, she sets her sights only on me.

Emma Jane knew that if she had to split her attention to protect others, she wouldn't be nearly as effective. She felt, more than heard, the hiss of the demon's voice as it whispered through the air.

"I've searched for both of you for a long time. But you've never been in the same place long enough for me to find you."

She rolled her demonic neck as if stretching, fixing her smoldering gaze on Emma Jane for a moment, before dismissing her and turning to Samuel. "You, I hold most responsible, but you have nothing to lose." She slithered the words out delicately, as though bestowing an endearment, then glided toward Emma Jane, Samuel, and Vanessa.

"All those whom you love have already passed beyond my reach, save for you."

She returned her dark gaze to Emma Jane, then a grimace that passed for a smile stretched her black cheeks wide, revealing row upon row of sharp, needle-like teeth.

Emma Jane kept her face expressionless as she blinked in response to the demon's words. She had no intention of conversing or acknowledging any weakness. Uŋȟčéǧila did not need to know who was important to her if she didn't already know. But Emma Jane waited nonetheless, ready for the demon to force her hand and make the first move. She allowed her to approach until she was standing directly across from the front row of seats, where only Evelyn and Robin now remained. Emma Jane's gaze flicked between Uŋȟčéǧila and her new friends, but she knew better than to worry.

Robin now sat alert, no longer bouncing his foot the way he had earlier, when Uŋȟčéǧila was merely fog. Instead, he rested his chin upon the palm of his hand, with his elbow on his loosely crossed knee. She could tell by his expression that he had absolutely no fear and wondered, not for the first time, just how powerful Evelyn and Robin must be to be able to sit stoically in the face of a demon as though they were watching TV. Well, Robin, anyway. Evelyn was still focused on everyone else.

Emma Jane looked back at Uŋȟčéǧila, who appeared not to notice the powerful beings beside her. Her tunnel vision remained completely focused upon Emma Jane and Samuel. He'd moved closer to her so that both Vanessa and Samuel were now within arm's length. She felt comfortable with her ability to protect them if need be and was now able to dedicate all of her attention to the angry demon in front of her.

Uŋȟčéǧila was only about five feet away and as Emma Jane readied herself for action, the demon opened her mouth and fire spewed forth. From out of nowhere, Cat jumped between the demon and Emma Jane and the fire harmlessly bounced off of her glowing figure. Emma Jane stared at her with surprise. She'd never seen Cat transform before and now understood why the legends spoke of the phoenix with such awe. Cat ignored Emma Jane, Vanessa, and Samuel, as she kept her hands in front of her, her wings open wide to protect them from the flames.

Uŋȟčéǧila stumbled back, but not for long. Once she'd regained her balance, she growled and leapt forward. Before Cat could react, the demon had wrapped one hidden serpentine-like tentacle around her waist, throwing her violently against the back door. Emma Jane's mouth flew open.

Vanessa cried out. "Cat!"

Emma Jane never took her eyes off Uŋȟčéǧila, but was relieved to hear the sound of the otherwise quiet and calm Cat swearing a blue streak from the back of the room. Without turning her head, Emma Jane spoke to whoever was behind her. "Jake? Zahara? I want you to take Samuel and get him to safety."

She half expected to hear Samuel object, but instead felt him briefly touch her back. "Remember, the seventh space."

Emma Jane dipped her head in acknowledgement, still keeping her gaze on the demon. "Vanessa, please step back. If she could do that to Cat, I don't want to think what she can do to you."

Emma Jane heard a huff from behind her, but no protest. The faint flutter of wings brushed the back of her hair and she knew that Vanessa had transformed into a raven. Good, she was stronger like that. And more mobile. With the area now clear, save for Emma Jane at the front of the room, she reassumed her boxer's stance and began to slowly circle the demon.

Emma Jane's powers were limited for use in close contact with others. Both her fighting skills and her ability to drain power from her opponents required touch to be effective, and she required full concentration in order to use both in battle. Locking out the sight and sound of everything but the

scaly demon in front of her, Emma Jane allowed her enemy
to approach. Once again, the evil serpent opened her mouth
to spit fire and flames, but Emma Jane quickly dashed to the
other side.

Uŋȟčéǧila whirled, growling with frustration as Emma
Jane moved to the other side of the room. She lunged, once
more meeting only empty space as Emma Jane continued to
circle her. Any hunter knew better than to allow a demon to
get hands on them. The legends said she could turn people
to stone with a look, but it was actually with a touch. If any
of the writhing tendril-like snakes emerging from her body
were to contact Emma Jane, she knew they could freeze her
in place and potentially kill her. At one time, she may have
even looked forward to it, for the chance to join her parents
and family. But now, she had Vanessa and her friends to consider. For the first time, Emma Jane's life was worth living
and she was in no rush to see her brothers, parents, or kokum
again.

Emma Jane was beginning to get winded as she tried to
keep out of reach of a demon who was much faster than she
was. Uŋȟčéǧila lunged again and this time, Emma Jane felt
one of the snakes brush her hair. Fear rose in her chest. She
wasn't sure if it was because she was flagging, or if it was the
same fear she'd felt prior to the demon's arrival. She realized
they'd moved closer to the front of the room and were now
near the bathroom entrance. From the floor, an unexpected
growl sprang forth.

Emma Jane's breath was coming faster by now and she
looked around, a flicker of movement from the other corner
caught her eye and distracted her. She squinted, wondering

if she saw something moving in the punch bowl, then shook her head and turned her attention back to Uŋȟčéǧila.

But it was too late. To Emma Jane's horror, she felt her left arm become trapped. As snakes wound around her she pulled her silver knife out of the sheath hidden on her leg and stabbed at the demon's obstructing snaky-tentacles. Before she could stop or remove them, a crash reverberated in the silence. The constriction released enough to allow Emma Jane to yank her arm free. While looking for the source of the noise, she saw shards of pottery on the ground surrounding the now stunned foe who'd fallen to the ground. Just behind Uŋȟčéǧila, looking shocked at the entrance to the bathroom just a foot away, was Mindy McLean, her hands over her mouth. When Mindy saw Emma Jane's expression, she apologized.

"Sorry! I was just checking to see what was happening and you appeared to need a distraction. I'll be in the bathroom if you need me."

With an impressed look, Emma Jane nodded. "Thanks. Now, go away. We're a little busy."

Mindy nodded, ducking back through the bathroom door and closing it firmly behind her. Two foxes barricaded the door, teeth bared and keeping their watchful eyes on the demon, who was rising up from the floor looking angrier than she'd been before, if possible.

Uŋȟčéǧila screamed with rage. "How dare you!"

Emma Jane shrugged. She hadn't actually done anything, but had no problem taking credit for it. "Because I'm like that?"

This time, the demon did not pretend to smile. With her needle-sharp teeth bared and her clawed hands reaching out, she lunged once more for Emma Jane. She was foiled in her attack again, only this time, it was by three small flashes of color. To Emma Jane's bewilderment, there were blue, brown, and orangey-red dragons now flying around the demon's head. Somehow, they remained just out of Uŋȟčéǧila's reach as they giggled with delight.

Emma Jane turned to give Jake and Mai a look, but when they merely shrugged, she turned to Uŋȟčéǧila again. The demon snapped her massive jaws as the red dragon flew past, then pulled back with a shriek as a pint-sized burst of flames emitted from its tiny mouth and caught her on the nose. Before she could retaliate, all three Dragons zoomed off chasing each other. Using the distraction to her advantage, while simultaneously thanking the Great Spirit for toddlers, Emma Jane ducked underneath Uȟčéǧila's massive head, avoiding the writhing snakes and coming up directly beside her thorax.

Samuel's voice echoed in her ears. *Remember the seventh space.* Frantically, Emma Jane assessed the unfamiliar anatomy and plunged toward what she hoped was the seventh space.

Capitalizing on Emma Jane's proximity though, Uŋȟčéǧila trapped her with the snakes, holding her in place. Emma Jane knew she wouldn't be able to get away until the monster was dead. She stabbed again and again, each movement causing more burning ichor to coat her hand. Uŋȟčéǧila shrieked, but didn't drop her hold. *Dammit.* Emma Jane knew she'd missed the space.

Taking a breath, she placed her left hand on the demon's chest and concentrated on absorbing her energy instead. She saw the darkness of the demon's aura traveling through her hand up to her elbow, the roiling black tinged with red as it overwhelmed her, and felt herself becoming hungry the more of it she stole.

She pulled the knife out, and stabbed again, but on the other side of Uŋȟčéǧila's body. This time, the injury, along with the power traveling out of her chest, caused the demon to stumble.

Emma Jane smiled, power flowing to her center as her satisfaction grew at the sight of Uŋȟčéǧila crumpling to the floor. But the demon still moved weakly, so Emma Jane sat on top of her, maintaining the connection to her body in order to absorb her energy. She stabbed a few more times, hardly even aware of the burning in her right hand as the blood ate into her flesh like acid. She felt someone pull her away and whirled on them, growling at the interruption. She bared her teeth at Cat, who was now sitting beside her and glowing with fiery brilliance.

The sight of her sister-in-law still in her phoenix form caused Emma Jane to snap back to her surroundings. She was horrified to realize how dark she'd become. Part of it was her connection to the demon, and the hunger she'd had to eat and destroy as she'd absorbed Uŋȟčéǧila's energy. But part of it had been her own, unfamiliar thirst for a kill. She'd never felt an urge that dark before.

Emma Jane stumbled back, breathing deeply as she fought to regain control. As she'd had to do every other time she'd killed, Emma Jane warred against the darkness within her. Focusing on her center and on forcing the evil leave her body, she was able to contain it and soon, she felt herself returning to normal.

That was when she noticed the excruciating pain in her arm. To her shock, she could see not only areas where the skin had been burned away by the demon's blood, but also areas where bone and muscle were visible through the damage the blood had created. Nausea rose in her throat along with the pain, causing Emma Jane to cover her mouth with the other hand. Shaking her head, she looked up to find Cat and Vanessa watching her.

"Oh, God!"

Emma Jane gulped, still covering her mouth with her left hand as she held the right one out in front of her, shaking with a combination of horror and pain. As she knelt on the floor, she realized a loose circle of her friends had formed around her, consisting of Samuel, Zahara, Omar, Jake, Mai, Cat and Vanessa. They watched her silently, cautiously, without stepping toward her.

Emma Jane didn't blame them. They'd all seen the darkness within her, and she was sure they'd want nothing to do with her from now on. But to her surprise, the expressions she saw on their faces were not those of disgust or fear. Emma Jane bit her lip, her eyes filling with tears as she recognized concern and worry, *for her,* on their faces. While she'd hoped Samuel and Vanessa would stay with her, she didn't expect anyone else to trust her after watching her turn into an evil-killing machine. But they seemed completely unfazed.

"Emma Jane? Can I..."

Cat's soft voice was the first thing to intrude on Emma Jane's swirling thoughts, and she looked up to see Cat standing beside her now, her hand inching toward Emma Jane's ruined right arm. At first, Emma Jane didn't understand what Cat wanted to do, until Vanessa's plea broke through the fog in Emma Jane's brain.

"Please, Emma Jane, *kisakihitin*. Let Cat heal you. You must be in pain. Let her take that away."

Emma Jane looked at Vanessa with confusion. "But it's not safe for anyone to touch me right now." She shook her head, adding, "I'm too open, I might hurt her. You might be safe with the talisman," Vanessa lightly touched the green stone around her neck as Emma Jane continued, "but I don't want to hurt Cat."

Cat protested. "You won't hurt me. Remember? My abilities are the polar opposite of yours. Allow me to help you."

Emma Jane looked at Cat with wonder. She still shone with the fiery radiance of a phoenix, but her face was her own, calm and reassuring, so Emma Jane held her arm out for Cat to take. A warm but not uncomfortable burning filled her as she watched Cat perform a miracle. In front of her eyes, the gaping, oozing places on her arm began to fill in, the damaged skin and tissue replaced by smooth and unblemished surfaces. She looked up at Cat, her mouth open as Cat smiled in satisfaction.

"There. That's better."

Cat exhaled, then almost faster than Emma Jane could blink, she shimmered back into her usual form, the dark blue bridesmaid's dress she'd worn the last time Emma Jane had seen her none the worse for the experience. Emma Jane looked at each face in turn as the entire group returned to their previous, human forms. Not a single one looked at her with anything other than relief and friendship. Except for Vanessa. With her eyes brimming with tears and love, she pulled Emma Jane into her arms.

THE WEDDING
CHAPTER 6

Vanessa shuddered against Emma Jane's hair. She wasn't sure if it was possible to hold onto her any tighter, but when she'd seen the look on Emma Jane's face and the damage to her arm, Vanessa had been devastated. For a moment, she thought she'd lost her love. Once Emma Jane had returned from her struggle to control the influx of dark energy from her defeated foe, however, the woman she loved reappeared behind the swirling thunderstorm-gray eyes. Then, Vanessa had been devastated at the thought that Emma Jane might lose her arm. Thank God her sister was a freaking miracle worker. Otherwise, she was sure Emma Jane's forearm would have fallen off by the time they could have gotten her to a hospital. She'd never seen that kind of damage before; she'd been able to see right through Emma Jane's hand.

Feeling another shudder of relief run through her, Vanessa kissed Emma Jane's forehead, eyelids, nose, and cheeks, before pulling back and holding her face in both palms. She searched the more diminutive woman's swirling, opaque eyes.

"Are you okay? I was worried that..." Vanessa's voice trailed away and she shook her head. She felt Emma Jane's warm and capable hands come up to hold her face in return, smiling with relief when she kissed her back. It felt as though a rainbow had come out after the storm and for the first time in two days, the last traces of her anxiety disappeared.

Vanessa looked at her friends, still standing awkwardly around them in a loose circle as they embraced. She smiled with everything in her heart as a collective sigh filled the room. When she gazed at the faces of her loved ones around her, Vanessa knew everything was going to be fine. She stood up, gently pulling Emma Jane with her.

Now standing together, Vanessa clasped Emma Jane's hand tighter. "Are you ready to finish this ceremony?"

Emma Jane beamed, her face lighting up. "There's nothing I'd like more. We should probably stand where we were when all this began."

Emma Jane pointed at the still dreamy audience and Vanessa nodded, raising her eyebrows as she looked back at her friends.

"You heard the lady. Places, everyone."

They all drifted back to the seats they'd been sitting in when the fog had filled the room. All, that is, except for the triplets, who were suddenly nowhere to be found.

"Freya, Peter, Gaia!" Mai scanned the room, but when none of the children responded, she began to look nervous.

Jake joined in, as did Cat. Just as Vanessa was becoming worried that the demon had done something to them after all, recalling the way they'd buzzed around her earlier, the faint sound of giggles emanated from the back of the room.

Vanessa tiptoed over, noticing the punch bowl was more than half empty. *Strange. No one had had anything to drink yet, except for a few glasses before we began.* But to her amusement, when she peered over the side of the crystal bowl she saw three small fairies sitting on ice cubes, laughing hysterically. When they saw Vanessa's face appear over the side of their little party, they shrieked and attempted to fly away. But instead of the usual graceful twirling movements Vanessa was used to watching them perform in Summerland, they took off erratically, crashing into the wall beside them and sliding down to lay underneath the table. Vanessa raised her eyebrows at the dazed looks upon their pointy little faces and shook her head.

"I did not just see that."

She looked at Robin, quirking an eyebrow, then double checked to make sure Evelyn hadn't let everyone out of their trance yet. The faces in the audience were as blank as they'd been a moment ago, so Vanessa looked at Robin again.

"You brought fairies to the wedding?"

Robin shrugged, unperturbed. "They snuck into my pocket. I put them in the punch bowl for safekeeping." He gave her a mischievous smile. "It's possible they may be a smidge drunk right now. They can't handle their sugar." He blinked his eyelashes, giving her an insincere smile of apology.

Vanessa burst out laughing. She may not have found the dragon triplets, but there was absolutely no way she'd ever forget drunk fairies at her wedding.

From across the room, a triumphant cry rang out. "Got 'em!"

Vanessa straightened up from where she'd been crouched watching the fairies, deciding they were better under the tablecloth sleeping it off, and turned in time to see

Mai leading her wayward offspring out of the bathroom, along with her mom, dad, and Marie-Jean. Vanessa returned to the front, looping her arm through Emma Jane's and holding her around the waist.

"What were they doing?"

Mindy raised an eyebrow, clearly amused. "Well, it just so happens that these three little ones decided they wanted to see what was behind door number two. Needless to say, we decided to keep them with us until after everything was all said and done."

Peter stepped forward to give Vanessa and Emma Jane a hug.

"I can see the danger is past. I hope you don't mind, but I may or may not have taken a few pictures of everyone in action while Mindy had the door open."

Vanessa's mouth dropped open. "Dad! Nobody can see those!" Then she stopped. "Did you happen to get a picture of me as a raven? I always wanted to see that."

Peter laughed, pulling out his phone and was about to start flipping through his pictures when Emma Jane cleared her throat.

"As much as I'd love to see the pictures, I think Evelyn may be getting tired."

Vanessa flushed as she remembered Evelyn, who was still sitting silently next to Robin with her eyes closed as she concentrated. "Sorry, Dad, I totally want to see those, but later. Okay?"

Peter nodded, putting his phone away. "Absolutely. We can look at them tomorrow, once everything is cleaned up. I'm pretty sure I'm going to have some great shots."

Vanessa nodded, giving him a kiss on the cheek. She waited for her parents to sit before turning to Emma Jane. Once again, they stood front and center at the end of the aisle, in the same place they'd been when the fog had first appeared.

Samuel, relieved of his protector, stood where he had earlier, seemingly unbothered by the events that had occurred. Once they were facing him, he nodded. "Excellent work, Emma Jane. Vanessa, it was a pleasure to see you in your true form."

Vanessa blushed, understanding without explanation that as Samuel was a man of few words, this counted as high praise from him.

"Thank you, sir. How are you?" she asked hesitantly. "Emma Jane was worried the demon would hurt you."

Samuel nodded, his face placid as he answered. "I am relieved. Together, you and your friends have finished a task I've long worried over. For many years, I have wondered when or if she would find us. Luckily for us, unluckily for her, she chose today, when we were at our strongest with powerful allies."

He glanced at the place the demon had fallen, now empty after Cat had quietly and efficiently destroyed any evidence by incineration. When he looked back at Vanessa and Emma Jane, he smiled, his teeth flashing white in the overhead lights.

"I can now officially retire, knowing the last of my loose ends have been tied up."

Samuel exhaled, as though a weight had been lifted off his back, then pointed his chin toward the still slumbering crowd. "Shall we continue where we left off?"

Vanessa smiled, turning to face Emma Jane and taking her hand. They waited until Evelyn gave the sign, then repeated the words as Samuel directed, this time, uninterrupted by anyone or anything.

With their vows spoken, they shared a sweet, loving kiss and turned to face the room. Accompanied by a standing ovation, they walked out of the ceremony and into the rest of their lives.

HONEYMOON
CHAPTER 1

Vanessa's bones ached. There was no other way to describe it. What should've been a regular day on set had instead turned into a crazy free-for-all. She yanked the door of her trailer open; her weariness causing her to groan at the strain on her tired arm muscles. Looking down, she groaned again when she noticed a tremble in her biceps.

"I never signed up for this," she muttered to herself, entering the trailer and letting the cheap metal door slam behind her.

She sat down in the chair in front of her mirror, grabbing makeup remover and wiping off not only her pancake makeup but actual pancakes. Vanessa had been surprised when she'd shown up to work that morning to find the director disturbingly gleeful. She'd expected to shoot a relatively tame living room scene that day, but when he'd informed the cast that he'd changed his mind and decided the episode needed more punch, she'd been certain she wouldn't like his good mood after all. When she found out they were going to do a breakfast food-fight instead, she should have known today would be a disaster.

Normally, getting messy wouldn't have bothered her. But unfortunately, they'd had to shoot the scene close to thirty times to get it right. That meant that plate after plate was thrown at her and by her, not to mention all the makeup, hair, and clothing changes that were required each time they'd had to do another take. Vanessa usually had energy to spare, given the extra 'oomph' that came from her ability to change into a raven and control air magic, but apparently, this had overwhelmed even her ample resources.

When she was convinced that she was as clean as she could get without a twenty minute shower, Vanessa changed back into her jeans and a plain T-shirt before throwing on her three-season jacket. The weather had finally started to warm up, but it was still chilly in the evenings and Vanessa knew her tired body would not appreciate being cold. A faint knock on the door broke her grouchy reverie and Vanessa moved stiffly as she pulled it open.

"Hey, you were late and didn't call, so I thought I'd stop by and see if you needed anything."

Vanessa smiled. Just like that, her fatigue and pain melted away at the sight of her beautiful new wife. "We just finished. Today was totally brutal."

Emma Jane tilted her head to the side, giving Vanessa a critical once over before stepping in and allowing the door to shut behind her. She leaned in, offering Vanessa her lips, which she accepted gratefully. A mixture of joy, love, and desire filled her instantaneously. For a moment, they stood there, clasped together in a tight embrace. When Vanessa felt her desire began to overwhelm all other sensations, she reluctantly pulled back to look at Emma Jane.

"You're exactly what I need right now. Amazingly, I already feel way better than I did a second ago. I'm glad you came. Does that mean you finished whatever it was you were doing?"

Emma Jane's expression transitioned through a series of emotions. While Vanessa could see the love, which she knew was mirrored on her own face, she also caught a faint flicker of guilt flash across her countenance before it was hidden behind Emma Jane's trademark stoicism.

Emma Jane nodded. "Yes, for now. And I missed you, so I thought I'd see where you were."

Vanessa pulled back, grabbing her purse and looping her arm back through Emma Jane's. "Well, your timing is good, because I'm ready to go. How did you get here?"

Emma Jane shrugged. "I walked. It was a nice evening, and I felt the need to be outside and reconnect."

Vanessa raised her eyebrows but didn't comment. After only a few short months together, Vanessa was aware of Emma Jane's need to spend time outside, preferably in areas that weren't developed by humans. She said it allowed her to meditate and contact the Great Spirit better and Vanessa hadn't questioned her reasons. Prior to grade twelve, when she'd discovered her own powers, Vanessa had been more of an indoor girl. But once she'd developed her ability to control the air and transform into the shape of a raven, she'd felt profoundly connected to nature as well. So the fact that Emma Jane had walked for almost an hour just to check on her didn't strike her as unusual, even though she had the sneaking suspicion Emma Jane had something else on her mind.

"I brought the car to work, so no walking for me tonight. Any ideas what you'd like to do for supper? We can hit up a drive through on the way home, if you want," Vanessa offered.

Emma Jane wrinkled her nose. "Let me think on it for a bit."

The two women walked out together as Vanessa waved absently at the few familiar faces they passed. On Fridays, the set usually cleared out within ten minutes except for stragglers like Vanessa, who preferred to clean up as much as she could prior to leaving. Then again, she'd also been getting interesting and complex makeup lately, while most of the behind stage people were free to leave after they'd put their equipment away.

Once in the car, Emma Jane answered Vanessa's earlier question. "Cat mentioned before I left that she'd like Chinese take-out tonight if we were interested. I can send her a text and let her know that's okay if you want? That way we don't have to stop anywhere."

Vanessa was learning how to wait, a new and weird experience for her. She had a tendency to blurt, but she found herself trying harder to be considerate and wait for Emma Jane to say something first. To her surprise, for the most part, it had worked. While quiet, Emma Jane had plenty to say if you gave her enough time to say it. She'd simply been raised to think first before speaking, which was a trait Vanessa was eager to learn.

Vanessa nodded, putting the car into gear and backing out of the parking lot. "Sounds good. The usual is fine."

Emma Jane sent a quick text to Cat, sitting back comfortably in the passenger seat as Vanessa drove the short distance. Due to her vision making her legally blind, Emma

Jane had never learned how to drive, but she was a surprisingly calm backseat driver compared to Vanessa's sister, Cat, who still occasionally tried to grab the wheel from her. Then again, Cat likely had bad memories from the car accident they'd been in back in high school, so it was understandable.

By the time they arrived home, Vanessa was relieved to find her muscles less sore than they'd been when she finished work. Thankful for her ability to recover quickly, Vanessa looped her arm through Emma Jane's and they walked up the stairway together. Vanessa paused at the landing, looking down at Emma Jane's shiny, dark hair that had fallen in front of her shoulders and went all the way down to the middle of her chest. Smiling, Vanessa brushed it back, letting her hand linger as it moved across her body.

Emma Jane's eyes began to swirl, their usual milky white darkening into thunderclouds. Vanessa watched with fascination as the evidence of her love's emotions became apparent. Unable to help herself, Vanessa leaned in, stealing a kiss on the doorstep of their house. Sure, Cat still lived there, but ever since they'd returned from the mountains as a married couple, Vanessa had thought of the apartment as *their* place. She wasn't sure how long they'd been standing there, lost in each other's lips, but the sound of someone awkwardly clearing their throat brought her back to the present with a jerk.

Turning around to find an uncomfortable appearing young man holding a large paper bag, she realized they must've been standing outside longer then she'd thought. Either that, or Cat had already ordered before Emma Jane had texted her back.

"I have a delivery, for Cat?"

The short young man held the bag out with shaking hands. Vanessa read all kinds of anxiety radiating off the man, even without having any superhuman abilities to do so.

Vanessa bit back a laugh as she nodded. "Yes, that's us. How much is it? I can take it from you."

The man nodded, eagerly accepting her money before turning tail and almost running down the stairs and into the night. The minute he was out of earshot, Vanessa let her laughter go. Emma Jane joined in, shaking her head.

"Well, he certainly seemed surprised," she stated, a soft smile on her face as she gazed up at Vanessa.

Vanessa found herself falling back under the spell of Emma Jane's eyes, until the door opened without warning.

"Are you guys having fun? I could hear you out here. Isn't it too cold to stand out here and do... whatever it is that you're doing?"

Cat leaned on the door, gesturing at Vanessa and Emma Jane with one eyebrow arched in amusement.

Vanessa laughed, brushing past her sister with the bag of food and placing it on the counter. "Whatever, Cat. I was just enjoying a goodnight kiss, then the food guy showed up and brought me a present."

Cat rolled her eyes. "Yeah, that's what you were doing. Anyway, I'm starved. I ordered all my favorites." Cat relented when she saw Vanessa's narrowed eyes. "And yours, of course. After all, it's a celebration."

Vanessa pursed her lips. "Celebration? What exactly are we celebrating?" She looked suspiciously at Cat, but when her eyes moved to Emma Jane in time to catch her covering her mouth, Vanessa lowered her head and crossed her arms.

"Oops?" Cat said, looking guilty.

Emma Jane just laughed, sitting down at the table after grabbing herself a plate of food. "It's fine, Cat. I was going to tell her over supper anyway. Now that we have food, technically you haven't spilled the beans."

Vanessa sat beside Emma Jane and put her plate down. "Tell me what, exactly?"

Vanessa wondered if this had anything to do with the hint of guilt she'd seen in her wife's face earlier at work. Emma Jane was usually an open book, so Vanessa knew something was up. Hopefully, it was something she'd enjoy.

Emma Jane chewed a bite of ginger beef, slowly, dragging out Vanessa's suspense until she was almost ready to snap before she finally responded, setting her fork down and looking earnestly at Vanessa.

"I wanted to show you how special you are. While I was trying to think of ways I could do that, I realized that we never had a honeymoon."

Vanessa sat back, floored. That wasn't what she'd been expecting at all. "What do you mean? We got married in Banff. I thought that was our honeymoon."

Emma Jane shrugged. "I considered it part of the wedding, myself. Now that we've had the family ceremony and party, I'd like us to go somewhere together, to get away from your work and everyone else."

Vanessa felt her excitement rise, remembering how stressful their second wedding day had been. "Okay, I'm listening. So far, I'm liking how this sounds. How did you manage to arrange this without me finding out?"

Emma Jane smiled, her bright white teeth almost glowing against her darkly tanned skin. "I had a helper." She tilted her head toward Cat.

Cat blushed. "Honestly, Vanessa, I only helped a little. I know you hate surprises unless you're the one doing them, but Emma Jane needed names and phone numbers, and well, a set of eyes..." Cat trailed off, the last words hardly a mumble as Vanessa's eyebrows rose even higher.

"I'm still listening. I'm not sure if I'm going to be upset or not yet. I need a few more details to decide."

Emma Jane nodded. "Fair enough. Well, I remembered you saying that you'd never had a chance to travel, as you guys moved around a lot growing up." Emma Jane looked at Cat, who ducked her head at Vanessa's mistrustful look. "So, with Cat's help, I contacted your work to find out when the best time to go away would be. It just so happens that it was possible to get a few weeks off once this week's scenes are shot. The director promised that we could take off after work is over on Friday."

Vanessa blinked in surprise. "You got him to make you a promise? After everything that's happened on set in the last few months?"

Emma Jane nodded and Vanessa knew she was also thinking about their run-in with the producer's late wife a few months earlier. She'd been a witch who'd targeted Vanessa's workplace, using it for a steady supply of young actresses to steal their beauty, along with their souls.

That was how Emma Jane had met Vanessa in the first place. Cat's best friend, Evelyn, had warned Emma Jane that Vanessa was going to be the witch's next victim unless she intervened. While Vanessa wasn't excited about having to fight evil, in this case, she felt she owed a debt of gratitude to the woman who'd tried to kill her. After all, if it hadn't been for the witch, Emma Jane would've never come into her life, and she wouldn't be the happiest she'd ever been.

Cat interrupted the shared moment, clearing her throat hesitantly. "I may have had something to do with that. I went with Emma Jane in person last week and kind of, maybe, put a little shine on his aura."

At Vanessa's shocked look, Cat blushed again. "I felt so bad for the guy, Vanessa. I mean, his aura was incredibly sad. It's been a tough year all around, and it's hard to have that many people die around you. I just took some of the sadness away. I guess he was so happy that when Emma Jane asked him for two weeks off for a honeymoon right after that, well, he had absolutely no problem with the idea."

Vanessa laughed. "Wow, Cat, I never thought you'd do that. Isn't that kinda my thing?"

Vanessa usually tried not to use her charisma, which was part and parcel of the set of gifts she discovered, but that *was* how she'd scored their apartment. Not only was she outgoing and generally well-liked, but if someone was being particularly difficult, she could always use her charm to influence them. She hadn't been expecting her almost completely Girl Scout-good sister to do anything of the sort, however.

Cat got a petulant look on her face but moved on. "Anyway," she paused while Vanessa smirked, then continued. "He was in such a good mood he agreed to two weeks off after Friday's shoot. Sounds like he's of the opinion that the entire cast and crew could do with a short break after losing four people in a short amount of time. Plus, you guys are close to the end of the season, so he wants to sit down with the writers for a week without anyone else there. He said something about planning next season?"

Vanessa nodded. "Okay, that makes more sense. You mean, he doesn't want to pay people to be on set while he's brainstorming."

Cat nodded, waving a hand. "Exactly. That's about where my involvement ended."

Vanessa looked at Emma Jane. "Did you say helper, or helpers?"

Emma Jane smiled, and Vanessa saw her mischievous inner child peek out. "Well, I may have spoken with Evelyn, as well."

Vanessa pursed her lips. "Interesting. And what did Evelyn have to say?"

This time, Emma Jane couldn't hold back a smile. "Well, the place I thought we should go involved a bit of a journey. I wasn't thrilled by the plane flight we took between here and Banff, as you recall, so I wasn't looking forward to the idea of doing something like that again so soon."

"Okay, I can't wait anymore. Stop dragging this out. Where are we going?"

Vanessa leaned forward, all thoughts of food completely forgotten as she rubbed her hands together and waited for Emma Jane to answer. Plane travel usually meant somewhere awesome.

Emma Jane now looked every bit as excited as Vanessa felt as she blurted out one word.

"France!"

Vanessa's mouth dropped open, then she jumped up and squealed.

HONEYMOON
CHAPTER 2

They finished eating eventually, but it had taken Vanessa a while to calm down after Emma Jane's big reveal. Now her biggest challenge was dealing with the fact that she still had an entire week to get through before they could leave. The biggest surprise and perk of the trip, which she'd found out once she'd stopped screaming, was that Evelyn had spoken to Robin, and he was cool with her taking them through Summerland instead of flying to France. Evelyn had even promised to show them her private entrance, where she met Robin for their visits.

Not only was Evelyn a goddess in her own right, but she frequently traveled between San Francisco, where she lived as herself, to other locations around the world, where she acted as a much more powerful being. Once she'd discovered who she was, she'd also found out that her powers were strongest in Africa, where her legend began. She'd been returning on a frequent basis ever since in order to recharge and rejuvenate, as well as to visit friends she'd made during her journey of discovery a little over one month earlier.

Normally, Evelyn didn't like to ask Robin for favors when it came to using Summerland to travel. It felt a bit presumptuous for the girls to ask him for anything unless it was truly important. But Evelyn had felt so bad about the debacle of their wedding that she'd wanted to make it up to them. Apparently, Robin had agreed, because she told them he planned to meet with them himself to say hello.

Vanessa smiled whenever she thought about Robin. He'd always been this cute, rambunctious little boy, right up until they'd traveled to Scotland when Cat and Evelyn had been in grade twelve. Looking back now, Vanessa felt strongly that was the trip when everything in their lives had changed forever, for better and worse.

Sure, they'd all known they had powers for a few years by then, but Scotland was when they had all matured, becoming who they were meant to be. That was when Vanessa had found out she could turn into a raven, when Evelyn had discovered she was a goddess, and when Robin had revealed himself to be her long-lost partner. Up until then, he'd been waiting for Evelyn to remember who she was and what he'd meant to her.

Vanessa smirked, remembering the first time Evelyn had told her that she was in love with Robin. She'd been pretty grossed out, until she'd seen the Robin who Evelyn was in love with, then everything had clicked. When he'd revealed himself to Evelyn, his form had also changed from that of a young boy to an model-hot young man. While Vanessa loved Emma Jane more than anyone she'd ever met and thought she was the most incredibly attractive person in the world, she could still appreciate a fine man when she saw one.

"As much as I'm enjoying the conversation, ladies, I think it's time for me to head to bed. I need to get some sleep so that I can be fresh to study tomorrow." Cat yawned, stretching as she matched her actions to her words.

Vanessa looked over at Cat, nodding absently and was about to say goodnight when she stopped. She squinted, giving Cat a suspicious look when her sister's eyes slid away.

"Wait. You have more secrets. What else should I know about?" Vanessa heard the warning tone in her voice and knew Cat did too.

Cat shook her head, deflecting. "No, I absolutely do not. You know everything now. You're going to France with Emma Jane for a second honeymoon, or first one, you guys are still arguing about that, and Robin is going to be your transport this time. I have no other secrets about you." Cat pursed her lips, still looking guilty.

Vanessa held Cat's gaze, not missing the fact she said *'about you'*.

"Is there something else you'd like to talk to me about?" Vanessa was curious, but Cat blushed and looked away as she waved her hand in an airy goodbye and disappeared into her bedroom.

Vanessa turned to Emma Jane, who was snuggled beside her on the couch. After the great revelation of the honeymoon trip surprise, the three women had retired to the living room to watch HGTV and had basically been chilling out until Cat had decided it was time for bed. Vanessa loved being with Emma Jane in a way she hadn't ever enjoyed being with anybody else, so while she knew they seemed to be settling into a boring married life, she didn't mind. In fact, she relished it. There had been enough excitement already in their relationship that she was treasuring each moment of sitting on the couch and doing nothing with her love. Vanessa bit her lip as she looked down at Emma Jane. She couldn't stop thinking about Cat, so she asked Emma Jane the question that had been plaguing her.

"Has Cat said anything to you?"

Emma Jane shook her head, drawing her eyebrows together. "About what?"

Vanessa wrinkled her nose. "I don't know. I just get the feeling there's something going on with her. I wondered about it when we were chasing that soul thief, but the feeling has gotten stronger over the last month or so. Do you think she could be seeing someone?"

When Emma Jane only shrugged, Vanessa frowned. "She'd tell me, wouldn't she? I mean, we're sisters. We're supposed to share everything."

Emma Jane gave Vanessa a hug. While patting her long, raven-colored hair, she tried to placate her. "I'm sure she'll tell you if there's anything going on, but only when she's ready."

At Vanessa's disgruntled look, Emma Jane took her chin gently in her right hand and held it so that she could look into her eyes. "Cat and I are a lot alike, Vanessa. It takes time for us to open up to people and to share our feelings. Even with those we love. I'm sure there's been many times growing up when Cat kept important information to herself."

Vanessa exhaled with a small huff. "Yeah, you're right. I mean, she knew about her powers for at least a month or two before she said anything to me. And she's never been one to share, let alone over-share. If there is someone bothering her or something happening, unless it's something she needs help with, she'll probably keep it to herself. It's just so frustrating! She always knows everything about me before I even understand what's happening."

Emma Jane dropped a kiss onto Vanessa's pouting lips. "It takes all kinds, Vanessa. After all, it's working out for us. Maybe Cat does have someone she's interested in. But if so, we'll find out at the right time. Try to be patient."

Vanessa let out a small growl, pulling Emma Jane down to enact a loving protest on her wife in response to her sensible words.

SATURDAY MORNING, EMMA Jane watched with a grin as Vanessa pulled everything out of her closet. After several minutes, she took a chance and commented. "We're only going for two weeks Vanessa. You don't really need that many clothes, do you?"

Vanessa scowled, gesturing at what Emma Jane was currently wearing. "Says the woman who wears jeans and boots almost every day and alternates T-shirts that I can't always tell the difference between."

Emma Jane shrugged, unperturbed by Vanessa's tone or words. "You knew what you were getting into with me. Clothing and possessions are not things I value. After two decades of traveling, you learn to pack light. Did you want me to give you some help?"

Emma Jane bit her lip as she waited for Vanessa to choke down the irritation simmering just beneath the surface. She didn't have a problem with Vanessa packing a lot of clothing but she knew Vanessa would complain bitterly if she had to carry luggage everywhere they went. Emma Jane had planned an itinerary she hoped Vanessa would enjoy wholeheartedly, but it did involve a lot of traveling between destinations.

To her surprise, Vanessa gave in instead of arguing further. She flopped onto the bed on several layers of shirts before rolling over onto her back and groaning. "Why is this so hard? I mean, I love clothes, but I know I don't need them all. I just can't decide what to wear. I want to look good for you."

Emma Jane melted at the look of tortured chagrin on Vanessa's face. "Vanessa, you look amazing in nothing at all. If it was up to me, you wouldn't need very much."

Vanessa's cheeks flushed, and her eyes turned a darker shade of blue as she processed Emma Jane's words. She seductively raised one eyebrow. "Oh yeah? Well in that case, maybe I will let you help me pack." She paused, adding one qualifier. "As long as you let me make sure that everything matches."

Emma Jane laughed. "Deal. I'll even let you pick something for me to wear, in case we go somewhere nice. How's that for a compromise?"

Vanessa rolled off the bed, bounding over to where Emma Jane leaned against the dresser and one smooth motion pulled Emma Jane in for a kiss which became intense the second their lips touched. Emma Jane felt the dark green stone, cool against her skin as it hung around Vanessa's neck, and lightly stroked it. It may not look like much, but it was because of this small green stone, simply set on a rawhide leather strap, that she was as happy as she was at this moment. Without it, none of this would be possible. Without it, a kiss from her could kill her true love.

Vanessa must have sensed Emma Jane's distraction because she pulled back, looking at her with concern. "Are you okay? You left me there."

Emma Jane smiled up at Vanessa, so tall and beautiful, and stroked a lock of her silky hair, moving the strands behind her shoulder then letting her hand trail down her wife's back.

"I was just thinking how amazing it is that we get to be together."

Vanessa looked at the green stone around her neck, then curled her fingers around it. "It is amazing, isn't it? Sometimes the simplest things can make the biggest difference in life."

After that, it only took a half hour to pack. Which was a good thing, because they'd just sat down to have a cup of coffee when the doorbell rang. Emma Jane looked at Vanessa.

"Evelyn." They said in unison, smiling with anticipation.

Vanessa got up to answer the door. Evelyn was standing there, with her familiar chocolate brown curls bouncing around her shoulders and a bright smile that flashed every single one of her teeth. While Emma Jane couldn't see Evelyn the way the other girls did, she felt like she saw her more clearly. Evelyn's spirit was more beautiful than anyone else's, except possibly Robin's. Her aura lit up an area of several feet around her, and that was while her powers were contained. Emma Jane had caught a mere glimmer of her true nature once, at the wedding, when she'd helped them take care of an old adversary of Emma Jane's who'd tried to crash the party. Even at that time though, Emma Jane knew she hadn't seen the full scope of her goddess-friend's power, as she'd been focused on keeping the entire audience in a trance instead of showing Emma Jane what she could do against an adversary.

"You don't have to do this, you know," Emma Jane said suddenly, causing Vanessa to look at her with confusion.

But Evelyn just laughed. "Of course I don't, silly. I know that. I'm doing this because I want to. I never gave you guys a wedding present. Plus, Robin's still embarrassed about the guests he brought to the wedding. Just think of this as a housewarming present, or a belated wedding gift. Whatever helps you to accept our help with an open heart."

Emma Jane nodded, relieved despite not wanting to rely on others. Although she hated to impose, the idea of flying wasn't something she'd been looking forward to.

"Thank you. I'm still not sure how I got so lucky to have such amazing women in my life. You've all been so wonderful to me."

Evelyn flashed a dimple before taking Emma Jane's hand and giving it a quick squeeze. "It's not like you don't deserve it, Emma Jane. You've had a rough life, through no fault of your own. You make a wonderful friend and I feel just as lucky to have you in my life. So there." Evelyn turned to wave a hand in Vanessa's direction. "Plus, I've never seen Vanessa so happy. Cat and I were getting pretty worried about her last year. Without Mai there to balance her, she seemed to be getting more down by the day. No one was happier than I was when I started to have dreams suggesting you two would have an important connection. And while I never expected this, it's turned out far better than I could've ever imagined, for both of you and everyone else as well."

Tears burned Emma Jane's eyes so she sniffed quickly, changing the subject. She wasn't a fan of letting her emotions get away on her. "Well, thanks again. Are you ready to go?"

Evelyn nodded. "Yep. Just waiting for you guys. Do you need any help carrying anything?"

A sullen look crept over Vanessa's face as her lower lip stuck out. She gestured to one small, hard-sided, leopard print suitcase on the floor beside the table. "This is all I'm bringing."

Evelyn's eyebrows shot up almost to her hairline. "Are you sure? You brought twice this much when we went to Scotland and that was to fight a witch, not go touring. You're only bringing this tiny little suitcase for your honeymoon?"

Vanessa looked down at the hard-sided leopard-print suitcase, while Emma Jane tried to bite back a grin.

"Yes. Emma Jane helped me pack."

Evelyn burst into a deep, belly laugh then raised her hand to give Emma Jane a fist bump. Emma Jane accepted, unable to keep her own amusement from escaping.

Evelyn shook her head. "Looks like you're quite the influence on our little clotheshorse. Next thing I know, you guys will be dressing the same."

"Hey! Watch what you say about me. I'm standing right here. And there's no way that's happening." Vanessa shuddered in mock horror. "I'd go crazy if I could only wear a few colors. I need more variety in my day-to-day apparel. I don't think I'd survive."

Emma Jane rolled her eyes. Vanessa talked a good talk, but she knew better. Vanessa wasn't nearly as obsessed with appearances as she pretended to be.

"Right, Vanessa." Emma Jane winked, causing Evelyn to laugh.

"Wow, you guys are already an old married couple. All right, before I have to break up an episode of the original *Honeymooners*, let's go."

As it turned out, the gate Evelyn had been using for her special visits to Robin was halfway between her apartment and where the girls lived, so they were able to walk over within minutes.

Emma Jane appreciated the quiet spot, which was almost completely hidden by bushes interspersed with wildflowers. With the notorious fog that always seemed to surround the Bay area in the early morning hours, it was unlikely that anyone would notice if a few girls seemed to magically vanish into the air. Because Emma Jane didn't see the world exactly the way others did, she was instead able to see a faint glimmer covering the entire area, as though someone had dropped fine glitter on everything.

She stepped closer, fascinated by the thought that the air itself was alive. She'd never seen her surroundings have this quality before, only living creatures, but it was her first experience with Summerland. She'd met Robin at their wedding ceremony, but as far as she knew, that had been the one and only time. She'd never visited him on his own territory. Robin reminded her of the tales of coyote, which had been retold throughout First Nations peoples for centuries. She wondered if he had a counterpart who lived in North America, or if maybe a younger Robin had been more of a traveler than he was now.

As Emma Jane walked into the shimmering air, she had a sensation of her body being draped in a cool fabric. It was light and not uncomfortable, but was appreciably different than the air she'd left behind. A moment later, the impression was gone, and when she looked around, the shimmer was gone as well. She'd somehow entered into a radiant woodland glade. It reminded her of Southern Manitoba in July, the way the grass was high and the trees luxuriant and green. She could almost taste the humid, fragrant air.

For a moment, she thought she saw dandelion seeds floating past, but when she examined them more closely she realized they were tiny creatures. If she wasn't mistaken, they were similar to the winged beings that had been in the punch bowl at the wedding.

Emma Jane looked at Evelyn, pointing with the index finger of her right hand between the small airborne creatures and herself. "Are those the..."

Evelyn grimaced. "Yeah, that was pretty much the first and last time they've ever been to a party. Don't worry, Robin's kind of ticked at them right now. They won't give you any trouble."

Vanessa snorted and Emma Jane whirled, raising her eyebrows pointedly. "What? You have to admit, it was pretty funny. I mean, how often do you see little drunk fairies? It's definitely a memory that I'll treasure," Vanessa protested, choking back laughter.

Emma Jane relaxed, now able to see the humor in the situation. She let out a dry chuckle of her own. "I guess you're right. After all, given everything else that happened that night, drunk fairies were kind of the highlight.

"Hello, my ladies."

Emma Jane turned in surprise, not having heard the arrival of the tall, attractive, dark-skinned man who was suddenly standing right behind her. It startled her and made her question her abilities as a hunter. Robin must have noticed her consternation, because he flashed a bright, dimpled smile and leaned over to kiss her cheek.

"Worry not, my wise hunter. It is through no lack of your abilities you cannot track my movements." He shrugged, brushing off one shoulder with false modesty. "I am a god, after all. I like to come and go as I choose, and generally, I like to do it in such a way as to create a lasting impression."

Evelyn rolled her eyes as she walked up to him then pulled him down for a much more personal kiss than he'd bestowed upon Emma Jane. Robin wrapped his arms around Evelyn, clearly enjoying the hello for a few moments before spinning her around once and placing her back on the ground with a small dip for a flourish.

"My dear, it has been too long. Will you be staying...after?" Robin tilted his head toward Emma Jane and Vanessa.

Evelyn returned his heated look with one of her own. "Of course. I have nowhere I need to rush away to at the moment."

Vanessa cleared her throat. "Hello? Still standing right here. If you guys are busy, we could totally be on our way. Not trying to rush you or anything, but you look like you have other things to...discuss."

Robin laughed then leapt over to give Vanessa a quick hug and whirl of her own.

"I do enjoy messing around here, but you are definitely one of my favorites, Lady Charisma. If you and your love would like to continue, head straight through toward those two trees right over there." Robin pointed to an area between two large oak trees. He waited until both Vanessa and Emma Jane nodded, then continued. "That is the path you will need for your journey. The door will take you to a place inside the city of Paris."

Vanessa narrowed her eyes. "Paris? Aren't there too many people there for a gate to remain secret?"

Robin shrugged. "The gates are always in places of power. Which is not necessarily tied to where the people are. In this case, the gate is well hidden. While technically in an area that people frequent, it is also a gate that few know about unless I wish them to."

Emma Jane shrugged, looking at Vanessa. "If Robin says it's okay, I believe him. Are you ready?"

Vanessa nodded, giving Robin one more hug. "Thank you so much. It means a lot to me that you'd let us go on a pleasure trip using the Summerland Express."

Robin smiled, tweaking Vanessa's nose. "It is my pleasure, little raven. I am sorry your last event was disorganized by everything that happened that day. But although this is meant to be a holiday, you must remember to keep your eyes open. As you know, things are never quite what they seem. You may get more than you bargained for from your honeymoon, in the end."

When Emma Jane and Vanessa both looked at him suspiciously, Evelyn rushed in with her own goodbyes. "You guys have a great time. Bring me back a souvenir and stay safe. You can always give any one of us a call if you need help."

She gave Vanessa and Emma Jane quick hugs, before pulling back and sharing another bright smile. "But if you're gonna call, try Cat first. Cell reception isn't always good where I am, and Robin lets everything go to voicemail." Evelyn shrugged, but shot Robin an irritated look that belied her nonchalant tone.

"What?" he asked, but before Evelyn could launch into the complaint that seemed to have been brewing for a while, Emma Jane interrupted.

"Thank you for everything, both of you. We'll definitely call if we need help." Emma Jane looked at Vanessa, who grabbed her suitcase then glanced uncertainly at Evelyn and Robin, who clearly had some things to discuss. Then without further ado, the couple walked together, holding hands, toward the giant trees that marked their path.

HONEYMOON
CHAPTER 3

Vanessa didn't expect this. She was never entirely sure where she'd end up when anything involved Summerland and gating, but when she'd walked between the two tall trees holding Emma Jane's hand, she'd fully expected to emerge somewhere else that had trees. Every other time she'd gone into and out of Summerland, there'd always been trees.

In Valleyview, the gate was at the park, and in Scotland, it had been the Khan's backyard. Even in San Francisco, there'd been a shrubbery or two involved. But now she was standing in the dark, blinking at a cement wall and wondering where the heck she was. Vanessa squeezed her wife's hand, letting go of a breath she didn't realize she'd been holding when she felt Emma Jane's warm hand squeeze back.

"This is interesting." Emma Jane's calm voice relaxed Vanessa. If Emma Jane wasn't worried, Vanessa would try not to be either.

Vanessa's eyes slowly became accustomed to the darkness, and she realized it wasn't pitch black like she'd first thought. While she didn't recognize their location, she could now see that they were in a tunnel that appeared to have a light at the far end. Turning to face Emma Jane, she gripped her suitcase tighter with her other hand. "Where do you think we are? I can't see much, but I feel like we're underground."

Emma Jane let out a humming sound, causing Vanessa to tilt her head with confusion.

"What is it?"

"Well, if we're in an underground tunnel and the gate has brought us inside Paris, then I'm guessing we're inside the catacombs. Not where I expected to gate to, that's all."

Vanessa's mouth dropped open but she shut it quickly, even though Emma Jane couldn't see her in the dark. "What do you mean, the catacombs?"

Instead of answering immediately, Vanessa was tugged along by the hand as Emma Jane moved toward the light. After a few minutes, Emma Jane spoke as though teaching a class.

"Paris has an extensive collection of underground tunnels. For centuries, people were buried below the city in catacombs. At times, these burials were official, but at others, they were definitely along the lines of unofficial and at other times were even body disposal by those who'd created the dead person in the first place. The graves in here range everywhere from elaborate to mass, and to quick and illegal burials."

Vanessa saw the flash of teeth in the dim light and knew that Emma Jane was smiling as she explained.

"In fact, they're quite popular with the tourists. And not just what we would consider dark tourists."

"Dark tourists?"

Emma Jane nodded, now becoming visible as they approached the end of the tunnel. "You know, people that travel the world seeking out macabre or dark stories. In fact, I'm pretty sure there's a documentary on Netflix about them."

Vanessa raised an eyebrow but didn't comment. As the light became brighter, she was able to make out a set of stairs at the end of the long tunnel. While not elegant, they were easy enough to ascend, even while dragging her wheeled suitcase behind her. When they emerged above ground, Vanessa discovered that the light she'd been following was a street lamp and it was nighttime. She looked at her watch, which had become completely useless within Summerland as always, and was surprised to find that it now read after two a.m. Apparently, jetlag from Summerland was a thing.

"I'm not sure what you had planned, but I'm thinking most of the tourist attractions in Paris are closed for the night by now. Did you make any arrangements for a hotel?"

Emma Jane shrugged, unconcerned. "No, I wasn't sure what time we'd arrive, or where, for that matter. But from the research I did with Cat I'm sure this time of year isn't too busy with tourists. Can you read a street sign for our location right now?" Emma Jane turned to Vanessa. While she may be able to use technology to help her with many things, ordinary street signs weren't something she could make out on her own, especially in the dark.

Vanessa squinted, but when she couldn't read anything in the dark from where they stood she headed to the nearest street-corner a few feet away, leaving her suitcase and Emma Jane behind. "I'm sure I'm totally butchering this, but it says we're on Rue d' Alesia."

Emma Jane nodded. "Ah, c'est bien."

Vanessa's eyebrows went up. "Um, what did you just say?"

Emma Jane smiled. "We learned French in school. I just said that's good."

Vanessa nodded. "Okay. Why is it good?"

Emma Jane closed her eyes, looking as though she was thinking for a moment, then opened them and pointed to the road ahead. "There's a Marriott, just down the street to the right."

Vanessa shot her an impressed look. "How'd you know that?"

Emma Jane smiled. "Because I did my research. While I wasn't sure where the Summerland gate would take us, I did look into Paris and its many attractions. I knew for certain we'd want to explore Paris for at least a few days of our trip. The catacombs are quite famous, and it was one of the places I'd looked to see which hotels were nearby, in case we visited and wanted to stay in the area."

"Cool. Shall we walk to the hotel and try to book, or should we call first?"

Emma Jane wrinkled her nose. "Walk. It's a nice night, and it's already two am. It will be easier to explain in person I'm sure, especially with a language barrier."

"Good point. Well then, Milady?" Vanessa offered Emma Jane her arm, which Emma Jane accepted with a mock bow.

As they walked down the quiet street, lit by quaint street lamps, Vanessa felt a tingle of happiness spread through her. They were finally starting their honeymoon adventure in the most romantic city in the world. She couldn't wait for tomorrow.

HONEYMOON
CHAPTER 4

Vanessa stretched out, enjoying the luxurious sensation of the cool, soft sheets of the bed against her skin. They'd arrived at the hotel only a few minutes after exiting the catacombs, and she'd been grateful when the front desk clerk hadn't acted surprised or put out by their appearance at that time in the morning. Maybe it was the Parisian nonchalance she'd heard so much about, or maybe it happened frequently enough that they didn't bat an eye.

Whatever the case, Emma Jane had handled the conversation while Vanessa had paid with her visa. Apparently, the combination of her money and Emma Jane's French had been enough to earn a smooth admission into a lovely room with a scenic view of the downtown, although all they could see were the lights in the darkness. While technically only afternoon at home, Vanessa and Emma Jane had been tired and had fallen asleep almost immediately after settling in.

The sun now streaming in between the slats of the supposedly blackout blinds told Vanessa it was at least morning, if not afternoon. When she checked her watch and found it was just after ten, she rolled over in bed to look at Emma Jane. To her surprise, however, she wasn't there. Sitting upright, Vanessa looked around the room with worry, then smiled when she saw Emma Jane sitting in the middle of the floor next to the bed, meditating. Vanessa rested on her elbows, watching Emma Jane with a sense of contentment. But the moment didn't last long. Emma Jane sensed Vanessa watching her and her mystical swirling white eyes opened, captivating Vanessa as always.

"You're awake," Emma Jane stated.

"Yes. I slept amazingly well last night." Vanessa smiled, still resting her head on her arms as she looked at Emma Jane. "I didn't know you spoke French. This is going to be an amazing trip. You can be my translator." Vanessa sat up in bed with excitement at the idea, but Emma Jane protested.

"Whoa there, don't get too excited. It's been awhile since I've spoken French with anyone. I'm pretty rusty. I'm not sure you could tell, but half of the conversation I had last night with the front desk was actually in English." Emma Jane stood up, dropping a light kiss on Vanessa's mouth.

"Mmmmm, you taste like coffee. Do I get to have coffee too?" Vanessa said, hope shining from her face.

Emma Jane laughed, then picked up a paper cup of coffee from the small table beside the TV. "Here you go, just the way you like it—not instant."

Vanessa clapped her hands, swinging her legs over the bed and holding her hands out like a child grabbing for a toy. "Gimme, gimme, gimme!"

Vanessa gratefully accepted the cup, inhaling the aroma of the nectar of the gods before taking a careful sip. They'd finally sprung for a decent coffeemaker at the apartment and ever since, Vanessa had been adamant she was going to drink better coffee.

"It's not a huge step above instant, but I found a tiny two-cup coffee maker in the room this morning. I figured you'd want a cup, so I made it before I began my daily meditation."

Vanessa opened her eyes, giving Emma Jane a look of such love and gratitude it made Emma Jane blush. "You literally saved my life right now. I'd do anything for you."

Emma Jane's lips quirked. "How's that different from a normal day?"

Vanessa shrugged. "I've got nothing. So, once I finish my coffee, where should we head first? I can't wait to explore Paris."

Emma Jane sat down and leaned into Vanessa's shoulder. She wrapped an arm around her, keeping her other hand firmly on her cup as she sipped.

"Well, since we're so close to the catacombs, we may as well start there. I think they open at ten, so if we're lucky, we might be able to snag tickets. I'm not sure how busy it is at this time of year."

Vanessa swallowed another sip of coffee. "That sounds great. I don't know anything about them other than what you said last night, but now I'm curious to see what they're all about."

Once they had dressed and Vanessa had finished her coffee, they headed back the way they'd come the night before. They kept the hotel room for another day, figuring it was as good a place to set up a base as any, but also because Vanessa had loved their mattress the night before. Since tourist sites everywhere in the world tended to get busier the later you went in the day, they proceeded straight to the catacombs instead of planning the rest of their time in Paris.

When they arrived at the main entrance on Avenue Du Colonel Henri Roy-Tanguy, Vanessa was instantly fascinated by the overall creepiness. But she became even more impressed when she discovered that most of the skeletons were not in their original resting places. During the Middle Ages in France, the city smelled horrible and fear of disease had spread through the city, partially due to all the cemeteries within the center that had begun to overflow.

At some point, the idea of moving all of the bodies into a single underground resting place became popular, and the catacombs were born. Some of the skeletons dated as far back as the Merovingian Empire, which Vanessa could hardly even comprehend. Thousand-year-old bones, some maybe even older. From the Cimetière des Innocents alone, historians estimated over two million bodies had been moved, which was completely unfathomable to her.

They stayed with the tour group they'd found at the entrance and listened to the guide, looking at the macabre exhibitions with a gruesome fascination. Skulls were stacked along the walls; femurs and various other bones lumped into piles together. Hundreds and thousands of them. If they were ever going to see a ghost, Vanessa knew it would be here. So many people not in their original resting place must make for a few uneasy spirits.

Vanessa waited until they'd fallen behind the rest of the group before leaning over to whisper to Emma Jane. "Do you think we're going to see any ghosts? It's so spooky down here; I can't even imagine what would happen if you moved that many bodies."

Emma Jane shrugged. "I haven't seen any yet, but I'll let you know if I do."

Vanessa was taken aback. "You mean you can actually see ghosts?"

Emma Jane shrugged. "Of course. I see spirit energy, which includes both the living and the dead. Most people don't stick around after the spark animating their body has left, though. I'm not really sure why. Anytime I've ever hunted a beast, it's been pretty much gone the minute I absorb its energy. So maybe I'm actually absorbing its spirit, or once its power is gone, it just dies. As for people..." Emma Jane paused, wrinkling her nose as she thought how to word it. "The minute a person dies, it's strange. I can say that I've felt the soul of a person depart their body. It felt almost like a bird wing brushing by my ear. But for the most part, spirits or souls go to a place where I cannot see them. Except, sometimes, in my dreams."

Vanessa pulled Emma Jane close. She knew from the sadness in her voice that Emma Jane was thinking about the family she'd lost when she'd been young. Emma Jane had shared a few stories about the forest where she visited with her family on rare occasions in her dreams; the place where Emma Jane felt the ancestors dwelled and waited for the living to join them.

It was very different from how Vanessa had grown up. Her mom had jokingly referred to their belief system as 'Christmas and Easter Christianity'. They'd gone to church for holidays when she'd been a child, but as she and her sister had gotten older, even that had tapered off. Emma Jane's experience had been much different. With her family dying when she wasn't even in her teens, then discovering she had unusual powers and being trained by an elder from her culture, Emma Jane viewed the world in an interesting mix of religious and earth beliefs that Vanessa felt more accurately reflected the world they lived in. After all, she knew two gods personally now and had seen terrifying creatures that weren't supposed to exist several times over the last few years. The Christianity of her childhood couldn't explain any of that as well as Emma Jane's belief system did.

And now they were walking through a place called the City of the Dead. A sense of unease crept over Vanessa and she was glad, not for the first time, that being overly sensitive and reading auras wasn't part of her superpower package. She wasn't sure she could handle that type of sensory input. But after they rounded the next corner, Vanessa rolled her eyes.

"Of course this is happening. Freaking Murphy and his laws. Please tell me I didn't do that," Vanessa groaned, pointing to a side spoke of tunnel that most of the group had already bypassed.

Emma Jane looked at where she was gesturing, her own groan of dismay following almost immediately. "No, probably not. But have you ever noticed the minute we start to worry about stuff, it happens? Let's try not to do that so often, mmkay?"

While Emma Jane tried to keep her tone light and joking, Vanessa could still hear the irritation which was directed toward the shape Vanessa had spotted in the otherwise empty tunnel.

At least it wasn't overly scary, Vanessa thought, as she stared at what appeared to be the ghost of a young girl. If anything, she seemed sad. Maybe her mood was related to the inappropriate amount of blood on the front of her old-fashioned dress, which suggested that her death hadn't been recent, nor easy.

Emma Jane approached the ghost cautiously, but without betraying any emotion. Vanessa knew she was in 'hunter mode', alert and ready for danger of any kind. Vanessa looked for their group, noticing they'd almost reached the end of the tunnel. If they didn't move fast, they might lose the group, which wasn't something Vanessa was eager to have happen. She hurried to stand closer to Emma Jane as she spoke to the apparition in French.

"Bonjour. Je m'appelle Emma Jane Cooper. Comment vous appellez-vous?"

The girl turned her head eerily, gliding closer as she acknowledged Emma Jane's words, placing a see-through hand on her chest.

"Moi? Vous pouvez me voir?"

Emma Jane nodded, stepping a few paces closer to the girl. Vanessa stayed back, wary of the ghost and guarding Emma Jane's flank, on the off-chance another ghost was lurking behind them.

"Oui. Je vois. Pourquoi est-ce que vous êtes ici? Avez vous besoin d'aide?"

Vanessa had no idea what Emma Jane was saying, but the tone of her voice as she spoke to the girl sounded pleasant and reassuring. Despite Vanessa's discomfort, the young girl didn't appear dangerous and hadn't made any move to hurt

Emma Jane. While waiting wasn't her strong suit, Vanessa took a deep breath and tried to be patient as she watched Emma Jane interview a ghost.

HONEYMOON
CHAPTER 5

Emma Jane was glad for her high school French, no matter how rusty it was. She hadn't been completely honest with Vanessa when she'd told her it had been a long time, but she definitely hadn't spoken French very often in the time since they'd been together. Occasionally, during her travels before Vanessa, she'd encountered people who only spoke French or Cree, so she'd had a chance to keep her skills at a basic level where she could converse enough to get her questions answered. But the French this girl spoke was not the modern, Parisian French she was accustomed to.

If Emma Jane wasn't mistaken, based on the condition and style of her clothing, this girl had died centuries earlier. Which made it even more interesting that her ghost had chosen to appear to them in a tunnel tourists frequented. She wasn't listed as one of the possible hauntings you could potentially see during a visit to the catacombs. Which meant, Emma Jane realized, that this particular spirit encounter was something only Vanessa and herself were meant to experience.

The girl looked at Emma Jane, a glimmer of hope shining behind her pale, transparent eyes. "I have been here a very long time," the girl said, still speaking an archaic French that Emma Jane was having a hard time understanding.

"What happened to you?" Emma Jane asked, gesturing at the girl's dress. The girl looked down, noticing the blood as though she was surprised to see it there. Emma Jane watched her face flicker again, before taking on a frightened expression then shaking her head in denial.

"No, no. It was all a dream. I thought..." The girl trailed off, her face crumpling as one silver tear trickled down her cheek. A faint wind blew through the tunnel, becoming more powerful until the girl took a deep breath and composed herself, then the wind died down again. Emma Jane knew the ghost had created it with her emotions and cautioned herself not to upset the spirit if she could avoid it.

"If it is too hard for you to speak of, I do not wish to cause you pain. But perhaps if you share your story with me and my wife, we can relieve your suffering so that you can rest with your family at last."

Once again, the girl's expression became hopeful as her eyes widened. "You would do that for me?" she asked, a faint smile curving the corners of her lips.

"I cannot promise, but if you tell me, I will try."

Emma Jane waited breathlessly, knowing better than to promise anything to a spirit that she couldn't guarantee. She'd heard tales of vengeful spirits dragging a person with them to their place of unrest between life and the afterlife. The place where the lost spirits wandered forever, where no one would ever choose to go voluntarily.

The girl nodded, accepting Emma Jane's words. "That is fair. My name is Jeanette Meniers. I am-was-ten years old. I lived with my mother, father, and brothers in Gévaudan. We had a farm there, with sheep. It was a lovely place. I had many friends and my two brothers to play with." Jeanette shook her head and Emma Jane could see the memories were becoming more painful.

"If it is too much..." Emma Jane started, wanting to reassure the wraith, but the girl shook her head.

"No. I need to tell you this. Maybe there is a reason why I am here now. You speak much differently and your dress is strange, but if you can help, I will share what I know."

Emma Jane nodded, certain it was no coincidence that this ghost had appeared now, but waited silently until she continued.

"I remember being out with my brother and the sheep one day. It was a normal day. The sun was high and the sheep were being sheep. We had started home for the evening when something large attacked us from the woods."

Jeanette's spirit became paler as the solidity of her form wavered. For moment, Emma Jane worried she would disappear entirely, but then her form sharpened and she spoke once more.

"I never saw what did this to me. I only felt a sudden pain and saw the terror in my brother's eyes." Jeanette looked at her dress, the remembered horror etching deep lines on the young girl's countenance before she looked at Emma Jane again, her expression one of soul-deep agony. "Before I died, there had been reports of other attacks. A beast was ravaging the countryside. They called it Le Bete de Gévaudan."

Emma Jane's eyes narrowed as she listened to the girl tell her story. The beast of Gévaudan? It rang a faint bell, somewhere deep in the recesses of her memories. But if it was the story Emma Jane recalled, it had happened as far back as the seventeenth century. Emma Jane crouched, lowering herself enough to be on eye level with Jeanette.

"What do you know about this beast? I am curious as to why you would be speaking of it now. It has been over three hundred years since that time."

Jeanette looked down, shaking her head. When she looked back up, Emma Jane saw tears sparkling in her eyes. "I do not know. I have been wandering, lost in the darkness for what feels like forever now. You say it is three hundred years? This does not surprise me. It has felt much longer than that. If you can find a way to send me back to my family so that I may rest, I would be eternally grateful."

Emma Jane pressed her lips together, exhaling through her nose as she considered the possibilities. She turned to look at Vanessa, standing behind her with an expression of blank confusion on her face. Emma Jane and the ghost girl had spoken French the entire time, so she knew Vanessa had no idea what they'd been talking about. Looking back at the girl, Emma Jane rubbed her chin then absently nibbled on her thumbnail.

"It's obviously important. I don't believe in coincidences, let alone coincidences over three hundred years in the making. If you say the beast is the last thing you remember, and you lived in Gévaudan at the time the monster rampaged, then that is where we shall go to find answers. Is there anything else you can remember which could potentially help us?"

Emma Jane spoke slowly, trying to be as clear as she could through the barriers of language, culture, and centuries. The girl shook her head, her sad eyes as wide and shimmery as anything Emma Jane had ever seen. Then, as though a light switch had been turned off, the girl abruptly disappeared, leaving only the darkness of the tunnel behind her. Emma Jane stood up, taking a step back to Vanessa's side where her love waited impatiently for a report of what had been discussed.

"Okay, two things." Vanessa said, holding her hand out before Emma Jane could speak. "First, you're totally lying about having rusty French. You sounded completely awesome just now. Second, what the heck was that all about? Was it just me, or did it get really windy in here for minute?"

Emma Jane tilted her head, acknowledging Vanessa's points. "Well, thank you for thinking my French sounded good. It does, if you don't speak French. As to what just happened? Well, for some reason, the ghost of a murdered girl from the 1700s chose to appear to us and mention the beast of Gévaudan."

Vanessa's eyebrows shot up. "What the who now?"

Emma Jane bit back a smile at Vanessa's irritated and bewildered tone, confident it was similar to how she used to speak to her mom when asked to do housework.

"The Beast of Gévaudan is a legend, or so I thought. It was said to be a werewolf that terrorized the French countryside back in the mid-1700s."

Vanessa groaned, tilting her head forward as she rubbed her forehead. "Now you're telling me werewolves are real?"

This time, Emma Jane laughed. "Yes. In fact, I remember fighting one with Samuel when I was still in my teens. I think I was fifteen, or maybe sixteen." Emma Jane shook her head. "Anyway, that isn't important. What *is* interesting is that this particular beast was supposed to have been captured. Several teams of hunters had been sent out, some of whom died, but one was able to capture a large wolf-like creature, which was taken to the French court to display for the King."

"Ha. Well that's interesting. So why are we seeing a ghost telling us about a werewolf that's already dead?"

Emma Jane nodded. "Exactly. You and I both know there's no such thing as coincidences when it comes to the supernatural. The odds of a seventeenth-century ghost girl who seems to have died by werewolf attack suddenly confronting us in the Paris catacombs in the twenty-first century stretches the imagination a little too far."

Vanessa looked thoughtful, then suddenly clapped a hand to her mouth. "Oh crap. We need to get back to the group. I don't want to end up lost in here. The brochure I picked up at the front said that in 2004, the police found an entire theater hidden and stocked with new movies. Who knows what kind of crazies are lurking? Let's catch up. We can talk about our next move after we get out. I'm hungry anyway."

Emma Jane nodded, turning away from the tunnel to follow Vanessa. The catacombs had proven to be far more interesting than either of them had anticipated. It looked like their honeymoon may end up being another hunting trip after all.

HONEYMOON
CHAPTER 6

Vanessa rubbed her eyes, looking around with exhaustion. Here she was, on day two of her French honeymoon vacation, sitting in a library next to her wife, surrounded by a stack of books.

"How did we get here again?" Vanessa asked, the bewildered tone of her question surprising even herself.

When Emma Jane looked at her blankly, Vanessa gestured at the books and the computer they were sitting beside.

"I mean, why am I in a library again? I feel like that's exactly what happened when I went to Scotland. Am I never going to get to go shopping in Europe?" Vanessa heard a solid whine in her voice and winced at how shallow she sounded.

It wasn't about the shopping so much as it was about the fact that she'd really only been two places in her entire life that could be considered foreign or exciting. And each time, her trip had involved more reading in a library than actually exploring the region. Although not personally opposed to libraries in general, they weren't her first place to head for fun while she was at home. Here they were in Paris, the City of Lights, and instead of touring the Eiffel Tower or the

Champs Elysee, she was stuck in a library. Granted, it was the library at the University of Paris and beautiful and historic in its own right, but it was still a library. She would've taken the Louvre over this and still could have been learning stuff.

Emma Jane reached over, patting her hand sympathetically. "We don't have to do this, you know. I mean, I did plan this trip for us to enjoy ourselves and relax. Why don't we go do something different?"

Vanessa sat back. She shook her head as she crossed her arms. "Absolutely not. I'm being a selfish brat. Look, I know as well as you do that we've been given more responsibility than the average bear. I just feel a little complainy right now. I'll try to suppress that until after we figure this out."

Emma Jane gave her a considering look before nodding slowly. "All right. As long as you're sure. The whole point of coming here was so that we could be together in a relaxed environment. I'm sorry the first thing we saw ended up being a ghost who pointed us to a supernatural legend that's almost three hundred years old."

Vanessa shrugged. "Yeah, me too. We've learned a few things that are interesting though, and that area of France is beautiful. The pictures online are quite lovely."

"Tell me what you've discovered." Emma Jane moved her chair closer to Vanessa, resting her chin on the palm of her hand and her elbow on the table.

While Vanessa hadn't helped Emma Jane with research in the past, it was proving to be quite advantageous. Although Emma Jane could use computers which had been adapted for people who were visually impaired, and on occasion, she'd been lucky enough to find books written in braille, for the most part, Emma Jane's research had relied heavily upon librarians. With this trip though, Emma Jane had been adamant about not wanting to bother them any more than necessary. Vanessa wasn't sure if it was insecurity about the way she spoke French, or because subconsciously she was trying not to find anything.

Instead of questioning her though, Vanessa had searched online. She'd focused on newspaper articles and legends, as well as more practical information, such as where they'd need to go to catch the train to Gévaudan and where to go afterward. While Emma Jane had been searching the items she was able to, Vanessa made their travel arrangements. She discovered the quickest way to get there would likely be the Train à Grand Vitesse, also called the TGV, which left Paris from the massive Gare de L'Est and arrived in Nîmes. From there, they could rent a vehicle and drive around the region. Gévaudan itself was barely a town, so Vanessa had also taken the liberty of booking a small hotel for a few nights until they figured out what was going on and where they needed to be. In the meantime, Emma Jane had uncovered more about the legend of the beast.

"Listen to this," Emma Jane said. "Apparently during the years 1764 to 1767, the countryside around Gévudan, an area of around eighty miles total, was plagued by many attacks. The accounts vary from a low of one hundred to as high as two hundred, although some of the injuries and deaths may have been due to attacks by other wild animals. One of the reports states that the beast was a hunting dog that had turned feral and bred with a wolf, but accounts differ wildly between articles."

Vanessa wrinkled her nose. "It doesn't seem likely that a hunting dog would've caused that many deaths."

Emma Jane shrugged one shoulder. "News reports back then were rather spotty. There was a lot of fighting during that time and superstitious beliefs were much more common. That was also around the same time the Huguenots were being persecuted and many resided in that area. Whenever religion gets involved, a lot of people are called demons." Emma Jane raised an eyebrow. "But realistically, people went missing for many reasons, so it's completely possible some of the deaths were actually just disappearances and may have been completely unrelated."

"I thought you said the beast had been killed?" Vanessa asked. "It sounds like the attacks didn't stop until 1767."

Emma Jane nodded. "The king's hunter shot and killed what they thought was the beast in September of 1765, but in December of that same year, two more boys were attacked: a six-year-old and a twelve-year-old. The twelve-year-old boy managed to fight it off and the beast dropped the six-year-old. He was quite injured, but he did live."

"Then what happened?"

Emma Jane lowered her voice. "Apparently, around Mont Mouchet, another hunter, who was also part of a hunting group organized by the king, managed to kill what was again thought to be the beast in 1767. This one was also taken back to Versailles, where it was mounted and displayed for quite some time. After that, the attacks stopped, but this time, for good."

Vanessa pursed her lips. "So, they thought the attacks were over more than once and caught more than one beast. Have there been any reports of attacks since then?"

Emma Jane shook her head. "No. The trail goes cold there. Then again, the French Revolution was brewing and things really got hairy all over France, pardon the pun. So it's possible that a smart person or beast, or whatever this creature was, could have hidden itself away somewhere. And of course, werewolf fever swept over France after that, so many of the common folk disagreed with the official party line that it was a large wolf that had been terrorizing the countryside."

Vanessa rubbed the back of her neck, thinking about what Emma Jane had said. "Nothing in that story sounds overly supernatural. Weren't there a lot of wild animals in Europe then?"

Emma Jane nodded. "Yes. Especially in that area. The mountains were nearby and the wilderness was lightly settled. It certainly would have been possible for wild animals, like a den of wolves for example, to have stalked citizens on the periphery of a town the size of Gévaudan. Even now, the town isn't a large one and is considered rural by French standards."

Vanessa nodded. "Yeah, I think it said it has about 3000 people?"

Emma Jane nodded. "That's tiny for Europe."

Vanessa agreed. "It's not even that big for the States."

Emma Jane leaned back, crossing her arms while she nibbled absently at her lip. Vanessa watched, wondering what was going on behind her swirling, inscrutable eyes. It was part of what she loved the most about Emma Jane. Her quiet thoughtfulness extended to everything she did. Not for the first time, Vanessa wished she was able to be a fraction as patient as Emma Jane was in her everyday life.

Emma Jane leaned forward again, this time looking at Vanessa with excitement. "What if whatever it was that did this to Jeanette is still there?" Emma Jane dropped the words like a bombshell, waiting with her palms flat on the table for Vanessa's reaction.

Vanessa shrugged. "With our luck, that's exactly why we saw her ghost. Even before doing research, once you'd told me about your conversation, I was pretty sure we were going to travel to Gévaudan. Like you said before, what are the odds of a supernatural coincidence finding us?" Vanessa gestured to the computer screen she'd been working on. "While you've been researching the important stuff," she said, tilting her head as she regarded Emma Jane, "I was looking at tickets for the train and nearby hotels. I knew that no matter what you found, we'd be going there to check things out. Before you ask, I didn't book the train until tomorrow morning."

Emma Jane looked at her curiously. "Why not?"

Vanessa crossed her arms with a stubborn expression as she defended her decision. "Because I've been in Paris for just over twenty-four hours. I want to see at least one more famous thing before we leave."

Emma Jane laughed, getting up from her chair and giving Vanessa a kiss. The sound of someone clearing their throat a short distance away brought them back to the present, and Emma Jane leaned back, keeping her arms around Vanessa's now relaxed shoulders.

"Of course. I've always wanted to see the Eiffel Tower with you. Why don't we leave now? Maybe we can have dinner there tonight, if the restaurant isn't too busy."

Vanessa smiled at Emma Jane. "That sounds perfect. I'll get the rest of our travel itinerary printed, then I'm ready to go. Did you need help putting anything away?"

Emma Jane shook her head. "No, I've got it. You just think about what you'd like to eat for supper."

HONEYMOON
CHAPTER 7

Emma Jane looked at the view below with a sense of wonder. Although she knew she was missing some of the beauty around her, being at the restaurant made her feel as if for once, she was seeing the grandeur that other people did. They'd managed to snag the nine o'clock seating at the restaurant, 58 Tour Eiffel. While the meal was pricier than any Emma Jane could remember enjoying in the past, the view alone more than made up for the cost.

She took another forkful of the decadent dessert in front of her, looking across the table at Vanessa as she did. Emma Jane smiled, happy to see that the look on her wife's face was one of rapture. Emma Jane had felt awful back at the library when Vanessa had complained, even though Vanessa had tried to downplay her disappointment as a character flaw. Emma Jane had been just as disappointed at how quickly they'd been drawn into a potentially dangerous situation when all they wanted was to spend some time together, alone and without being worried about something trying to kill them. She knew Vanessa wasn't as shallow as she pretended to be, but sometimes it was hard to convince her self-deprecating wife of that fact. Vanessa's eyes returned from the view below to catch Emma Jane staring at her.

She smiled, tilting her head. "What? Do I have something on my face?"

Emma shook her head, allowing her own wonder at her love's joy to shine out. "No. I was just marveling how beautiful you are. You look happy, which is all I ever want you to be."

Vanessa leaned forward and Emma Jane met her in the middle, the fork left forgotten on her plate. There, on top of the Eiffel Tower and the world, they shared a lingering kiss. Everything was so magical that Emma Jane never wanted the moment to end.

"Pardon?"

Emma Jane and Vanessa broke off their kiss, giving the waiter who'd silently crept up on them sheepish smiles.

"Is there anything else you wish for tonight? Perhaps un café? Or peut-être un nightcap?"

Emma Jane shook her head. "Non, merci. Je prendrai l'addition, s'il vous plaît. Everything has been wonderful. "

The waiter gave them a debonair half-bow then removed a few dishes before departing. Remembering the dessert in front of her, Emma Jane lifted her fork again, this time offering it to Vanessa. Vanessa closed her eyes and leaned over, savoring the last bites of Emma Jane's Baked Alaska.

When Vanessa was done she leaned back and rubbed her stomach before sighing. "That was amazing. No wonder the entire world raves about French cooking. Everything was perfection."

Emma Jane agreed. "I've never had cod cooked quite like that before. I've eaten a lot of fish growing up, although mostly fresh, and often over a campfire. Whatever they did with it here," Emma Jane shook her head, lost for words, then kissed her fingertips dramatically. "It was magnifique!"

Emma Jane and Vanessa looked at each other and Vanessa reached out her hand. Emma Jane took it and together, they sat in silence gazing out at the Parisian skyline below. Emma Jane was fascinated by the flickers of lights she could see moving everywhere. Although she knew Vanessa was getting a more traditional experience, she felt that her version of this night in Paris was something she'd remember just as clearly.

The waiter reappeared with their bill and they reluctantly paid, leaving the Paris skyline behind as they descended to the ground. But Emma Jane had one more surprise to share with Vanessa before the evening was over. Waiting at the exit, decorated in an over-the-top fashion specifically geared for tourists, was the horse and carriage ride that Emma Jane had secretly procured.

"Oh my God!" Vanessa shrieked, squeezing Emma Jane's arm the moment she spotted the carriage. "Is that for us? How did you do that?"

Emma Jane simply tilted her head and gave Vanessa a mysterious smile. But when she saw her wife becoming irritated at her non-answer, she relented and told the truth. "I spoke with the concierge at the hotel when we returned from the library. I wanted to do something special that you wouldn't expect. Since you'd already booked supper, I was rather limited in my options. But then, I thought what would be better way to end a romantic dinner in Paris than with a moonlight carriage ride along the Seine?"

Vanessa squeezed Emma Jane tightly again, this time adding a heated kiss. The faint stamping of the horse behind them caused Emma Jane to smile, breaking the kiss and the moment as Vanessa stepped back.

"You first," Emma Jane said, gesturing for Vanessa to enter the carriage. Vanessa smiled, resembling a kid on Christmas morning as she hopped in, then clapped her hands. Emma Jane moved more gracefully, shutting the door behind her before she wrapped her arm around Vanessa and snuggled close beside her.

The driver turned around, waiting politely until Emma Jane spoke.

"Nous sommes prêts. We are staying at the Marriott along Route Blanc, but we would like to go along the Seine before heading back. Is it possible to go the entire way with you?"

The man nodded. "Absolument. Now relax. I shall do the work with the help of my friends in the front, Jacques et Henri."

Emma Jane was positive that her heart was as full as it could be. As the night passed behind them with the flicker of the lights of Paris in between kisses and embraces, Emma Jane knew this was exactly what a honeymoon should be. The most romantic city in the world with her true love to keep her warm on a chilly spring evening. Life couldn't get any better.

HONEYMOON
CHAPTER 8

Vanessa sat down beside Emma Jane on the train, curious to see what exactly the TGV experience was all about. She couldn't help but admire the French for naming their train 'the very fast train'. It seemed promising for any transportation, especially if it lived up to the bravado. She'd been impressed with herself as well. Although she didn't speak any French, the tickets she'd purchased online had worked without a hitch in person.

When they'd arrived at the huge train station, Gare de l'Est, in the heart of Paris, Vanessa had been overwhelmed by its enormity. The juxtaposition between grandeur and function was something she'd never experienced before. When they'd found their train, she'd been more than a little relieved as she'd begun to worry about getting lost.

Emma Jane had taken everything in stride, as usual. With the exception of her unexpected nerves during the two plane flights they'd taken together, Vanessa had rarely seen Emma Jane look worried about anything. At first, she'd been similarly sanguine about the train ride, but once it began moving, Vanessa was surprised to notice Emma Jane looking uncomfortable.

"Are you okay, Emma Jane? You're a little...pale."

Emma Jane was seated beside the window with her eyes closed and her face turned to the inside of the train car. She swallowed hard, giving Vanessa a fake and somewhat shaky smile. "It appears that fast-moving trains are also not on my list of favorite ways to travel."

Vanessa frowned. "But why? I mean, we're still on the ground. There's no flying involved."

Emma Jane shook her head. "It's not that. I'm not afraid—in fact, I think I may have motion-sickness. The sight of everything flashing by outside at the rate we're going..." Emma Jane swallowed hard again, her face becoming more green than pale as she looked at Vanessa anxiously. "I might throw up."

Vanessa rushed to help her. "No, don't do that! Here, let's trade seats. Maybe if you're not beside the window, you'll start to feel better."

Emma Jane nodded and Vanessa helped her switch places. Once they'd resettled themselves, Vanessa watched Emma Jane carefully. She felt somewhat responsible for her wife's condition, but at the same time, she wasn't eager to have to help someone else throw up. She looked around the small space, peeking inside the back of the seat folders in front of her then exhaled with relief as she pulled out a vomit bag.

"Here. Hold onto this. And maybe don't look out the window anymore, okay?"

Vanessa practically shoved the bag into Emma Jane's hand as Emma Jane nodded sickly.

"Don't worry, I'm not going to. I'll just sit here with my eyes closed and try to meditate until we get there. How long did you say this trip is?"

Vanessa grimaced. "Three hours, give or take."

Emma Jane groaned, leaning back in the chair as she closed her eyes. "Wake me up when we get there."

Vanessa bit her lip, but noticed Emma Jane's color began to improve almost immediately once her eyes closed, and let out a sigh. Hopefully, there'd be no christening of any of Vanessa's clothing or shoes before they arrived in Nîmes.

True to Emma Jane's word, she spent the remainder of the ride with her eyes closed as she meditated in an attempt to get through her motion sickness. Vanessa thought it was strange that Emma Jane could handle riding in a car no problem, but as she had no idea what Emma Jane was able to see of the world, it was difficult for Vanessa to understand why the train would make her motion-sick.

Either way, the quiet left Vanessa with plenty of time alone with her thoughts. For the first time, as Vanessa watched the rolling plains turn into more elevated areas, she considered the possibilities ahead and found herself becoming excited. True, she wasn't keen on the idea of potentially fighting a werewolf, but on the other hand, she'd never been to the south of France. Wasn't that where all the movie stars went on vacation? Where people didn't look at you no matter how famous you were and everyone seemed to have a chalet somewhere?

Vanessa daydreamed about where they were headed. Perhaps she'd fall in love with a quaint little place there and they could join the never-ending legions of people who vacationed in France. Vanessa glanced at Emma Jane, smiling fondly at her wife's still firmly closed eyes. It wasn't what she'd expected from the train ride, but at least they were together.

Vanessa checked her phone, ensuring that the rest of the details for their trip were easily accessible. The train station had a car rental place, so once they arrived, Vanessa planned to have Emma Jane do most of the talking to acquire a car, then she'd drive it from Nîmes to Gévaudan. She'd found a reasonably decent looking hotel online, with the exception of one report of bedbugs. She'd hesitated when booking it, the idea of bedbugs simultaneously making her wince and have phantom itching, but at the same time, there were limited accommodations in the area and the trip advisor report was from two years earlier. Vanessa figured if the bedbugs were still around, they were going to be hunting werewolves anyway. They were just as likely to get fleas or die, and in that case, bedbugs would be a non-issue.

Vanessa felt the train begin to decelerate and noticed it was pulling into a city. It slowed to regular train speeds then to a crawl. Vanessa shook Emma Jane's arm gently and when she opened her eyes, Vanessa pointed out the window.

"I think we're here, Emma Jane. How do you feel now?"

Emma Jane stretched, raising her arms over her head and yawning. Her color had improved and Vanessa was hopeful the worst was over.

"Much better, thanks. We're here?"

Vanessa nodded. "I believe so. I haven't seen a sign yet, but it's been over three hours and the train is slowing down. When we get there, I'll need your help to get the car, then I'll drive. I've already downloaded a map into my phone, so basically, all we need to do is grab our luggage and the car then we can hit the highway."

Emma Jane leaned over to give Vanessa a kiss. "Aren't you little Miss Organized. Thank you so much for taking care of this."

Vanessa blushed. She'd never been the one who made arrangements for anything before now and she was rather proud of herself. In her family, it was always her dad or Cat who did the planning. Then when she'd moved to San Francisco, she'd been so busy working that she'd never needed to organize a trip anywhere. It made her feel mature, somehow, which was nice.

Things went smoothly once they arrived. They collected their luggage, successfully rented a car, and headed off down the road. While the signs were in French, so were most of Vanessa's instructions and she found it easier to navigate than she'd expected. Emma Jane sat in the passenger seat, occasionally looking at the passing countryside. For the most part, however, she seemed content to lay back in her chair with her eyes closed.

It wasn't until they arrived at Gévaudan that Emma Jane truly perked up, becoming aware of her surroundings in the usual, vigilant way Vanessa was accustomed to. As though a switch had been flipped, Emma Jane became alert; every inch of her body tuned to the world around her. She'd worn her sunglasses, as no one looked askance at a woman wearing sunglasses on a sunny day, but as usual when she did, Vanessa missed catching glimpses of her tantalizing eyes.

"Vanessa, can you feel that?"

Vanessa glanced over at Emma Jane curiously, then back at the road. She tried to open her senses to see what it was Emma Jane was asking her, but the road was unremarkable, as was the town they were entering.

"Feel what?"

Emma Jane wrinkled her brow, then shook her head. "I'm not sure. I feel something," she responded, thoughtfully drawing out the last word. Vanessa could almost feel her frustration. "Remember when I told you how everyone leaves an imprint of themselves behind, like a fingerprint, and how I can track them based on that?"

Vanessa nodded, vaguely recalling the discussion where Emma Jane and Cat had compared what Cat had called aura vision to what Emma Jane called spirit vision, back when they'd first met Emma Jane.

"Yes, I think so. Are you seeing someone's fingerprints?"

Emma Jane pursed her lips, tilting her head as she searched for words before shaking her head again. "I don't know. I've never felt this particular signature before. But if it isn't what we're looking for then we most likely have another thing to worry about. It feels like a very dark, very old soul. Whoever I'm sensing is not what I would consider a benign entity, but I can't tell who or what it is."

Vanessa nodded. "So, you're sensing something dark and evil, but it could be something new that's also dark, or something old. Did I get that right?"

Emma Jane let out a dry chuckle. "Yeah, for the most part. It sounds kind of crazy when you say it like that."

Vanessa shrugged. "Hey, I call it like I see it. So, something dark and evil with a fingerprint you don't recognize is in the neighborhood. Check. If nothing else, that tells us we're probably in the right place."

"Yes, I think we are. Let's check in and put our stuff away. It's still early enough that we can go out and try to find the trail of who or what I'm sensing."

At that moment, Vanessa's phone navigation interrupted and told them to turn right. After a few more bossy directions, Vanessa pulled up outside a nondescript, two-story hotel. They checked in and threw their bags down in a completely ordinary hotel room and then, remembering the potential for bedbugs, Vanessa flipped the sheets and examined them thoroughly, earning an odd look from Emma Jane in the process.

"What? I want to make sure that I don't get all itchy. I've had bedbugs once and that's something I never want to experience again. In fact, I make sure that I always travel with antihistamines now, just in case."

Emma Jane laughed but didn't say anything else as Vanessa satisfied herself the room was free of tiny dead bug bodies or blood specks on the sheets. The review had been a few years old, but it never hurt to double and triple check.

Once that was done, exploration began in earnest. Vanessa had to remind herself more than once not to squeal like a dewy-eyed tourist but knew that she was the definition of what people talked about when they said tourists were unsophisticated. The town itself wasn't touristy though, so she felt as though they were getting a true impression of the lives of ordinary, semi-rural French people. Even though she was basically tagging along with Emma Jane while she hunted for an energy signature, Vanessa was able to pretend they were out walking for their own enjoyment.

Vanessa had eaten a light snack on the train, but soon found herself becoming hungry from the activity, so when she spotted a sign that said *Boulangerie*, she tugged on Emma Jane's arm. "Can we stop and get a croissant or some sort of French bread-stuff? I'm hungry, and apparently, we're supposed to eat as much flaky bread as we can while we're in France."

"Sure," Emma Jane said, absently, as she stared at a police car at the end of the street. Vanessa considered Emma Jane's expression, unable to decipher it. It was partially her usual stoicism but was mixed with something else that she couldn't read.

"What are you looking at?" Vanessa leaned over, wrapping her arm around Emma Jane and bringing her face closer Emma Jane's. To anyone passing, it simply looked like two women embracing. Vanessa was actually leaning into Emma Jane to try and glimpse whatever it was Emma Jane was watching.

"What do you see beside the police car?" Emma Jane kept her voice low and her tone deep.

If they'd been alone and Vanessa hadn't been trying to concentrate on whatever it was Emma Jane was observing, her tone was the same one that normally gave Vanessa warm shivers. She still had shivers, but this time, they weren't the good kind. As Vanessa followed Emma Jane's gaze, she noticed an elderly man standing to the left of the police car in conversation with an officer who was emerging from the vehicle. To her average, unmagical eyesight, nothing about the situation appeared odd.

But because Vanessa knew Emma Jane was watching something, she squinted her eyes and tried to see beyond the ordinary. Then she felt it. She couldn't see what Emma Jane saw, but as she opened her senses, trying to use every ability she had, Vanessa sensed a disturbance in the air. It was subtle, and she knew that if Emma Jane hadn't been worried, Vanessa would never have noticed anything wrong. But now that she was focusing on the air, she felt the faintest tingle of magic. It was wild, as though it belonged somehow to nature, and yet, it didn't feel natural at all. Instead, Vanessa could felt a strong and dangerous darkness swirling in front of them.

Vanessa leaned down, dropping a kiss on Emma Jane's face without letting her eyes stray from the ordinary but not-so-innocent scene in front of her. "Something is off with those two, isn't it?"

Emma Jane nodded, moving her head so that Vanessa could see better while ostensibly sharing a mild public display of affection.

"Yes, although I'm not sure which man the darkness is coming from. It could be the old man, or it could be the policeman. Either way, one of them could be who we're looking for."

Vanessa pulled back, looking at Emma Jane with surprise. She hadn't expected that. "What should we do next?"

"Well, you said you were hungry, correct?"

Vanessa nodded. Emma Jane gestured not to the bakery, which Vanessa had been salivating over, but to a small restaurant beside the two men, who were still talking. Feeling a twinge of disappointment that she quickly shoved down, Vanessa agreed. "Sure. We can get breakfast from the bakery in the morning."

Emma Jane raised her eyebrows. "Are you sure? You sound sad. I'd hate to get between you and pastries. I've seen that end badly for people in the past." Emma Jane delivered the sentence completely deadpan, causing Vanessa to laugh and shake her head.

"I'll be fine. Besides, I'm sure that they have some other traditional French food there. Like frog legs, or even pâté de fois gras."

Emma Jane laughed, then wrinkled her nose. "I'm not so sure you should be ordering the paté fois gras. Pretty sure you'll end up with reflux. You should stick to the frog legs, or maybe snails would be more your speed."

Vanessa shuddered, not understanding why anyone would ever want to eat anything that slimy. "I'll stick to the steak tartare. At least I know that it had legs at one point in time."

Emma Jane laughed again, then wound her arm through Vanessa's as they walked across the street to the restaurant.

EMMA JANE WAS ON HIGH alert. While she'd managed to laugh at Vanessa's comments when appropriate, she knew that she wasn't giving her the attention she deserved. It wasn't because Vanessa wasn't engaging. Emma Jane always enjoyed her dry and somewhat snarky sense of humor. But the darkness emanating from the corner where the two unas-suming men stood made it hard for her to focus on anything else.

She tried to separate the energy of the two men. The police officer was younger by at least a decade, maybe more. He stood about six feet tall, with brown hair and a small goatee. His face was attractive, although relatively average. She wasn't sure if it was a face that would have caused her to stop and take note, even prior to meeting Vanessa. But the darkness surrounding him was another matter. It was atypical, how it almost appeared to flow between the two men instead of belonging to either in particular. She couldn't remember seeing anything like it before.

Flipping her attention to the older man, she examined him in detail. He was balding, with what hair he did have being almost entirely white, more salt than pepper, although she could see faint threads of a darker brown at the back and along the edges. He had a lean build with average height and was slightly shorter than the younger man, but impeccably dressed. While not the best at matching colors with her eyesight, the shade of his belt and shoes was identical and blended nicely with the shadows of his shirt and pants. He had a pipe in his mouth and Emma Jane smelled the soothing fragrance of tobacco, flavored with hints of cherry and rose, even from where they were. She didn't approve of smoking, but held tobacco itself in the highest esteem. She knew that the blend the man was smoking was one that her mentor, Samuel, would appreciate.

As they approached the men, Emma Jane gripped Vanessa's arm more tightly while maintaining the same leisurely pace, doing her best to appear unhurried and relaxed. But instead of continuing into the restaurant, Emma Jane stopped and turned to the two men, who regarded her with surprise.

"Pardon. J'aimerais savoir où vous avez acheté le tabac?" Emma Jane winced, knowing she'd butchered the accent as she'd asked where they'd bought the tobacco.

The older man smiled, pulling his pipe out of his mouth to examine it with a bemused expression. The pipe itself was lovely and Emma Jane could still sense a hint of the life energy in the wood it had been carved in. If she wasn't mistaken, it was redwood and had most likely originated in California.

"A fine question. I buy my tobacco at the tobacco shop: down the street, and one store to the right at the end of the rue." He smiled as he responded in English, which immediately confirmed her suspicions about how much she'd murdered the accent.

Emma Jane looked to where the man was pointing but focused on the energy signatures of the men instead of the tobacconist sign which was clearly visible a few hundred yards away. Now that she was closer to them, she realized that she'd thought she saw the darkness flowing between the two men because it actually was shifting between them.

Emma Jane's brow furrowed with confusion, wondering what it meant. She'd never encountered that before. She wished she could ask Samuel, but with the time difference, he'd most likely be asleep and she hated to disturb him. He was getting on in years, and his hearing when they spoke on the phone wasn't always great lately. Pushing her emotions aside, Emma Jane looked back at the men.

"Merci beaucoup. I will go and look at the store later, after we have a bite of lunch. I am much obliged at your kindness indulging a stranger's curiosity."

Vanessa stood watching the entire interaction with a look vague confusion on her face as Emma Jane spoke in a mixture of French and English, so she tried to include her with a smile. Vanessa smiled back brightly, including the two men in her usual, charismatic fashion as Emma Jane explained herself.

"I was just asking them where they got the tobacco. It smells lovely and I'd like to buy some for Samuel."

Vanessa nodded. "I'm sure that he'd like that." Vanessa hesitated, looking between the two men again before speaking. "Emma Jane, I'm wondering if you'd be able to ask the men if they're related?"

When the men looked at Vanessa curiously, she smiled brightly again and asked them herself, since they'd obviously understood her. "I'm sorry, but I couldn't help noticing you look very similar. Are you family?"

The police officer inclined his head, flashing a charming look at Vanessa, which caused Emma Jane's gaze to sharpen on him. *Interesting. For an average, nondescript police officer, his smile is a little too charming.*

"Mais oui. This is my father. I am part of the local police force in Gévaudan." The man gave her another smile, speaking with heavily accented English that Emma Jane thought was much better than her own French. "We were on our way to have lunch together as well, as I am on my break."

Vanessa batted her eyelashes, causing Emma Jane to wonder what she was up to. "Well, what a coincidence! My friend and I have just arrived in your lovely town and we're absolutely starving from our travels. Maybe a nice officer of the law, such as yourself, could give us pointers on the best places to visit while we're in the neighbourhood?"

The police officer winked. "Bien sur, Mademoiselle. You've come to the right men. Why don't you join us for lunch and we can discuss everything you should do while you are in the south of France."

Vanessa tittered, causing Emma Jane to groan inwardly. She never heard Vanessa simper in such a vacant, girly fashion before. She wasn't sure what Vanessa was trying to pull, but for some reason it appeared she'd decided the best way to get more information was to charm the men. Emma Jane couldn't deny Vanessa had a special kind of magic when it came to interacting with others. Although Emma Jane knew what they were doing could potentially be dangerous, they were in a public place, during broad daylight, and things were as safe as they could possibly be. For now, anyway.

HONEYMOON
CHAPTER 9

Vanessa kept her arm around Emma Jane as they entered the restaurant. It was mostly empty, which seemed odd until she checked her watch and realized it was already after two o'clock. Obviously, the lunch rush was over. Keeping a fake, professional smile on her face, Vanessa was careful to maintain just the right amount of eye contact with the officer as he showed them to a table.

While she knew Emma Jane could see darkness around the two men, if Vanessa had been an ordinary person, she would've been flattered by their attention. After all, two French gentlemen escorting them to lunch without either Emma Jane or Vanessa asking them to was within the realm of what she considered gentlemanly, even wish-fulfilling, for many women. But Vanessa still remembered another man who had been equally gentlemanly, so she wasn't letting her guard down, yet. Her first encounter with the supernatural had been in her last year of high school with Declan Boyer—a charismatic, soulless creature who'd been masquerading as a high school student. Even now whenever Vanessa thought about Declan, she was filled with a mixture of regret, sorrow, and fear.

He'd captivated her mind and emotions in a way that no one else had until she'd met Emma Jane. Then again, he'd also taken small parts of her soul every time she spent more than a few minutes with him. At least until the Christmas party, when he'd tried to kill her by taking all of her soul for himself. Vanessa was positive he'd played a large part in why she hadn't been able to have a relationship until she'd met Emma Jane, when her attraction had finally overwhelmed her fear of being hurt by getting close to another person. In one of life's great ironies, however, it had turned out that Emma Jane was another person who could take her energy and spirit, although not because she was evil the way Declan had been.

Vanessa fingered the smooth, dark spring-green stone around her neck. She wore it at all times, whether prominently on display or tucked into her shirt, or even occasionally wrapped around her wrist. She never took it off. While it technically gave her the ability to resist any magic directed against her for the purpose of stealing her soul or her own magic, the aspect Vanessa cherished most was that it allowed her to have a relationship with Emma Jane without the risk of her losing herself, something she hoped never to experience again.

The police officer noticed Vanessa toying with her necklace and tilted his head as he watched her thoughtfully. "That is a very pretty bauble."

Vanessa realized what she was doing with a start, dropping the stone then spreading her hands innocently on the table as she gave him a coy smile and tried to downplay its importance. "This? Oh, it's not valuable, other than for sentimental reasons." Vanessa looked down, batting her eyelashes just enough to seem innocent, before looking up at him with a self-deprecating smile. "It's an heirloom that was recently passed down to me by an distant relative."

Vanessa gave them an altered history of her necklace, technically telling a partial truth, although the spirit of Big Bear wasn't *her* ancestor. "But I'm sure you have things like that as well." She watched with interest as the two men exchanged a quick glance then smiled blandly, their expressions almost identically blank.

"But of course. What family doesn't have special items? We all have our own..." The old man smiled cryptically as he paused, then continued. "Legacy, you could say. But I just realized I have not introduced myself. How remiss of me." The older man stood, giving Emma Jane and Vanessa a courtly half-bow before extending his hand first to Vanessa then to Emma Jane.

"My name is Pierre de Bourbon, and this fine upstanding young man of the law beside you, who has also neglected proper introductions, is my son." Pierre gave him a look, causing him to stand abruptly and offer his hand as well.

"My name is Jean François. Also de Bourbon."

Vanessa allowed each man to take her hand in turn and bestow a small kiss upon it, giggling a smidgen before putting her left hand on her chest as though she was a debutant, then responded with the only French she knew.

"Enchanté."

Emma Jane was more subtle and laid-back, but Vanessa could tell the men's old-world charm and manners were not completely wasted on her.

"It's a pleasure to meet you," said Emma Jane, nodding as the men sat down again. A waitress came to take their orders, then the foursome began to discuss the must-do's that the women needed to accomplish prior to leaving the region. Vanessa wondered what Emma Jane was picking up from the men. The air still felt unsettled around the de Bourbons, but she lacked the ability to tell what their inner motivations were.

"The area around Gévaudan is quite lovely, although not as tourist-centric as some of the other regions in France. The town itself is fairly old, even for European standards. It was founded almost a millennium ago by monks, although there were people in the area prior to that. You must check out the original buildings while you are here. There is a museum in the center of town that will provide you much more information, should you choose to take a historical perspective for your trip," offered Pierre.

"Absolutely. My sister is a history major. I'm under strict instructions to bring back anything that could be of historical interest. She's looking for a final project for one of her classes, and while she has a few months left, she's becoming nervous that she doesn't have a topic yet. Maybe I'll come home and save the day for her." Vanessa raised an eyebrow, pursing her lips coquettishly.

Jean François laughed. "Well, if history isn't the only thing that piques your interest, the scenery is quite beautiful as well. The town is built around the Tarn River and is surrounded by rolling hills. The river system has more than enough variety to keep you busy on long walks or picturesque drives. The mountains are not too far away, either."

This time, Emma Jane piped up. "What about Mount Mouchet? I've heard it's lovely this time of year."

The two men exchanged a wary look before Pierre answered Emma Jane's question.

"You need to be careful around the mountains. They are prone to unexpected...weather disturbances."

Jean François agreed. "I do not recommend hiking too close to the mountain, especially later in the day. Most of the danger happens after dark."

A tingle went over Vanessa's back when Jean François said the word *dark*. While his words were light and his tone friendly, something about the way his eyes had tightened when he said it caused her internal antenna to perk up. She may not be able to read auras or tell what someone was by their spirit, but she knew what someone who was hiding something looked like better than most.

Vanessa giggled, playing dumb to hide her true reaction. "Don't worry. I'm not the most athletic person. Unless you count shopping as a sport."

Emma Jane laughed dryly but didn't add to the conversation. While not exactly the backup she was hoping for, Vanessa knew it was as close to charming as Emma Jane ever got with strangers. She may be a good tracker and a good hunter, but she was absolute crap when it came to finessing people. That was Vanessa's job, so she turned to her wife with imploring eyes.

"What do you think, Emma Jane? Should we explore the city tomorrow, or should we check out the mountains and the area beside the river first?"

Emma Jane pursed her lips, considering her options while the men looked on curiously. After a few moments, Emma Jane smiled at Pierre.

"I think I would enjoy learning more about the history of the town first. Perhaps if we explore the past, we'll have a better sense of where we should go in the present."

Vanessa bit back a groan. Although there was nothing wrong with her words, she couldn't help think that Emma Jane sounded remarkably like Robin, with his irritating doublespeak whenever he didn't want to tell the girls what he knew. At least in this case, the men shouldn't see anything unusual in Emma Jane's reply. When Vanessa looked at Pierre, she could see that he'd relaxed at Emma Jane's decision and also that the strange tightness had left Jean François' eyes.

Interesting. Definitely something we'll need to discuss later.

"What do you think we should look at today? By the time we're done eating, I'm sure that most of the facilities will be closed, will they not?" Vanessa asked, ensuring that the tiny dimple she had was present as she looked at Jean François with wide, guileless eyes. She knew her ploy had worked when he had to clear his throat before answering.

"Well, I believe many of the exhibits close by four, but perhaps if I give you ladies a ride to the monastery they will allow you extra time."

Vanessa clapped her hands. "That would be fantastic! Is it safe to leave our car on the main street, or should we move it back to the hotel?"

Jean François shook his head. "Everything you need to see in town is within walking distance. You may as well park it back at your hotel and I can pick you up from there. If you wish me to take you, of course."

Emma Jane smiled, causing Vanessa to swallow hard. She knew that look. Emma Jane had her hunting face on. But of course, the man couldn't see it, as blinded by Emma Jane's bright smile in the beautiful, tan face with impossibly high cheekbones as Vanessa had been the first time she'd seen her.

Emma Jane could've been the actress, not me, Vanessa thought, not for the first time. She had that elusive mixture of exotic and girl-next-door good looks that often made one a superstar, especially with the way social media could elevate an unknown to celebrity overnight.

"I'd love to have a local show us around. If you could give us ten minutes to freshen up at the hotel, we'd be more than happy to have a police escort."

Jean François bowed. "It would be my pleasure."

HONEYMOON
CHAPTER 10

Neither Emma Jane nor Vanessa ended up eating much for lunch. Vanessa had been hungry, but her stomach was too keyed up to follow through. Perhaps it had been the steak tartare. It had sounded amazing and so quintessentially French that she'd been unable to resist trying it. While the taste had been acceptable, the idea that she was actually eating raw meat had turned her stomach after only a few bites.

Both Pierre and Jean François had ordered the steak tartare as well, but they'd devoured theirs. For men who had such polished manners otherwise, she'd been put off by how fast they'd eaten. Glancing at Emma Jane, Vanessa saw a contemplative look slide over her wife's face briefly before being replaced by her normal, impassive expression. Was it possible that they were looking for *both* men? Or was there something else going on she didn't understand? Perhaps they were just French men being French.

Once they'd finished the shared meal, Pierre had insisted on paying the entire bill. After a brief, obligatory protest, Vanessa and Emma Jane had graciously accepted. They returned to the hotel as Jean François drove his father home; apparently, he had other matters to attend to that evening and couldn't be late. Vanessa had expressed her regret and thanked the man again for a pleasant afternoon. The moment they were back at the hotel however, both women dropped the façade. As the door closed behind her, Emma Jane turned to Vanessa. "Did you catch any of that?"

Vanessa grimaced. "I'm sure I didn't get nearly what you did. I saw enough to make me suspicious though. They both acted odd when we mentioned Mont Mouchet, which was weird. I mean, weather is weather. I'm sure anywhere we go we can check a weather report prior to hiking. Surely it can't be as dangerous as the Rocky Mountains in winter."

Emma Jane nodded. "Yes, that's one thing I noticed. But more than that was strange. Remember when I told you about the darkness that I saw?"

Vanessa nodded. "Yeah, I was wondering about that. Were you able to figure it out?"

Emma Jane shook her head, absently running her hands through her long, mahogany hair. "No. At times, it seemed as though they had normal auras. Or at least, there was always one normal aura around them at any given time. The darkness was still there, but it almost seemed to pulse, like it was waxing and waning and shifting between them."

Vanessa's eyebrows raised. "That's an interesting choice of words. Waxing and waning? Shifting?"

"Actually, Vanessa, you're right." Emma Jane pursed her lips.

Vanessa knew she was thinking about something but wasn't sure what until Emma Jane looked at her with eyes that swirled with intense dark clouds trapped inside.

"Vanessa, can you check your phone? I'm curious where we are in the lunar cycle."

Vanessa blinked and her heart sank as she realized where this was headed. "Lunar cycle? Yes, I can do that. Just a sec." Vanessa took her phone out, flipping to her calendar app, which had tiny little circles indicating the position of the moon. When she went to the present day, her mouth instantly went dry and she looked at Emma Jane.

"The full moon is tomorrow night." Vanessa spoke quietly, but the impact of her words in the silent room was as loud as a bomb.

"Shit, I was afraid that may be the case."

Vanessa blinked. Emma Jane wasn't given to swearing often, which more than anything else that had happened during their trip to France convinced Vanessa that they may, in fact, be up the creek without a paddle. She watched as Emma Jane began to pace across the narrow room, deciding it was best to sit on the edge of the bed while she waited. It could be exhausting to watch when Emma Jane got like this, so she'd long ago decided she didn't need to stand as well. But after she'd bitten her tongue for several minutes, she grew tired of being patient.

"Okay, while I understand pacing helps you to come up with ideas, we have a semi-handsome French policeman who is likely waiting downstairs to take us somewhere. If he's the bad guy, this is a terrible idea. But if he's a werewolf, we should be okay until night time at least, right?"

Emma Jane stopped pacing long enough to answer, resting her fists on her waist as she nodded. "If he's a werewolf, yes. Technically speaking, we're fine until after dark when the full moon is out. But the moon is almost full tonight and the night after the full moon, so we have at least three days where we'll need to be extra-careful. Assuming he's a werewolf, of course."

Vanessa leaned forward. "What do you mean, assuming he's a werewolf?"

She was confused. Hadn't Emma Jane been interested in Jean François and Pierre because the swirling darkness surrounding them meant that they were werewolves?

Emma Jane shook her head. "We're assuming Jeanette was killed by a werewolf in the 1700s. But remember, there are many creatures which have a similar method of attack. We don't know for sure what we're up against. Even superstitious peasants in the 1700s couldn't agree who'd perpetrated the attacks: whether it was a large animal, a werewolf, or something else entirely. We always need to keep other possibilities in mind, including the potential that the Bourbons aren't even why we were led here."

Vanessa sighed, not fond of uncertainty, particularly the idea that there could be something else out there as well. "It makes sense. Is there anything we can do to stay safe if Pierre or Jean François *are* werewolves? What if they aren't who we're looking for?"

Emma Jane shrugged. "For the most part, silver is pretty effective with most magical creatures. Iron isn't bad either. And then of course, fire is always our friend." Emma Jane raised an eyebrow. "In terms of who or what we're looking for, something is wrong with them, so we may as well start there."

Vanessa exhaled loudly. "Okay. Plus, we have magic, so that's nice. I guess my biggest question for you is whether or not you think Jean François is dangerous."

Emma Jane shook her head, shifting to cross her arms as she looked blankly at the ceiling, a slightly water-stained pressboard with one dingy round light in the center of the room, which Vanessa knew she couldn't even see.

"He's not quite right, whatever he is. But that could mean anything from him being a dirty cop, a murderer, or several other unsavory things that aren't remotely supernatural."

Vanessa gave Emma Jane a baleful stare. "Emma Jane, we know they aren't natural. Whatever led us here to help Jeanette's ghost must have something to do with one or both of those men." Vanessa paused, waiting for Emma Jane to nod, then asked again. "Do you think it's safe for us to get in the car with a police officer in broad daylight to travel to a historical building within town limits?"

Emma Jane raised a shoulder. "Probably. I mean, the sun is up for a few more hours. But you're right, maybe I'm being naïve when I say I want to go with him. If nothing else, we can keep an eye on him while he's with us and if we're lucky, maybe we'll even discover something helpful in the process."

Vanessa placed her arms around her wife's shoulders and stared into her swirling eyes. "We'll figure it out. After all, he doesn't know who we are. That's one point in our favor."

Vanessa saw worry reflected up at her instead of Emma Jane's normal confidence, so she leaned down to give her a soft kiss, pulling back only after she'd relaxed against her. Cupping one hand beneath Emma Jane's chin, Vanessa winked.

"Are you ready to confront the beast in his lair, or more accurately, his car?"

Emma Jane's face smoothed out, the worry she'd briefly allowed Vanessa to see replaced by her confident hunter's stare. "Bring it on."

HONEYMOON
CHAPTER 11

J ean François was waiting in the lobby. He stood up on seeing them, an easy smile on his face as he waited for them to approach. He inclined his head slightly then gestured to the door. "Mademoiselles, aprés vous."

Vanessa responded with the same light, engaging smile she used whenever she wanted to get time off work. When his face brightened in response, she bit back a chuckle. Apparently, it worked on Frenchmen as well as directors.

He led them to his police car and while opening the back door, he gave them an apologetic grin. "I'm still on shift, otherwise I would have traded vehicles. The doors lock from inside, so unfortunately you won't be able to get out unless I let you out. I hope that isn't a problem?"

Vanessa's eyes flicked to Emma Jane, but she managed to keep her face inscrutable, betraying no concern whatsoever. Vanessa followed her lead, holding up a hand to reassure him. "I'm sure we'll be fine. As long as you promise to let us go, of course?"

Jean François laughed, placing his right hand over his heart. "On my honor as a police officer and a de Bourbon."

Vanessa smiled, but didn't miss the same, barely noticeable tensing around his eyes. Something dark lurked behind the friendly brown eyes, that she knew for certain. He was hiding something. It was just the *what* which remained to be seen.

As promised, Jean François delivered them to the monastery and had a few words with the woman at the door. She nodded, blushing, then Jean François returned with a satisfied smile.

"Marguerite says if you need extra time, she'll stay open a half hour longer. Unfortunately, this is where I must leave you. I need to get back to my paperwork at the station."

Vanessa gave him a mock bow. "Thank you so much for your hospitality, Jean François. It's been wonderful to have met you. Maybe we'll see you around town before we leave."

Jean François tilted his head gallantly. "I would be more than happy to see you ladies again, mais desolé; today is my last day in Gévaudan this week. I will most likely be out of town on family business until after you leave. It has truly been my pleasure. I hope you enjoy our lovely town and countryside. I'll bid you adieu."

Vanessa gave him a disappointed pout. "Oh, darn. I'm sorry to hear that. I was hoping to get to know you better. I must thank you for giving us a wonderful day at least. I'll be happy to go home and let all my friends know that everyone in France was utterly charming and polite, and that their men are every bit what the movies tell us they are. They'll be so green with envy."

Jean François took her hand, bestowing a light kiss upon it before raising his head with a smile. "I shall tell everyone that the beautiful Americans I met today were absolutely lovely as well. Good luck in your travels. Remember to be careful around the mountains. The weather can be quite deadly, and it is better to look at them from a distance."

"We will, thank you."

Emma Jane came to stand beside Vanessa and she wondered if her wife was trying to protect her, or displaying a jealous side. Either way, Jean François appeared oblivious as he bid them a final goodbye, then turned and walked away. They entered the exhibit and waited until they were out of earshot of anyone before speaking. They'd left the entrance behind and Jean François was long gone. The exhibits were closing in twenty minutes, which meant they didn't have much time to explore, but any interest they'd had in history had all but evaporated by that point.

Vanessa looked around, narrowing her eyes at the exhibits. "I don't think Cat will mind if I don't bring anything back for her. Right?"

Emma Jane shook her head with a wry smile. "What she doesn't know won't hurt her. However, I don't think that we'll find what we need about the attacks in here. I do, on the other hand, think it's suspicious that both Pierre and Jean François suddenly have things to occupy their attention tonight."

Vanessa raised one eyebrow. "A coincidence? Or maybe they actually do have a family event."

Emma Jane looked at her, disbelief written all over her face.

"What? It could be." Vanessa rolled her eyes and admitted defeat. "Okay, let's say it's not a coincidence. Our working hypothesis is that the next three nights are going to be very dangerous to be wandering the countryside, yes?"

Emma Jane nodded. "Yes. I'm also starting to wonder if there's a genetic component I'm missing. That's the only thing I can think of that would explain the way the aura/spirit shifted between the two men, almost as if it was a shared property."

Vanessa scratched her chin as she thought. "Interesting. You mean being a werewolf is an inherited trait, the way eye color or height is?"

Emma Jane nodded. "Exactly. I mean, you and your sister are great examples of that. Your entire family is packed with people who have power. Why couldn't something like lycanthropy travel through the family tree as well? That would make sense. I mean, think about it. What if there's been lycanthropy in France for centuries, just flying under the radar since the 1700's?"

Vanessa pursed her lips. "Go on, I'm listening."

Emma Jane leaned on a display case, waving her hands in front of her as she reviewed the history. "The first accounts we have are tied to the attacks between 1764 and 1767. There were several occasions when they'd thought they had the beast. What if they actually did? What if every time they killed a beast it *was* one that was responsible, but because there were multiple beasts, the attacks never stopped?"

"I get it. So it wasn't just one beast they were fighting, but an entire family?"

Emma Jane nodded. "Exactly. But due to the attention the attacks garnered and the beasts that were killed, the rest became smarter and went into hiding. They could have easily continued their hunting as the population grew if they'd been more careful about it. Then the French Revolution happened. Civil unrest throughout the country was up-and-down for at least a century following that. By then, the population was much bigger so it would've been easy to hide an occasional missing person."

"How come there haven't been any reports of werewolves since then though? Surely with how superstitious people were, someone would have reported a sighting somewhere."

Emma Jane crossed her arms. "Because, the age of reason and enlightenment arrived then. People began to attribute natural causes to everything that happened in the world around them. Within a really short period of time, even an ordinary, uneducated person went from attributing bad things that happened from supernatural causes to logical explanations. Demon possession became a rare event, exorcisms fell out of favor, and medicine and science took their place."

"Makes sense to me. I mean, prior to grade twelve I would've thought you were crazy if you'd said any of this to me," Vanessa said. "In fact, I'd still prefer to attribute stuff to logical explanations, but sadly, that option doesn't seem open to me very often these days."

The corner of Emma Jane's mouth quirked. "You and me both, you and me both. I haven't been able to do that since I was twelve. Man, for once I'd love epilepsy to be the reason why someone's convulsing in front of me with foam coming out of their mouth, instead of an actual demon possession."

Vanessa laughed. Then, when she realized she was laughing at a joke about demon possession, she laughed even harder. At Emma Jane's blank look, Vanessa stopped laughing. "I just realized how messed up my world is. I found your happiness about seeing a real seizure hilarious. Man, have I changed since finishing high school."

Emma Jane chuckled as well, giving her an admiring look. "It's all for the best, Vanessa. Now, let's go back to the hotel. I'd like to take the car and cruise around. Maybe we can find a trace of where Pierre or Jean François went. Before dark, if possible."

HONEYMOON
CHAPTER 12

E mma Jane's thoughts were turbulent. The day had gone well, in fact, far better than she'd anticipated. Not only had they discovered something dark in the small town within moments after arriving, but the possessors of said strange darkness had invited them to lunch and given them advice on the best places to visit, as well as what to avoid. It was the advice on what to avoid which Emma Jane had paid particular attention to. When the subject you were hunting tried to deflect or make something seem unappealing, Emma Jane had almost always found that was the direction you needed to look. Unless it was a double-fake, of course, in which case they'd need to look in the opposite direction.

As Vanessa drove around the town and its immediate environs, Emma Jane's thoughts turned to the ghost of Jeanette. She'd been so young. In fact, she was the same age as Emma Jane's younger brother, the oldest one of the three she'd lost when they'd died so long ago. While she'd looked nothing like him, Emma Jane felt as though Jeanette had the same spark, like a flash of Paul's spirit, when she'd spoken with the girl. Maybe it was the Great Spirit guiding her, but she'd felt a sense of familial duty toward Jeanette. Emma Jane couldn't recall that sensation with any of the others she'd helped over the years and wondered if the same darkness which had taken Jeanette had also destroyed her family. But the moment she thought that, Emma Jane shook her head. *No, I took care of that evil long ago*. But still, the nagging thought wouldn't leave her alone.

"What's going on in that busy upstairs of yours?"

Vanessa's soft, soprano voice broke into Emma Jane's musings, and she turned with a forced smile. "I was just thinking about Jeanette. And my family. And the nature of good versus evil."

Vanessa glanced at Emma Jane then turned back to the road. "Wow, deep thoughts for the night before the full moon. I hope that doesn't bode ill for us."

Emma Jane shrugged, turning to the passenger window. Objects went by at a pace that she could handle now; the light in the trees, the animals, the grass, and all the living things reassured her as they passed. No matter what happened, life would be there, with or without her. With or without her loved ones. But until she was gone, she knew she'd continue to fight to protect each and every single one of those little lights that filled the world with beauty.

Emma Jane looked back at Vanessa, finally admitting the truth. "Something about this situation hits close to home for me."

When Vanessa looked at her, forehead wrinkled with confusion, Emma Jane tried to explain. "Jeanette's ghost made me think about my brother. I'm wondering how families play into this. Maybe there's a connection we're missing."

Vanessa pursed her lips. "Maybe. Just to clarify, do you think this has something to do with the death of your family?"

Emma Jane shook her head. "No, not that. I caught and killed the monster who destroyed my family. But I'm wondering if something about this situation has a link to Jeanette and her family."

"There's an interesting thought. Jeanette said she couldn't remember what happened, but the ghost we saw was covered in blood, mostly around the head and neck of her dress. From what we read, that was consistent with the attacks, correct?" Vanessa arched an eyebrow.

Emma Jane agreed. "Yes. And we know that she died, because she's the ghost of a ten-year-old girl. But I wonder what happened to the rest of her family."

Vanessa faced forward as she drove, turning a corner onto a quiet cul-de-sac. "I don't think we should count on finding out any of those details. I mean, the trail is 300 years old. We'll make better use of our time if we focus on figuring out what's going on now with the father-and-son combo we had lunch with."

Emma Jane sighed, knowing Vanessa was right. She looked out her window again, searching for a hint of the darkness that seemed just out of reach. "I know. Let's keep driving. Hopefully, I'll find the trail soon."

But Emma Jane was beginning to get frustrated. They'd been driving for what felt like hours already, although she was sure it hadn't been that long. It wasn't quite dark yet, so there was still time. The closer nightfall approached though, the more she worried they wouldn't discover what was happening in time to prevent something bad. Emma Jane let out a groan as Vanessa turned onto streets Emma Jane recognized from earlier during their drive.

"We might as well stop for tonight. We've started to repeat streets and I still haven't seen anything."

Vanessa checked Emma Jane's expression then wrinkled her nose. "Are you sure? It's only five-thirty. We still have lots of time."

Emma Jane bit the inside of her cheek, trying to keep her exasperation to herself. Then Vanessa reached over and patted her hand, before lacing her fingers through Emma Jane's and giving them a reassuring squeeze.

Emma Jane deflated. "This is worse than trying to find that soul thief. At least when I was tracking her, I knew where to look, for the most part. I don't suppose you've got any idea about where two Frenchman would hang out if they're hiding evil secrets from the world?"

Vanessa narrowed her eyes. "I wonder," she started, then shook her head. "Never mind, it's silly."

Emma Jane looked at Vanessa hopefully. "No, tell me. It doesn't matter how silly it is, it's an idea, and I'm fresh out."

Vanessa tapped the index finger of her left hand on the steering wheel as she drove slowly down the street. "What if the thing Pierre is planning is the same reason Jean François is on vacation? Could they possibly be headed to Mont Mouchet for the next few days?"

Emma Jane raised her eyebrows. "That's actually a really good idea, Vanessa."

Vanessa shot her an affronted glare. "Next time could you say that like it's not so crazy that I've got a good idea?"

Emma Jane shook her head, apologizing. "I'm sorry, that wasn't what I meant. I mean, it's a fantastic idea. I'm not sure why I didn't think about that earlier. You're absolutely right-the way they tried to warn us away from the mountain at lunch and then again, right before Jean François left. That's exactly where we should look."

Emma Jane bit her lip at another thought. "But not tonight. I don't want to be in an isolated forest or mountain region without being prepared. We need to make sure we have equipment with us, in case we get lost or attacked. At the bare minimum, we need to go back to the hotel tonight, to pick up a few extra weapons."

Vanessa shot her a surprised look. "Wait, you have weapons in your suitcase?" Then Emma Jane's declaration fully sunk in. "Wait, you have weapons on you right now?

Emma Jane looked at Vanessa guiltily. "After twenty years of hunting, I can't go anywhere without my weapons. It was convenient for more than one reason that Robin helped us get to France. I wouldn't have been able to bring nearly as much of my arsenal as I did if we'd had to clear customs." Emma Jane added a nervous smile, wondering if Vanessa was angry that she'd brought weapons on their honeymoon.

Vanessa laughed. "Well, I'm not worried about anything happening to me as long as you're around. My very own personal bodyguard."

Vanessa's eyes were warm and Emma Jane knew she was thinking about how they'd first met, when Emma Jane had come to warn Vanessa she was in danger.

"I will always guard your body, Vanessa." Emma Jane wiggled her eyebrows lasciviously, which caused both of them to burst into laughter. As the laughter died a natural death, Emma Jane's mood lifted. Vanessa turned the steering wheel to head back to the hotel, but just then, Emma Jane felt something.

"Vanessa, wait a minute. Stop here."

Vanessa glanced at her just as she put the turn signal on. "What's here? The aura fingerprints you're looking for?"

Emma Jane nodded. "Yes. Pull over."

Without question, Vanessa pulled over to the side of the road and parked the vehicle. Emma Jane closed her eyes, centering herself with the breathing she always used to put herself into a deep meditative state. Soon, she opened her eyes and scanned the area around them, searching for the darkness which had triggered her to stop.

"There."

Emma Jane pointed to a nearby house. It appeared to be several centuries old and was made out of a dark yellow stone, with vines and trees providing privacy and shade. Emma Jane was sure the house looked lovely in the bright light of day, but with her unique vision, the darkness swirling around it now gave it a sinister air.

"Nice house. I wonder if that's what they call a 'château,'" Vanessa mused.

Emma Jane answered her absently. "I think everyone calls their house a chateau over here. This house looks very old though. I wonder..." Emma Jane bit her lip, letting her sentence trail off as she thought.

Vanessa poked her arm. "You wonder what?"

Emma Jane shook her head, looking past Vanessa. "I wonder if that house was here originally. I mean, at the time when the beast was supposed to have roamed." Emma Jane turned her head again, narrowing her eyes as she considered the house. "The fingerprint I'm seeing is too large to just be attached to one person. The house itself feels almost alive."

Vanessa leaned over, putting her head almost into Emma Jane's lap as she tried to get a better look at the house. She squinted at it then leaned back and shook her head.

"I don't see it. Is that something that happens often? Can houses be alive?"

Emma Jane shook her head. "Not usually. I've only seen it a few times, and then only under the darkest of circumstances. For a house to have an aura, a lot of bad things have happened inside it. Usually death, and almost always more than one violent or spiritually charged death."

"So what does that mean? Is this where Pierre and Jean François live? Or could it be something else?"

Emma Jane shrugged. "I don't know. All I can say for sure is that there's a dark aura here. Pierre and Jean François also have dark auras. But I can't pinpoint theirs well enough to tell you if this one is the same or not." Emma Jane shook her head, her irritation at her inability to tell for certain increasing.

Vanessa nodded. "Okay. So, the house needs to be checked out. What's the plan?"

HONEYMOON
CHAPTER 13

While it made Vanessa uncomfortable, they waited until dark to make their move. She'd moved the car from their initial parking place to a better spot underneath a large, old oak tree which provided more privacy and hid the car from view of the house they were planning on breaking into once the sun went down.

Vanessa watched Emma Jane, thinking that she would have made an excellent undercover officer. Her lips curved in amusement as she pictured Emma Jane dressed in a form-fitting black suit, wearing sunglasses and carrying a gun. She could see the heading now – Emma Jane Cooper, Undercover Agent. Coming soon, to a big screen near you.

"What are you laughing about?"

Vanessa startled in her seat. "Oops! I must have been daydreaming."

Vanessa gave Emma Jane a searing look which raised fire in her love's cheeks, then shared her thoughts. "I was picturing you as a hot FBI agent working a case."

The flush on Emma Jane's face deepened and her gaze warmed on Vanessa in response. "I want you to hold onto that thought until after we're finished breaking and entering.

If things go well, we can see how undercover agents celebrate a successful mission."

Vanessa licked her lips. "That sounds very, very tempting. I'm definitely holding you to that."

Emma Jane held Vanessa's gaze, giving her a look of such promise that Vanessa's heart rate climbed and her breathing quickened. Then just as quickly, Emma Jane blinked, her stoic hunting mask returning as she shifted her gaze back to the house. By now, night had fallen. Emma Jane surveyed the area for a few moments then turned back to Vanessa.

"Okay, here's what we're going to do. We'll approach the house from behind, meaning we'll walk around the block and approach it from the other side of the street. I'm anticipating more of these giant trees, which should provide us with some cover. If we see a good one near the house, I'd like you to bring us both up so we can survey the target from above. We can figure out the best entrance point from there. Unless you have another idea?"

Vanessa shook her head. "No. If you hadn't suggested it, I was going to. It worked out pretty well for us one other time."

Emma Jane raised an eyebrow. "You've done stakeouts before?"

Vanessa made a seesaw motion with her hand. "Well, kinda. Once. In grade twelve, the first time I encountered a soul thief. We watched him one night, and I floated myself into the tree to scope out the backyard first."

Emma Jane nodded. "Well, there should be no problem for us getting in then. Let's go."

Vanessa and Emma Jane linked arms, walking around the block as though they were a couple out for an evening stroll.

Which to be fair, they were. They just happened to have an ulterior motive. They were relieved to see they'd been correct in their assumptions. The backside of the street was equally shaded with trees, and it was easy to see that the houses and plots were very old, as they were much larger than yards in other areas of town they'd been through.

Vanessa eyed their options for which tree to use, and when she was sure Emma Jane was watching but no one else was around to witness it, she used the air to float into a perfect tree. From the well-leafed branches, Vanessa could see the house better. Most of it was shrouded in darkness, with the exception of two rooms on the main floor where soft lights shone from the windows. She looked down through the trees for Emma Jane, surprised to find that she'd already started climbing and had almost reached the branch Vanessa was perched on.

"Hey," Vanessa whispered, slightly put out that Emma Jane hadn't waited for her. "I thought I was going to look, then float you up?"

Emma Jane shook her head. "I got impatient. Plus, I'm good at climbing trees."

Emma Jane moved closer to Vanessa, both of them hidden within the branches and resting on a large branch which leaned toward the house. Upon seeing the same lights Vanessa had, Emma Jane nodded. "The darkness is congregating in those two rooms. Something bad has happened there, and more than once is my guess."

Vanessa narrowed her eyes. "Not to be macabre, but if that house is laid out in the same way most houses are, that's probably the kitchen and the dining room area."

Emma Jane nodded grimly. "Which would go along with my suspicions."

Vanessa grimaced. God she hated finding out people were possibly being eaten. She couldn't help thinking back to the cannibals she'd encountered in Scotland with a feeling of revulsion.

"So now what?" Vanessa asked, trying to sound calm and less grossed out than she actually felt. "I'm not looking forward to seeing someone dining on long pig."

Emma Jane looked at the house again her gaze swirling and mysterious as the shadows played across her face. Vanessa wasn't sure what she was looking at, but a moment later, Emma Jane nodded.

"I want you to float us over there, to that part of the roof. Do you see where I'm pointing?"

Vanessa followed Emma Jane's finger. She was singling out one of the peaks on the roof, which appeared to have a small window beneath it. She closed her eyes, concentrating on the movement of the air, then held her arms out for Emma Jane.

"It'll be easier for me if I'm holding you while I do this. Also, more fun," she added, a smile growing on her face when Emma Jane raised an eyebrow.

Emma Jane stepped closer and Vanessa wrapped her arms around her as she concentrated, feeling the wind lift them. It was almost as though she was on a moving sidewalk, using the air to move her without having to do any of the work of walking. Vanessa set them down carefully on the roof while Emma Jane took another look at the house from their new vantage point. Once Emma Jane was satisfied with their location, she pointed to the room now beneath them.

"I'm going to lower myself down to the ledge. If the window is unlocked, which I'm hoping it will be, I can open it then you can follow me."

Vanessa nodded. Without another word, Emma Jane gracefully slid over the side. For a moment, Vanessa worried she'd fallen but when she looked over the edge of the roof, she caught the tail end of a gracefully executed flip. Emma Jane held onto the windowsill with one arm, pushing the windowpane open with the other. Vanessa hadn't realized how strong Emma Jane was until that moment and was even more impressed with the quiet and competent woman beneath her. When Emma Jane disappeared inside, Vanessa wasted no time and floated through the window to join her.

HONEYMOON
CHAPTER 14

E erie silence filled the air, as crushing and heavy as if an elephant was sitting on top of her chest stealing her ability to breathe. Emma Jane normally loved silence. It helped her do her best work. Prior to Vanessa entering her life, Emma Jane had mostly worked that way, rarely speaking with others unless in pursuit of information. She could go days, sometimes even weeks, without talking to another human. But this silence was oppressive. She could see darkness swirling around and was now certain that the house itself had a spirit. She could only hope that it wasn't sentient and able to warn the people she was sure had created the abomination in the first place. She scanned the room, finding nothing of interest. It was simply a dusty attic room, without any objects of concern or value. Emma Jane walked toward the door, intuitively knowing where not to step to avoid making the wood creak.

Looking back, she put a finger to her lips. Now that they were in the house, silent was the only way to move. Vanessa nodded and Emma Jane watched with approval as Vanessa levitated an inch off the floor. Blowing her wife a kiss, Emma Jane turned to focus on the door itself. Closing her eyes as she breathed slow and deep, she placed her hands on the knob and let some of her energy run through it. She focused on the energy difference between the metal and the empty spaces, feeling the locking mechanism beneath her fingers ease and give way to her spirit. Samuel had taught her many ways to get through a locked door, but this was her favorite. For the cost of the small amount of energy, she could move silently through any lock humans had invented.

Emma Jane opened the door so slowly that even though the hinges were rusted, they remained silent under her gentle ministrations. Moving into the hallway as smooth as smoke, Emma Jane concentrated again. She waited, watching to see what the darkness would do next. As it moved around them, it began to coalesce at the end of the hall. She followed it, allowing it to lead her to their next destination.

Occasionally glancing over her shoulder to ensure Vanessa was keeping up, Emma Jane focused most of her attention on the darkness roiling through the hall. As it swirled and shifted, Emma Jane wondered if it was trying to communicate, or if it was just moving in response to changes in the air. She'd never spoken with a house before and wasn't sure if it was possible, but she did know the darkness was getting deeper the further they went. They came to a set of stairs wide enough for three people to walk abreast and she immediately knew that they were the main stairs. She paused, looking into Vanessa's sapphire eyes, recognizing awareness of the danger ahead of them within their depths. She tightened her mouth, giving Vanessa a short nod, then continued a slow creep into the darkness.

The stairs looped around, becoming more ornate as the couple entered what was clearly the front hallway. This was where they would have entered the house from the side of the street where the car was, had they been invited in. Even in the darkness with her decreased vision, Emma Jane could tell that the house was elegantly decorated with an eye toward harmony. Appearances could be deceiving though, which she knew all too well. She kept her ears open and her eyes wide, alert for any sign of danger. The house remained oppressively quiet, with only the sound of their breathing to lift the weight of the air around them.

Emma Jane felt a tug on her arm and saw Vanessa pointing down the hallway away from the light. Emma Jane squinted, then her mouth dropped open with sudden comprehension. The room that she'd thought was the kitchen with a light on was in fact a large dining room, which continued the length of several rooms. But no sound emitted from there. Emma Jane heard the unmistakable sound of a knife being sharpened, coming from the room which Vanessa had indicated.

Emma Jane centered herself, preparing for whatever lay behind the door as Vanessa did the same. Emma Jane edged forward, slowly craning her neck once she'd reached the door where the noise had emerged from. Peering around the edge, she kept the rest of her body hidden behind the protective wood.

There, in the light of an almost full moon, was the shape of a man with his back toward her. The light reflecting off metal in the moonlight was evil in its sharpness, sending a shiver down her spine. The man looked familiar, but not exactly the same as either of the men they'd seen earlier. When he turned around, she realized what was different. While he was the same general size and shape as the officer they'd met during the day, his hands were now covered in dark brown fur with elongated, bone-colored nails. His right hand was clasped around the handle of the blade, while the other held a sharpening stone. The knife was long and curved, with strange letters glowing blue in the moonlight along the edges of the blade. This was no normal knife, and whoever was holding it was most certainly not a normal human.

Emma Jane took a deep breath, glancing over her shoulder to assess how Vanessa was faring. She looked good, but Emma Jane knew she'd seen what was lurking in the kitchen and once again, put a finger to her lips. With her other hand, she pointed in the room as she mouthed the words 'Jean François'. She knew that Vanessa understood when her eyes widened and she mimed claws and vampire teeth. Emma Jane nodded. Vanessa shuddered, but threw her shoulders back as soon as she'd finished, a resolute look on her face.

Emma Jane didn't know what he planned to do with the knife but feared they'd walked in on a ritual of some sort. She needed to stop him before he did any damage, but before she could act, he made the decision for them, putting the sharpening stone down on the counter and stepping away from the light of the window.

As he did, Emma Jane noticed the excess hair disappear. The hand wrapped around the knife still displayed wicked claws, but they'd regressed in size. The further he moved from the window and the moonlight, the more obvious the changes became. With surprise, Emma Jane realized his transformation was completely dependent upon being touched by the light of the moon.

Emma Jane pulled back, almost bumping into Vanessa, who managed to move just in time to avoid a collision. *How strange*. Everything Emma Jane had ever experienced or learned about werewolves included a dependence on the moon in order to transform, but it wasn't a back and forth thing like what she saw before her now. This was completely different. Not only was it partial, it also seemed painless, which didn't fit.

But Emma Jane didn't have time to ponder the strangeness of what she'd just seen. The man/werewolf/whatever it was still had the knife and had just left the kitchen through another doorway. She sucked in her breath then slid soundlessly through the half open door into the kitchen. Vanessa followed, narrowly fitting through it herself while she shot Emma Jane an incredulous look. Emma Jane knew she was going to hear about it later but was too preoccupied with what the creature, who may or may not be Jean François, was about to do next to react.

As they slunk forward, following the man/beast into the lit room, they remained as unobtrusive as possible. The light they'd seen from the room, which had seemed so bright at a distance, was the result of hundreds of candles which had been lit and placed in various locations; the floor, the windows, and shelves. The whole place looked like it was ablaze at first glance until she noticed the candles were not arranged randomly. As the pattern organized itself, Emma Jane realized that the candles were in the shape of a star within a circle. And in the very center of the circle lay the unconscious form of a child.

HONEYMOON
CHAPTER 15

E mma Jane heard a gasp behind her. Even as she turned to glare, Vanessa was already covering her mouth. Luckily, Vanessa had been quiet enough that the noise went unnoticed as the man began to chant. Emma Jane didn't recognize the words but knew he was beginning a ritual that was unlikely to have a good outcome for the figure lying motionless in the center of the circle. The man began to dance around the still form of the child, moving the blade in elaborate figures in the air as he traced shapes in and out of the circle.

She quickly examined the rest of the room. Emma Jane had thought it was a dining room on initial inspection, but on further examination it became apparent that it was actually a wide-open salon-type space, with chairs along the walls and a wooden parquet floor. Like a ballroom, only smaller. The symbol on the floor was drawn into the shape of a star on top of an intricate circle by a steady, artistic hand. If Emma Jane wasn't mistaken, someone had put a lot of time and effort into that design, but it hadn't been created in the recent past.

Moonlight spilled into the room through a large row of windows at the front, lighting up the areas that the candles couldn't touch. As it shone on the man, he once again began to transform, sprouting hair out of all visible skin while his nails lengthened into claws. His nose elongated as well and Emma Jane saw the resemblance to a wolf, but what she was seeing didn't make sense. He now appeared every inch as much a werewolf as the one she'd fought many years earlier, but once again, the transformation was too smooth and too painless for it to be via the usual mechanism through which lycanthropy worked.

The moon ducked behind a passing cloud and the room was shrouded in darkness once more. Jean François was now recognizable, without a hint of the wolf visible. As he continued to dance around the body of the child holding the tip of the blade aloft, the letters along the edges glowed with the same blue light she'd seen in the kitchen. This time, even though the moon was hidden behind a cloud, he transformed easily.

Illumination dawned and Emma Jane understood what was happening. Whatever ritual he was conducting involving the knife, its symbols, and the sacrifice within the center of the floor was also what was giving him the power to switch back and forth with the moonlight. Somehow, he was gaining the power to become a wolf. Emma Jane turned to find a look on Vanessa's face that reflected surprise, shock, and horror. When she caught her eye, Vanessa pointed toward the child with her chin. Emma Jane knew exactly what she meant and nodded without hesitation. *Yes, they were going to stop the ritual, one way or another.* This was no normal werewolf, bound to transform under the full moon. Instead, he was a human who had stolen powers of the creature for himself, through dark magic.

Vanessa raised her eyebrows. "*Now*?" she mouthed.

Emma Jane nodded, replying with a whisper. "*Now*."

The time for stealth was over. They entered the room, standing just outside the boundary created by the symbol carved into the floor, and waited for Jean François to notice them. It took a moment, but once he'd completed another round of flashy circles in the air with his knife he ended facing them, starting with surprise at the sight of two women staring at him. His elongated snout shortened, returning almost completely to that of a human as he growled.

"What are you doing here?" he snarled.

Emma Jane stood still, examining him with a cool expression from the bottom of his half-dressed, half-human figure, to his face, where she stopped her perusal and glared at him.

"I could ask you the same thing." She gestured toward the body on the floor. She couldn't tell if the child was alive or dead from where she stood, but hoped that Jean François required a live victim for whatever sacrifice they'd interrupted. Emma Jane trusted that if she could distract him long enough, Vanessa would be able to get the child and herself to safety before the real fight began.

"You have no right coming here. This is private property." He stepped closer, stalking toward her with his lip pulled back in a warning.

Emma Jane raised an eyebrow. "Isn't that interesting," she said, tapping her chin as she moved around the periphery of the room. She made sure to stay a safe distance away from him as she spoke. "If this is private property and you're an officer of the law, how much trouble would you get if this little situation was to make it back to your place of work? Perhaps we can call the police, or even better - we can put these pictures online. I'm sure before you could do anything to stop us, we could have them posted to every social media outlet there is. Do you think this would count as private property then?"

As Emma Jane spoke, keeping Jean François in her crosshairs, she caught Vanessa take her cellphone out of her back pocket and snap a few shots to accompany her threat. *Good girl.* Vanessa would likely know where to post the pictures for maximum effect. But that wasn't her true goal. Proof of a recognizable man, dressed oddly with what appeared to be an unconscious child in front of him on the floor as he held a knife above them was completely incriminating. If there wasn't anything supernatural going on, the pictures alone would land him in jail.

But Emma Jane had a larger goal. Jeanette had sent them to Gévaudan to right an ancient wrong. Emma Jane couldn't be sure Jean François was the same beast who'd done so much damage centuries before, not without more information first.

"Are you the beast?"

The question was a simple one. Emma Jane hoped his answer would determine what happened next, but when he narrowed his eyes and wrinkled his forehead, she knew that he had no idea what she was talking about.

"Beast?" He scoffed. "I'm not a beast. I'm a god. With the help of moonlight and this ritual, I will be able to control my transformation between human and wolf whenever I want. I will be invincible."

Emma Jane raised eyebrows and dropped her arms to her side, readying herself. "Really? Is that what you think?"

Vanessa moved closer, gesturing at the girl on the floor. "What about her? Is this something you've done before? Just curious, but did she get a say in whether or not she wanted to help you become invincible?"

Jean François looked at Vanessa as though she was stupid. "A god doesn't ask. A god merely takes what is his due." His eyes narrowed as a cruel smile spread over his face. "I wonder how much more powerful the ritual would be if I multiplied the sacrifice by the power of three?"

Raising the knife in his hand, Jean François transformed again. Hair sprouted as his nails elongated and his snout lengthened. Within seconds, the only thing resembling a human were the pants covering his canine back legs and the grip which he'd maintained on the knife.

Emma Jane shrugged, then assumed her familiar fighting stance and began to circle him, bringing her own knife out of the sheath she kept at the small of her back.

"I have one of those, too," she said, smiling as she glided around him. She successfully avoided the symbol carved into the floor, which was now glowing with an unnatural light. While she wasn't sure it could hurt her, she didn't feel like taking a chance.

Jean François leapt toward Emma Jane with a growl. She neatly sidestepped his lunge, planting a powerful front kick on his backside as he landed in the spot where she'd been a split second earlier. She kept her eyes trained on him as Vanessa floated overtop of the sacrificial circle and scooped the girl away without Jean François noticing.

"That was rather clumsy of you," Emma Jane taunted, making sure his attention remained on her and not on what Vanessa doing. By now, he was enraged and only had eyes for her. The dark fingerprint, which the house had displayed earlier, flickered then rose up, completely eclipsing its previous forbidding energy. Whatever was happening, she was now positive that he'd done it all himself.

Jean François leapt again, stabbing with the knife in his right hand while slashing at her with the claws on his left. Emma Jane was too fast for him to catch though, and using her favorite move, she slid closer to him then thrust both palms into his chest. He flew backward, sprawling on the floor with a stunned look on his face. The knife flew from his hand as he hit the ground. With a flick of her wrist, Vanessa flung the knife into the wall behind him with a solid thump.

Jean François's eyes widened when he noticed her carrying the girl in her arms, removing her from his sacrificial circle.

"No!" He shouted. He attempted to rise but Emma Jane stopped him, kneeling down as she thrust the heel of her right hand into his throat, cutting off any further conversation. She knew she'd found her mark when she felt a crunch underneath her hand. Tightening her lips with sadness and determination, Emma Jane wrapped her hand around the area she'd struck and absorbed the last bit of energy he had. Even as the familiar rush of power filled her, tears welled in her eyes as she witnessed his energy fade, his skin collapse, and finally, the light drain forever from his eyes.

"You do not deserve to be a god," she whispered. Once satisfied he'd never get up again and that she was in control of her increased power, Emma Jane stood and faced Vanessa.

HONEYMOON
CHAPTER 16

Tears streamed down Emma Jane's face and Vanessa looked at her with an expression of such understanding it caused more tears to join the ones already there.

"You did what you needed to do, Emma Jane. We both know he was going to kill this girl and would've transformed into a monster if he'd had the chance."

Emma Jane sniffed, wiping the tears off her cheeks as she took a deep breath and set her jaw. "I know. But it never gets easier."

She looked down at the floor, where the dried-out husk of Jean François lay, motionless and lifeless. "He was human. He just made the wrong choices."

Vanessa looked at Emma Jane's flat expression, knowing without words the worries that filled her wife's heart. After leaving the girl on the floor beside the windows for safety, she moved closer in case Emma Jane wasn't able to control herself.

Vanessa held out her hand until Emma Jane tentatively accepted it then she pulled the weeping woman in for a tight embrace. Safe in the knowledge that as long as she wore her amulet Emma Jane couldn't accidentally hurt her, Vanessa stroked her wife's mahogany hair and whispered into her ear, alternating words with light kisses along Emma Jane's cheek.

"You don't have to worry you'll go down that path, Emma Jane. I'm here to stop you, just in case you ever become tempted enough to consider going to the dark side."

Emma Jane gave her a watery smile before she let go. "Thank you. Hold that thought for later, please. Right now, we need to get this girl to a hospital. I'm also concerned that we haven't seen Pierre yet. I'm positive he's up to his eyeballs in this."

Vanessa bit her lip. "Do you really think it was both of them? Or is it possible only Jean François was responsible for tonight?"

Emma Jane grimaced. "That symbol in the floor? It's old. As old as the house is my guess. With the darkness of the shadows I can see surrounding this place, my best bet that the entire family has been responsible for many atrocities over the centuries. If Jean François was involved, there's a one hundred percent chance his father is, as well."

Vanessa was practically gnawing on her lip, her gaze landing on the girl she'd placed beside the wall. She hadn't done much more than take a pulse to make sure she was alive, but now that the imminent danger had passed, she went back for a more thorough assessment. Vanessa couldn't see any obvious injuries, but she was certain there must be something seriously wrong with the girl; otherwise with everything that had just gone down in the room, she should have woken up already. Vanessa looked at Emma Jane, worried she was missing something.

"Can you see if there's anything wrong with her? I mean aura or spirit-wise?" Vanessa wished Cat was with them, as she would have been able to tell the exact location of the problem, but at least Emma Jane could see the broad strokes.

Emma Jane nodded and stepped closer but not near enough to touch the girl, just in case. Vanessa knew Emma Jane always worried about the possibility of draining someone immediately after she'd opened herself enough to absorb the energy from her prey. Vanessa had noticed it seemed to take Emma Jane less time to recover each time she'd seen her do it, although maybe that was specific to the fight, she wasn't completely sure. In this case, Vanessa wasn't concerned about the girl's safety but she could understand why Emma Jane would be.

Emma Jane tilted her head, her hair falling in a dark sheet over one shoulder. She narrowed her eyes as she looked the girl over from head to toe. After several moments, she finally looked at Vanessa, shaking her head.

"She looks like she's okay. We need to get her to the hospital, but I don't see any darkness in her aura. In fact, it just looks pale. Hopefully, whatever he did to her isn't permanent."

Vanessa exhaled with relief, looking down at the diminutive figure. She appeared frail, probably not even five feet tall and very thin, with pale blonde hair and a complexion that at the moment seemed waxy and almost doll like. Vanessa wasn't sure if that was her natural coloring, or a result of whatever Jean François had done to get her here. Vanessa leaned over and scooped her up into her arms, suddenly intensely sad as she felt her slight weight. She was so tiny.

Vanessa couldn't help but wonder if her parents were somewhere frantically searching for her at that very moment. She looked up to see Emma Jane regarding the girl, an odd expression on her face.

"What is it?" Vanessa looked down, trying to determine what was making Emma Jane so pale and shaky all of a sudden. Then it struck her.

"Oh my God, Emma Jane. Is it possible?"

Emma Jane shook her head slowly. "I don't know. It..."

Emma Jane trailed off, and Vanessa finished her sentence. "She looks like Jeanette, doesn't she?"

Emma Jane nodded, opening and closing her mouth a few times before swallowing then closing her mouth without saying anything. Her eyes met Vanessa's, as if she was unable to understand or believe what her eyes were telling her.

"Either this is Jeanette's long, long, *long* lost great-niece or relative, or..."

This time, Emma Jane finished Vanessa's half-sentence.

"Or somehow, it wasn't a ghost we saw in the catacombs yesterday."

Vanessa shook her head, adjusting the weight in her arms unconsciously.

"But how? I mean, that ghost was covered in blood, this girl looks fine. And Jeanette said she lived in the 1700s, so it can't possibly be the same child."

Emma Jane shrugged. "I don't know. I guess we'll have to wait until she wakes up to ask. But what if?"

Vanessa nodded. "What if? What if this child was reincarnated, and during her out of body experience, her past life came to tell us she was in trouble?"

Emma Jane pursed her lips. "No way to know for sure. It's possible, but one thing is certain - the similarity in appearance is uncanny."

"Well, that answers my question about why Jeanette appeared to us yesterday, when she wasn't listed as one of the ghosts known to frequent the catacombs."

Emma Jane agreed. "Yes, that part makes more sense. But we're not done yet. We still need to find Pierre. Whatever Jean François was up to tonight wasn't the first time this has happened." Emma Jane shook her head. "I think the entire Bourbon family has been involved with shady side of the supernatural for centuries."

Vanessa started walking, the slight weight of the girl hardly weighing her down. "Let's get her to the hospital. We can talk more along the way."

Emma Jane took one last look around the room. Her eyes locked for a moment on the still, wizened figure of Jean François sprawled beside the ancient symbol of evil on the floor. Whatever the Bourbons had been up to would soon be over forever if Emma Jane had her way.

HONEYMOON
CHAPTER 17

Vanessa drove carefully after googling the location of the hospital in Nîmes. She hadn't wanted to take the girl to the hospital near Gévaudan, because although it was a longer drive to Nîmes, it avoided the possibility of running into any locals who may have been involved in the kidnapping. Luckily, it was within an hour's drive so it gave Vanessa and Emma Jane a chance to plan what they should do next. Emma Jane hadn't sensed anyone else in the house after she'd defeated Jean Francois, so they'd left without searching further for Pierre, certain that there was second location and he was likely elsewhere, planning another atrocity.

"What if Jean François was changing back and forth between human and wolf because he wasn't able to fully transform yet?" Vanessa mused, keeping her hands on the steering wheel as she cast a brief side-glance at Emma Jane, who was in the backseat, keeping an eye on the girl.

Vanessa's eyes moved down to the frail figure beside her wife. She hadn't woken up yet, but as her breathing had remained steady and she didn't appear to be in any distress, they'd agreed it was safe for them to take her to the hospital further away. It avoided any unnecessary contact with local police or authorities, which made the slightly cynical Emma

Jane more comfortable, while even the less paranoid Vanessa wasn't confident it wouldn't look suspicious if an American and a Canadian were found with the body of a missing ten-year-old while vacationing in France.

"Yeah, I think you may be right. Jean François was nowhere near as strong as I expected him to be. Frankly, he couldn't fight worth a damn. I think that he was pretty new to his powers. In fact, I'm wondering if sacrificing this girl was supposed to give him the full whatever that he was going for."

Vanessa nodded, keeping her eyes on the road. "Makes sense. Remember when he said that he could supercharge the ritual if he sacrificed us, as well?"

Vanessa heard Emma Jane humming thoughtfully behind her and glanced in the rearview mirror again, to catch her absently biting her thumbnail. Their eyes met in the mirror and Vanessa smiled. It wasn't the honeymoon she'd dreamed of, but she couldn't deny the thrill of excitement she'd felt working with Emma Jane to save the girl from Jean François.

"I still feel like this has something to do with Mont Mouchet," said Emma Jane, maintaining eye contact with Vanessa in the mirror.

Vanessa nodded. "Yeah, both Pierre and Jean François warned us a few times about the weather being bad. They didn't seem worried about the weather anywhere else, but warned us about Mont Mouchet at least twice. What if they were warning us away because Pierre went there to prepare another ritual? He did say he was going to be out of town for a few days."

"Wasn't that also the place where the local hunter caught the beast, when the attacks finally stopped in 1767?"

Vanessa snapped her fingers. "Of course! What if that's where the family came from?"

Emma Jane continued, warming up to her theory. "And when that beast was killed in the seventeen hundreds, they went into hiding in town, instead."

"The entire family must've been involved." Vanessa watched the pieces fitting together smoothly in her wife's logical brain and felt a tingle of pride sweep through her.

Emma Jane smiled at Vanessa's conclusion. "That would also explain why the beast was caught more than once."

"Because it wasn't one beast, or a pack of wolves. It was the entire Bourbon family," Vanessa said, triumph making her almost shout the last word.

Emma Jane smiled, the cool look of a hunter back in her eyes. "That means once we drop the girl off, we'll be heading to Mont Mouchet."

Vanessa looked at the road and the dark night around them. The moon was bright but hidden behind passing clouds, and the road was nearly deserted except an occasional vehicle going the other direction. "We'll leave tomorrow, in the morning, right? I don't think it's a good idea to explore unfamiliar territory when there's a possibility of being ripped to shreds by werewolves or shifters or whatever else they are."

Emma Jane seemed to deflate, but reluctantly agreed. "You're right. By the time we get her settled at the hospital and back to Gévaudan, it will be after midnight. We'll go back to the hotel tonight and get some sleep; then first thing in the morning, we'll pack for a few days of hunting. Let's end werewolf fever in France, once and for all, and track the beast back to his lair."

HONEYMOON
CHAPTER 18

E mma Jane woke up the next morning as energized as if she'd already had several cups of coffee. At first, she didn't remember where she was or why she was so alert, but when she rolled in bed and felt a warm soft body next to her, the events of the previous day flooded back. She rolled back over, absently scratching her arm as she snuggled closer to Vanessa's warmth. She wasn't ready to get up yet, so instead, let the soft tingle where their skin touched soothe her as thoughts of the girl from the night before intruded.

She wondered how she was doing. When they'd arrived at the hospital in Nîmes, Emma Jane had tried to explain with her awkward French that they'd found the girl near Jean François' house. As expected, they'd been bombarded by questions. Emma Jane had done her best to answer them, but it quickly became apparent to the doctors and nurses that neither her nor Vanessa knew anything about the girl. The police had subsequently been summoned and taken over the interrogation from the health care professionals. Emma Jane had given the officers the address of the house, hoping they'd bought her reason for not taking the victim to the hospital in Gévaudan, and that they'd left nothing incriminating behind.

One of the police officers had been shocked, but then his face had hardened and his mouth had become a thin line as he diligently took notes. Emma Jane had worried he was friends with Jean François at first, but upon examining his spirit, she'd seen his horror at the events she'd described and knew his anger was channeled into a determination to make things right. Whatever else he may be, this officer was an honorable man who didn't like hearing about bad things happening to children. Emma Jane had been relieved to know that the girl was in good hands and they'd left shortly after, giving their contact details to the police as well as their plans to hike around Mont Mouchet the next day.

Instead of receiving another warning about bad weather, the police officer had merely nodded and said he'd check in with them when they had more information about the girl or if they needed to ask them any more questions. Emma Jane had found that interesting. With her suspicions about the de Bourbons' repeated cautions about the weather on the mountain thus confirmed as bogus, Emma Jane and Vanessa had taken leave of the girl. Pressing goodbye kisses on her forehead as she slept, they prayed for a speedy recovery for the slumbering waif.

Emma Jane wasn't positive, but she had a feeling that the girl wouldn't, couldn't, wake up until they'd accomplished their task and taken care of Pierre as well. Her last look at the comatose young woman had been what had caused her to wonder in the first place. While there wasn't even a hint of darkness on the girl, her spirit was barely a shadow of what it should be. It had been more of a pale silver than the expected bright aura that a girl that age should have. With her thoughts firmly revolving around the girl and the events from the night before, Emma Jane didn't notice Vanessa was awake until she heard a low, rumbling purr coming from beside her.

"Good morning, beautiful," said Vanessa, snuggling closer. "Did you sleep well? Your eyes are dark thunderstorms right now. What are you thinking of that's causing you such distress so early in the day?"

Emma Jane smiled sheepishly. "Caught me. I was just thinking about the girl we found. And Mont Mouchet." Emma Jane stared into Vanessa's deep sapphire-colored eyes, voicing her fears out loud. "I don't think Jeanette is going to wake up until we get to the bottom of this."

Vanessa's expression became pensive as she rested her head on Emma Jane's shoulder and pulled her into her embrace. "I think you're right," she said, mumbling the words into her shoulder. They lay there for a few minutes, silently considering the poor girl who was alone in a hospital bed, without even a name or loved ones to care for her. After a few minutes, Emma Jane forced her sadness down, replacing it with the more useful determination to make things right. She pulled away from Vanessa, eliciting a small moan of protest as she sat up in bed.

"Let's help her wake up. We still have the hotel room tonight, so we can leave our unnecessary stuff here. We'll pack enough supplies for twenty-four hours. Food and weapons only, unless you think there's something else we need to bring?"

Vanessa rolled over to lie on her side, resting her head on her hand as she watched Emma Jane pace around the room.

"No, that should work. It's not like we're going camping. I'm eager to get this done as well- we have a girl to save and a honeymoon to get back to. The sooner we take down this asshole, the better."

Emma Jane smiled with approval then continued preparing. After a quick breakfast at the bakery, which Vanessa had insisted upon, they got in the car and drove. Mont Mouchet was in the Cévennes mountain range and while it wasn't heavily populated region, it was a tourist destination with a decent hiking system and plenty to see and do. In a little over an hour of driving, they'd arrived near the base of the mountain and parked the car at a well-labeled trailhead.

They'd both packed sturdy hiking shoes for their trip, as Vanessa had hoped they'd find a few hikes she could brag about to Mai and Jake the next time she spoke with her friends, and Emma Jane always wore sturdy shoes. Despite the repeated warnings from the de Bourbons, they were greeted with a lovely day. The sun was out, a light breeze blew the sweat from exertion off their skin, and the scenery was beautiful. As they approached the base of the mountain, they searched the area carefully. They knew it wasn't likely that what they sought was something an average tourist would stumble over, which meant they were either looking for something hidden by supernatural means, or tucked out of the way by nature.

It was early afternoon by the time they reached a place that matched the description of what they were searching for. As Emma Jane had suspected, the mountain itself had been altered by magic. She wouldn't have noticed it at all if it hadn't been for a small squirrel running across the field. One moment, it had been scurrying across the green backdrop of the mountains, and the next, it had disappeared beneath her amused gaze. Startled, she looked more closely at the spot where it had vanished, then noticed an odd shimmer covering the side of the gentle slope.

"Vanessa, do you see that?"

Vanessa looked where Emma Jean was pointing, squinted, then looked back at her and shook her head. "What am I looking for? I just see mountainside."

Emma Jane bit the inside of her lip. "Look closer. Here, I'm going to stand where I was pointing. Tell me if anything happens."

Vanessa nodded and Emma Jane walked toward where she'd last seen the squirrel. She could sense the shimmer in the air and wondered if it was a gate, because it reminded her of what she'd seen when they'd passed through Summerland. But instead of the beautiful forest glade she remembered, the shimmer abruptly gave way to a deep darkness. Emma Jane stopped, looking around with surprise as she found herself inside a large cave. She took a step back then breathed a sigh of relief when she saw the sun, as well as a startled Vanessa staring back at her.

Vanessa's eyes were as wide as saucers. "What the what? You totally disappeared."

Vanessa came over to where Emma Jane stood then gingerly waved her hand in the space Emma Jane had just emerged from. While Emma Jane watched, Vanessa's hand instantly vanished, as though cut off at the wrist. Vanessa pulled her hand back, looked down at it, and shook it out.

Vanessa stared at Emma Jane for a moment before either woman was able to speak.

"I think we found the entrance," said Emma Jane, after a long pause.

Vanessa nodded, putting her hand in front of her to test it again before pulling it back and shuddering. "Do we really have to go in there?" Vanessa looked at Emma Jane, pleading with her eyes.

Emma Jane nodded, her own reluctance obvious. "I'm afraid so. If we want to end this, we need to confront Pierre."

"Okay, but what if it's more than just Pierre in there? We could be walking into a huge ambush, or a dark mass, or something. We don't know how many people are in the family, after all."

Emma Jane exhaled deeply. "You're totally right. There could be an entire town in there, or maybe just Pierre. We have no way of knowing until we look. Either way, we need to cut the head off the snake. Pierre is almost certainly the head of the family, so regardless of what else we find inside, in order to save our Jeanette-doppelgänger we're going to need to stop him."

Vanessa winced then extended her arm to the strange space again. "As long as we both understand that we're flying blind. But you first. I'm not fond of caves, especially after our last experience in one."

Emma Jane grimaced at the memory. Considering that she'd almost been killed by the last monster they'd encountered in a cave, she wasn't eager to go in herself. But they both knew they had to, so Emma Jane took a deep breath and held out her hand for Vanessa.

Vanessa sighed, accepting her hand and squeezing it tightly. "After this is over we're going back to Paris and I'm going shopping. Pretty sure I'm going to need a lot of retail therapy once we're done here."

Emma Jane squeezed back. "Sure. I think I can handle a little shopping after we deal with Pierre."

Holding onto Vanessa's hand, Emma Jane stepped into a completely different world. As she adjusted to the darkness around them, she realized she could actually see, which was strange. Normally, Emma Jane's vision made everything look like vague, grey shapes, shades of darkness and light, but the strange symbols glowing along the rock wall lit the room in a way that was clearly supernatural. Although she couldn't read them and had no idea what language they were written in, they appeared to be the same symbols that had glowed such an eerie blue on Jean François' knife the previous night. Now regretting that she'd left the knife behind, Emma Jane made sure not to touch any of the symbols in case they were dangerous. She caught Vanessa's eye and pointed to them, then shook her finger. Vanessa nodded, stepping away from the wall that she'd almost brushed up against.

They glided like ghosts down a narrow yet arching entranceway. If Emma Jane hadn't known better, she would've thought they were inside a house the way it was laid out. *Perhaps we are. Perhaps this is the original château chez Bourbon.*

The hallway twisted and turned before they encountered a set of stairs that descended into an unseen darkness. Emma Jane was reminded of the stairs in the house in Gévaudan the night before. The niggling sense of familiarity made her wonder if this was a dark mirror of the more elegant home, and if perhaps the darkness that had seemed to pulse last night had its origins here. Emma Jane rubbed her chin thoughtfully as she looked down the dark staircase that led into an abyss. If that was the case, then she knew where these stairs led. Emma Jane looked at Vanessa, raising her eyebrows as she pointed down the stairs.

Vanessa stuck her tongue out, showing her opinion clearly, before her shoulders drooped with acceptance. Emma Jane felt her lips twitch with amusement in spite of the heavy atmosphere, then she padded down the stairs as quietly as if she was tracking a forest animal, while Vanessa used her air magic to levitate and avoid the possibility of her footsteps creating noise altogether. Emma Jane was relieved to see light filtering from around the corner to the right by the time they reached the bottom of the stairs. As she'd expected, the layout was the same as the house from the previous night, with the exception of the walls, ceiling, and floor being composed of stone instead of the more sophisticated appearing wood and marble.

In front of them, Emma Jane knew they'd find the kitchen. And, if she was correct, it was where they'd find Pierre and the altar where legend had begun. Taking a deep breath, Emma Jane stepped toward the light.

HONEYMOON
CHAPTER 19

Vanessa followed closely behind Emma Jane, grateful for the faint glow coming from around the corner - at least until she heard a creepy humming sound originating in the same place. Inwardly cringing, Vanessa stayed close on Emma Jane's heels, ready to use her air magic at any sign of danger. *Weird*, she thought, noticing how the hallway was almost a carbon copy of the house they'd been in the night before. Emma Jane peeked around the first doorway they came to and Vanessa held her breath when she caught a glimpse of what was on the other side.

If she'd thought there'd been too many candles in the open room the night before, this room outdid that to nth degree. There must've been over a thousand candles. Some hung from the walls, on the floor, some were even arranged in a chandelier. They covered every single available surface as far as she could see, but instead of making her feel comforted by the light, her heart dropped somewhere into the bottom of her stomach. The humming intensified but it was hard to make out where it was coming from until they entered the next room.

In the center was a man, but it wasn't humming she heard. It was singing. The words were so guttural she'd thought he was humming at first because she couldn't make out any syllables. When he turned and she glimpsed his face, her confusion evaporated. She clearly remembered the suave older gentleman from the day before; his salt-and-pepper hair, his resemblance to his son. But this individual was completely altered. Much as how Jean François had appeared barely human last night, Pierre now seemed feral, more wolf than man.

Instead of the thinning, receding hairline he'd had earlier, he was covered with hair on every visible part of his body. His fingernails closely resembled claws and in his hand was the twin of the knife Jean François had been dancing around with in the house. Vanessa hadn't a clue what was up with the symbols in the cave or on the knife, but they glowed with a creepy blue light that frankly scared the crap out of her. Whatever was going on here was so far from normal she couldn't even explain it. Luckily, it appeared that only Pierre was in the cave, which gave them an advantage.

Emma Jane seemed to think that the de Bourbons weren't a true werewolf family, but some sort of hybrid shifters who used magic in order to gain their powers. Vanessa didn't know what to believe, but the wolf-man in front of her was neither man nor fully a wolf, which went along with Emma Jane's hybrid theory. She didn't know mythical monsters as well as Emma Jane did, but she could tell that the creature in front of her wasn't natural the second she saw him.

He hadn't spotted them yet, but when Vanessa caught a glimpse of his eyes, she knew without a doubt that if Emma Jane had seen a normal aura on him at one time, it was long gone now. His eyes were dark, endless pools that glowed with the same blue fire reflecting off the walls and the knife. Vanessa bit her lip and looked at Emma Jane, hoping for guidance. When Emma Jane pulled out her knife, her plan became obvious. She wasn't taking any prisoners. Not that they'd had success with that in the past, but still. Vanessa would have liked just once to have been able to tie someone up for the police to deal with. In this case, however, Jean François had *been* a cop, so it wouldn't have worked this time anyway.

Taking a deep breath, Vanessa closed her eyes to tune herself to the air, so that she'd be aware of any sudden shifts. She knew instinctively that Pierre would be more powerful than Jean François had been due to his age, but also because he wasn't flickering in and out of his human form the way his son had. Vanessa followed Emma Jane's lead, making sure that the space around them was large enough to transform to a raven. After all, if Pierre was going to fight as a wolf, she'd be damned if she didn't get her chance to be a raven.

As they snuck closer, she was satisfied to note that the ceiling was higher here than in the hallway they'd passed through. Whatever this room was for, it had been designed with the soaring ceiling of a cathedral. With the candles that spilled down the walls it almost looked like Notre Dame in the heart of Paris. *Maybe it had been built around the same time.* They'd almost made it all the way into the room when Pierre looked up and saw them approaching. But instead of being upset, Pierre greeted them with a wolfish smile.

"Mademoiselles! I have been waiting for you. How lovely you could join me tonight, and on such an auspicious night at that! You see, tonight is a full moon. But not just any full moon." He laughed as though he'd just told a joke and was impressed with himself. "Tonight is the Blue Moon, which means that my power is at its peak." He leered at them with canine teeth double the size of any human teeth Vanessa had ever seen. "Your presence here at this special time means that you will be lucky enough to have the opportunity of making a very unique donation to my family."

Vanessa's mouth went as dry as toast as he stepped toward her. In the darkness, his eyes glowed with the same cold, evil nightmare she'd only seen once before. When she'd been confronted by the god of darkness himself.

HONEYMOON
CHAPTER 20

Emma Jane watched with an impassive expression on her face as the new, unimproved version of Pierre de Bourbon sauntered toward them, his pace unhurried and his not-quite-human face alight with dark joy. She knew if he had his way, they'd never leave the cave alive. It was up to her and Vanessa to ensure that he couldn't achieve his vision and that he never hurt anyone else again.

Emma Jane raised an eyebrow. "I'm happy that you're happy to see us. But before we go any further, I should tell you that you won't be having company, other than the two of us, of course."

Emma Jane grimaced with mock-chagrin, hoping that she was correct in assuming that only Pierre was present in the cavern they'd walked into. She watched as his face ran through a gauntlet of emotions: dark pleasure at their apparent capture, surprise, then finally, to comprehension.

"You lie." He spat, shaking his head in denial as he advanced another step. "Jean François is running behind. He often does, with all of the work he must do to maintain his cover."

Emma Jane shrugged, trying to hide her relief at the confirmation they were only dealing with the two men. She looked at Vanessa. While her eyes appeared frightened to her perceptive gaze, her wife's face was a smooth mask which betrayed nothing.

"Vanessa? Do you remember the last thing Jean François said to us when we spoke with him last night?"

Vanessa made a show of trying to remember before dramatically hitting the side of her head with her hand. "Oh! Yes, I do. I believe he said..." Vanessa gripped her throat dramatically, making a gurgling sound.

Emma Jane bit back a laugh at her wife's demonstration. She hadn't thought Vanessa would do that and was a little horrified at her graphic acting, but looking at Pierre's face, she knew that Vanessa had succeeded in inciting him to anger, and perhaps, to committing a mistake.

"You shall die for that!"

Emma Jane yawned, covering her mouth with her right hand before dropping it down behind her back to her waist, where she kept her knife. Drawing it out in one smooth motion she gave him a wicked smile. "Yes, I'm sure you will." When he appeared confused, she chuckled dryly. "No, I didn't make a mistake when I spoke. I'm not paying for anything tonight, but you will. You'll pay for everything you've done to everyone you've harmed over the last however many years you've been around. You see, before Jean François could finish the ritual he'd planned for that poor girl, we stopped him. So, if you're planning on making me pay for anything, now's your chance. Because when I take my turn, there won't be enough of you left to do anything."

Pierre's lip curled and he growled. Although he had no way to know if what Emma Jane said was true, she knew he believed her by the way his wrath had intensified as she'd taunted him.

Emma Jane glanced at Vanessa, noting that she'd already transformed into her other form. Emma Jane had wondered if she'd change, knowing that Vanessa preferred to fight evil as a raven whenever possible. Emma Jane was familiar with the Celtic legends of the Morrigan, so now whenever she saw Vanessa in her glossy, powerful bird form, that was who she thought of- her own personal goddess of death and war.

Pierre hadn't seen what Vanessa was doing until after she'd shifted, and Emma Jane watched his mouth drop open in surprise at the sight of the large black bird who flew safely out of his reach. Instead of merely a defenseless girl, she'd suddenly become an unknown quality. Emma Jane smiled as his manner changed. He'd gone from being angry to wary as he was confronted by something other than the two helpless victims he'd planned on. The moment he'd seen that Vanessa had changed, he looked at Emma Jane as if expecting her to have another form as well. She used the distraction to see if she could glean any more information.

"How long has this been going on?" Emma Jane asked, stepping in a sideways pattern around him, keeping him safely in front of her with her back to the wall in the same manner she'd done the night previous with his son. When she moved deeper into the room, she observed a second, larger, sacrificial altar on the floor. The same blue symbols glowed between the points of the stars and the intersections where the circle crossed through them.

"For much longer than you've been alive, you fool. You should never have come here. We warned you. Or did we?"

Pierre's smile became hungry and once again, he flashed sharp, white teeth.

Emma Jane nodded. "Of course. You weren't warning us away, you were hoping you'd whet our curiosity so that we'd come and explore the mountain in time for your ritual." She made quotation marks in the air as she said the word ritual, causing him to laugh.

"Foolish child. Stupid Americans. So easy to manipulate two wide-eyed tourists. All I had to do was chat with you over one lunch and you'll be enough of a meal to last me a decade." Pierre threw his head back, chuckling with an evil rasp that apparently passed for laughter. "Women are always so much easier to trap than men. As much as you ladies like to think you're so smart, such good judges of character."

Pierre sneered at Emma Jane before casting a suspicious glance at Vanessa, who was perched behind his head looking down at him. "It was too easy. Buy you lunch, tell you to stay away from the mountain because of the weather, then just wait and let you do the rest."

Emma Jane bit her lip, trying to suppress a smirk. While she found his words irritating, she knew things hadn't worked out as well as he'd planned. "Wow, then it must really grind your gears to find out that two 'stupid Americans' managed to kill your son so easily. I bet that wasn't part of the plan, was it? Oh, and FYI, I'm not American."

His face hardened, but it was the titter of laughter from behind his head that finally threw him over the edge. At first, he seemed torn, unsure who he should attack first. He whirled, searching for the source of the laughter, but Vanessa moved further out of his reach so he snarled and spun to face

Emma Jane instead. This time, she knew she was in for a real fight. Her adrenaline rose like an old friend who'd been gone too long and she loosened her muscles in preparation as Pierre took a deep breath and completed his transformation.

He grew as he shifted, almost doubling in size. The knife fell forgotten onto the floor while he completed his conversion into a wolf. In moments, she was face to face with a white wolf flecked with patches of dark brown. His snout was crisscrossed by old scars and dark yellow fangs, the likes of which she'd never seen on a human before, were bared beneath it as he stood on all fours, now almost six feet tall. Emma Jane knew he outweighed her by at least two hundred pounds if not more and quickly assessed her options. This was not a battle she'd be able to win through sheer force. Although she was stronger than she looked, she was still at least a half a foot shorter and much lighter.

Even though she didn't believe he was a natural werewolf, she ruled out close contact as an option. At least, until after she'd disarmed him, which meant disabling his claws and his teeth. Or killing him, whichever she could accomplish first. It was two against one, but Emma Jane wasn't counting on that being a enough of an advantage to win. If Pierre truly was the beast of Gévaudan, it would take everything in her arsenal to beat him. Closing her eyes, she took a deep breath. Sending out a prayer to the Great Spirit, she prepared for the fight of her life.

HONEYMOON
CHAPTER 21

Vanessa watched from her perch, terrified from the second she'd watched Pierre transform into the largest, most ferocious appearing beast she'd ever seen. He made the sásq'ets who'd tried to kill them in Banff look like a furry, playful puppy. This was a monster from her darkest childhood nightmares. His eyes were full of hatred and fixed firmly on the love of her life, while Emma Jane pranced around him, looking as though she was at a bar in a dance-off. There wasn't even a shadow of fear on Emma Jane's face as she focused on the giant wolf a few feet away from her. She wasn't sure how she did it. Vanessa's love and pride for Emma Jane doubled. But even though she was sure that Emma Jane was more than capable of taking care of herself against Pierre, Vanessa wanted to make sure she didn't get hurt in the process.

Vanessa snapped her beak as she thought, candles filling her peripheral vision with their fake cheeriness. What could she do to distract or injure him enough so that Emma Jane could deliver the killing blow without being injured herself? At first, nothing came to mind until she remembered Emma Jane's earlier words from the hotel room. *Silver, iron, and when all else fails, kill it with fire.*

Vanessa smiled as much as her avian face would allow, then swooped down and picked up a candle with her claws. Unseen and unheard in the darkness of the cave, she glided behind Pierre as Emma Jane and Pierre focused solely on each other. Vanessa loved watching Emma Jane move around an opponent and took a moment to admire her wife. The way she wove around the wolf was almost magic in itself, and although Pierre was less graceful due to his mass, he moved with his own animalistic power.

So when he cried out without warning, both Pierre and Emma Jane searched for the source of the noise before realizing he'd been what had made it. The stench of burnt hair filled the stagnant air of the cave, but Vanessa was gone, already reaching for another candle. Moving like a ghost in the darkness, her wings were soundless in the air which she controlled. By the time she dropped the next candle, Pierre had lost sight of her. If it hadn't been so tense below, Vanessa would have laughed at the fury on his face.

After the second candle hit its target, Emma Jane became a blur. Pierre tried to focus on Vanessa, but when he wasn't able to see above him, he let out a howl, which reverberated from the walls of the cave. Vanessa waited until he spun in the other direction, then nosedived with another candle. At that instant, Emma Jane made her move. Vanessa could hardly see her and if it hadn't been for the glint of her silver knife in the candlelight, Vanessa would have thought nothing had happened. But in concert with the third candle landing on Pierre's back, Emma Jane plunged her knife into his rib cage, tearing along the right side of his chest, then rolling out of reach of his claws.

This time the sound that echoed through the cave was a yelp of pain, oddly truncated as his lungs filled with blood. It ended in a weak gurgle as Pierre ran out of air. Vanessa looked away, unable to watch but also not yet confident he would stay down. Sailing to the other side of the cave, she reached for one more candle. It wasn't over, not until he didn't get up again. She returned a fourth time as he struggled to his feet, his teeth bloodied but his eyes glittering and defiant. She dropped the last candle. As the fire reflected in his eyes, she caught a flash of quicksilver to his left. This time, there was no noise as he collapsed with a strangled gasp, then lay still on the cave floor.

Nausea rose in Vanessa's throat, the bitter taste churning with adrenaline into a painful acid as she realized Pierre's other lung had been pierced and that was why he was unable to make a sound. Emma Jane's aim had been true. She landed on the floor, remaining out of reach in case Pierre had one last burst of energy, then transformed into her human form. Emma Jane was covered in blood, although Vanessa was happy to know that none of it was her own.

Holding the knife protectively in front of her body, Emma Jane placed her left hand over Pierre's head then plunged the silver dagger into him once more, this time into the black heart of the beast of Gévaudan. His eyes flickered once then went dark with the filminess of death. A blue glow surrounded Pierre then traveled into Emma Jane. Throwing her head back, she began to absorb his power.

Vanessa bit her lip. Something was different about this time, but she wasn't sure what, or if she should do anything to help. As she had each time before, she waited helplessly while Emma Jane fought through the influx of power. She'd never seen her fight this hard before, and didn't know if it was due to Pierre's age or power, but she could see Emma Jane struggling to regain control. She dropped to her knees, panting and arching her back as her hands curled and uncurled against the floor.

For a moment, Vanessa was filled with horror at the thought that Emma Jane was about to transform into a wolf. But when the hair and claws she feared failed to materialize, Vanessa released her breath. After what felt like an endless battle, Emma Jane's eyes finally opened.

Vanessa backed up a few paces at the sight of her usual swirling white clouds replaced by a blue glow, snapping and crackling as though she had lightning trapped inside them. Reflexively, she grabbed onto the green stone she wore around her neck and tried to remind herself that Emma Jane wouldn't, couldn't hurt her.

"Emma Jane? Emma Jane!"

Vanessa didn't know what to do. Was Emma Jane going to attack her next? She remembered Emma Jane's sadness and fear about the darkness calling to her when she'd killed Jean François, and how she'd naïvely reassured her that she'd never let her turn to evil. But, for the first time since she'd met Emma Jane, Vanessa wondered if stopping Emma Jane from going rogue was something that was even within her power to promise. She took another involuntary step backward, holding her breath as Emma Jane closed her eyes and stood up, then remained motionless and hardly breathing for several moments while Vanessa waited, ready to bolt if need be.

Emma Jane's eyes snapped open. Vanessa almost passed out with relief at the sight of her love's beautiful, magical white eyes that had enchanted her from the moment she'd first seen them.

"Wow. Sorry about that." Emma Jane rubbed the back of her neck, rolling it as she stretched the muscles out.

"What happened, Emma Jane? What was that?" Vanessa wasn't sure she was prepared to hear the truth, but couldn't keep herself from asking.

Emma Jane shook her head. "That, my dear, was the worst fight I've ever had against the darkness."

"I don't understand. Why was this time harder?"

Emma Jane shrugged. "Honestly? I don't think I've ever encountered a creature as strong as Pierre was. He wasn't just a werewolf. He was what my people sometimes call a skin-walker. An ancient, powerful skin-walker. But I've never heard of any living in Europe, and his power was different than what I'm used to."

Vanessa wrinkled her nose, confused. "Skin-walker? What's that? Is it like a shapeshifter?"

Emma Jane nodded, but didn't answer. Instead, she slowly approached Vanessa as if expecting her to bolt. When she didn't move, Emma Jane smiled and relief lit her face with a healthy glow.

"I can't believe how lucky I am to have you, Vanessa." She smiled with amazement and love in her eyes. "I'm not sure what it looked like, but based on how I felt, I wouldn't have thought less of you if you'd left me here. I don't know why you haven't left already, after seeing how weak I am against the darkness each time we fight it."

Vanessa heard the wonder and the pain in Emma Jane's voice. The rest of her questions could wait. Right now, Emma Jane needed to know just how much she loved her. Vanessa pulled Emma Jane into her arms, channeling all of her love, fear, and relief into the most powerful kiss she could as she lifted her up and spun her around. For a moment, they celebrated in a way that only two people deeply in love can when they find their partner safe against all the odds.

She'd nearly forgotten their surroundings when the first rumble intruded into their bubble. By then, she'd lifted Emma Jane up against the wall as they clung to each other. Emma Jane was pressed tightly against her, breathing hard as passion overwhelmed them. At first, Vanessa ignored the sound, unwilling to let go of her wife long enough to investigate. She'd just gone back in for another kiss when she the noise came again. This time, she almost lost her balance as the ground shook. As though a bucket of cold water had hit her, Vanessa realized the cave was moving.

"Emma Jane." Vanessa tried to speak, but had to clear her throat and repeat her name twice before she said it loud enough for Emma Jane to hear her. Her vocal chords were thick, rusty from disuse and desire, but she managed to get Emma Jane's attention a split second before another rumble pierced the silence.

Moving swiftly, Emma Jane dropped her feet to the floor, moving Vanessa behind her as she assessed the risk. Candles had already begun to tumble off the walls as rocks and dirt clouded the air. Vanessa coughed, her lungs suddenly tight.

Emma Jane tugged her hand. "Come on. We need to move!"

Vanessa nodded, not needing encouragement beyond that of the cave collapsing around them. Together, they raced through the hallway in the direction they'd entered. Whatever magic had kept the cave a secret for the last several hundred years was to breaking apart now that Pierre was dead. First small rocks, then boulders rained from the ceiling of the cave as they ran. Several times Vanessa or Emma Jane pushed the other out of the way as rocky projectiles narrowly missed them. When they reached the staircase, Vanessa knew they'd never make it unless she took control.

"Emma Jane!" Vanessa shouted over the deafening noise. "Drop your backpack and hang on. We're going to fly this popsicle stand."

Emma Jane nodded and dropped the bag, keeping her knife as she jumped on Vanessa's back and held on for dear life. Calling her air magic to her, Vanessa lifted them up the staircase and through the hall, bursting into the daylight on a beautiful spring day just as the side of the mountain collapsed behind them. Vanessa looked at Emma Jane, lying on her back after falling off into the grass when Vanessa had tumbled out of the cave into reality, and began to laugh.

HONEYMOON
CHAPTER 22

Emma Jane sipped the absolute best mug of hot chocolate she could remember having as she listened to Vanessa animatedly discussing a dress she'd bought at the last store they'd been to. The day after they'd finished up their business at Mont Mouchet and Gévaudan, they'd returned to Paris. Emma Jane had accompanied Vanessa to every store that caught her eye, as promised.

Vanessa was currently on a roll, saying something about ruching and layers. Or was it a hemline? Emma Jane shook her head. To be honest, whenever Vanessa started to go on about fashion, she had a tendency to tune her out. It wasn't as though she hated it, but when she literally couldn't see what all the fuss was about, it ranked lower on her list of interests than it might for another woman. Or maybe it was her minimalist nature that didn't find fashion overly practical. Either way, Emma Jane's mind had a chance to wander back to what had happened after they'd made it out of the cave in one piece.

SHE'D BEEN FULL OF the usual conflicting emotions and feelings that followed on the heels of a killing and had found the Beast of Gévaudan more difficult than her other encounters. On the one hand, her blood and every single molecule of her being still vibrated with the power she'd absorbed. She'd been terrified at how close she'd come to accepting the call of the darkness, knowing that it was the furthest she'd travelled toward that path.

Even now, she wondered if the only reason she'd regained her willpower was because at the exact moment she'd felt the most out of control, she'd seen Vanessa's pale face watching her. It was the first time she hadn't thought of her loved ones waiting for her after death, and Emma Jane was certain that if Vanessa hadn't been in her life, she would've fallen without her to anchor her to the light.

But, because of Vanessa, she'd managed to fight back the seductive pull of evil once more. When Vanessa had rewarded her with love, acceptance, and kisses, Emma Jane's desire had overwhelmed her. If it hadn't been for the cave falling down around their ears as they kissed, she would have been more than happy to celebrate a successful mission right then and there. Instead, they'd had to race for their lives out of a collapsing cave. When they'd finally emerged into the sunshine, they'd taken one look at each other. Relief and joy had caused them to burst out laughing before Emma Jane finished what Vanessa had started back in the cave. As they'd lain in the grass, still breathing rapidly, her heart almost exploded with joy. Emma Jane had turned to Vanessa and answered the question she'd asked what seemed like hours ago.

"It was him, Vanessa, all this time.

"What do you mean?" Vanessa asked, moving close enough to rest her head on Emma Jane's shoulder, absently stroking her heart. Emma Jane felt a tingle of desire rise up and stilled Vanessa's hand long enough to finish what she'd been trying to say.

"When I absorbed Pierre's energy and his spirit, I caught flashes of his past, his memories. It was him, Vanessa. All along. He was the creature who killed Jeanette back in the 1700s, but he's also the one who captured the girl we rescued from Jean François' house."

Vanessa shook her head. "But how? Why?"

Emma Jane shrugged, not entirely sure herself. "I don't know. Maybe it was because he recognized her. Maybe she was the original victim whose murder gave him the power to live this long as a skin-walker. Or maybe it was just dumb luck, synchronicity, or destiny. Either way, it was probably that symmetry which started this whole mess in the first place."

Emma Jane waved her hand in the air, gesturing to the destroyed cave, which now resembled an old rockslide on the side of the mountain.

"Damn," said Vanessa, shaking her head. "I think this just goes to show that once again, when it comes to us, there's no such thing as a supernatural coincidence. It felt like something pointed us in this direction. Maybe there *is* a bigger plan."

Emma Jane nodded. "That's what I've been telling myself, ever since my family died. I've got to believe that the Great Spirit has a plan for me, that I'm one of its warriors for the light, and that my work here on earth will be important. It gives me something to work for, to hope for."

Vanessa leaned over to kiss Emma Jane. "Good. You keep telling yourself that, whenever you feel down, or think you're going fall to the dark side."

Emma Jane gave Vanessa a wry smile. "I do. But even so, I was worried today. I don't think it would have been enough if you hadn't been there. Thanks for saving me, Vanessa. I don't know what I'd do without your love to keep me on the bright path."

Vanessa snuggled closer. "I'm not sure who saved who this time but I'm pretty sure that the whole point of being married is to save each other. So, if you want, how about we just say you owe me one?"

Emma Jane smiled, meeting Vanessa's lips as all conversation stopped and emotion took over once more.

"SO, WHAT DO YOU THINK?"

Emma Jane almost spilled her hot chocolate on her shirt as she startled, her eyes opening wide as she realized Vanessa had asked her question. She grimaced without replying.

Vanessa rolled her eyes. "Aright, alright. Apparently, my love of fashion is not as scintillating for you as it is for me. Where were you just now?"

Emma Jane wiped hot chocolate off her hand with a napkin then looked into Vanessa's amused eyes. "I was thinking about yesterday."

Vanessa arched one eyebrow, her sapphire eyes sparkling with interest.

"Oh? Which part? The part where we took on a 300-year-old skin-walker, or the celebration of our successful secret-agent mission afterward?"

Emma Jane chuckled. Trust Vanessa to get to the heart of the matter. "Both, actually." She shook her head, a sense of wonder at everything that had happened over the previous few days filling her. "I'm still amazed I have you in my life, Vanessa, and even more stunned at how much you ground me."

Emma Jane's eyes met Vanessa's, trying to convey the depth of her admiration as she leaned over, taking her hand. "You are my everything, Vanessa. I hope you know that."

Vanessa squeezed Emma Jane's hand. "I know. But I'm not sure you understand that you mean just as much to me." She shrugged one shoulder. "I guess I'll just have to keep trying to make you understand. Maybe when we're in our nineties you'll finally believe me."

Emma Jane smiled, her heart full as they shared a quiet moment.

Vanessa snapped her fingers. "I just remembered! When I was in the change room, I got a phone call from the police officer in Nîmes."

Emma Jane cocked her head to the side. "Did he have any news about Jeanette?" Emma Jane winced. "I mean, whatever her name is?"

Vanessa nodded excitedly. "Yes! It turns out that she woke up yesterday. Shortly after four o'clock, according to him."

Emma Jane raised her eyebrows. "Did she? How...interesting."

Vanessa agreed. "Yeah, it seems that after the nurse got back from break, she found the girl awake in bed. And not just awake," Vanessa drawled, dragging out her words to build suspense. "But awake, talking, and in full command of all her senses."

Emma Jane leaned forward, squeezing Vanessa's hand tighter. "Who is she? What did she tell them?"

Vanessa's eyes sparkled and widened. "Get this. Apparently, her name is Ginette, pronounced the same, and her family's been in the area for centuries. She confirmed what you said about Pierre being the one to take her. I guess she was walking home from school when she saw an old man looking for his dog."

Emma Jane groaned. "When will children learn to stop helping old men find dogs?" She shook her head as her irritation spilled over. "I can't even count how many times I've heard that story when there's been a kidnapping."

Vanessa shrugged. "Apparently, the ruse works just as well when you need a sacrifice as when you're a pedophile." Vanessa shuddered, then waved her hand and spoke again. "Either way, Ginette has been reunited with her family, and it sounds like she'll be fine. She doesn't remember anything after looking for the dog, according to the officer."

Emma Jane was relieved. "That's good. No one needs to remember being in the center of a sacrificial altar while a half-man, half-wolf dances around you with a knife. I'm not sure that's something you'd be able to get over."

Vanessa nodded. "No doubt. But it sounds like things turned out well in the end."

Emma Jane smiled, relief flooding through her. She'd hoped by stopping Pierre that Jeanette's spirit would go back into her body, but she hadn't been sure. She'd never heard or experienced anything like what had occurred in Gévaudan. She had a feeling she needed to do a bit more research about the nature of skin-walkers, in case of future encounters. Although they hadn't found any other family members at the house or in the cave, it wasn't impossible that Pierre and Jean François had other relatives. Taking another sip of her hot chocolate, she pouted when she realized it was empty, then looked up at Vanessa with a mischievous smile.

"I think this super-secret-agent needs something else that's rich and sinfully delicious. But as my hot chocolate is gone, I was thinking of something along...another line."

Vanessa's eyes darkened as Emma Jane's intentions swirled in her eyes and she knew that Vanessa had caught her meaning.

"Check please!" Vanessa shouted, urgently looking for the waiter while Emma Jane laughed at the promise life held for them.

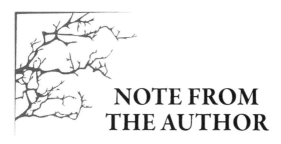

NOTE FROM
THE AUTHOR

Thank you for reading the adventures of Vanessa and Emma Jane! I hope that you've enjoyed reading them every bit as much as I've enjoyed writing them. I have more in store down the road for my ladies, but for now, I wanted to tie things up a little. I'm not a fan of cliffhanger endings as a reader, and have been know to become somewhat grouchy when tricked into one. Which is the reason I like my stories to have a nice ending of course :)

Reader reviews are incredibly important to Indie authors like myself, so it would mean so much if you could take a few minutes to leave an honest review wherever you buy books online. Even a few words can make the difference in helping a future reader to discover a book, as every review makes a novel more visible in the vast ocean of literature.

If you're interested in receiving updates, giveaways, or advanced copies of upcoming books, sign up for my mailing list at books@hmgoodenauthor.com, or through my web-page at https://www.hmgoodenauthor.com. You can also follow me on Facebook, Instagram, Twitter and many other places. I love to hear from readers and do my best to answer every comment and question. I hope you will join me in my next adventure!

COPYRIGHT INFORMATION

2019 by H. M. Gooden
Cover design by Franzi Haase
Edits by Muddy Waters editing

is much appreciated. Published in Canada by H. M. Good-en.

Don't miss out!

Visit the website below and you can sign up to receive emails whenever H. M. Gooden publishes a new book. There's no charge and no obligation.

https://books2read.com/r/B-A-POWE-YPBX

BOOKS 2 READ

Connecting independent readers to independent writers.

Did you love *The Raven and the Witch Hunter Omnibus: Volumes 2-4*? Then you should read *The Raven and the Witch Hunter* by H. M. Gooden!

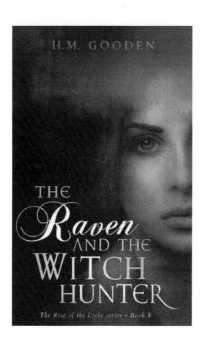

Vanessa lives a charmed life as the rising star in a hit new TV series. She has family and friends that love her, as well as the secret perk of having air magic and being able to turn into a raven and fly away if things get stressful.

But when her best friend moves away and a mysterious woman enters her life warning her of impending danger, her perfect life takes an unexpected turn.

Not only is Vanessa confronted with the very real threat of someone trying to kill her, but her own emotions will become inexplicably tangled.

What is it about this Witch Hunter that breaks every rule Vanessa has for herself? And what the heck is she supposed to do about it?

Read more at https://www.hmgoodenauthor.com/.

About the Author

H. M. Gooden has always loved the world of books, but over the last few years a new story has begged to be told, and as a result, this series was born.

In between dealing with children and work, the majority of the actual writing happens between four and six am and involves multiple cups of coffee for inspiration.

You can always find me on Twitter, Facebook, Instagram, Bookbub and Goodreads.

I always love to hear from readers!

Read more at https://www.hmgoodenauthor.com/.